Dine and Die on the Danube Express

Also by Peter King

The Gourmet Detective

Spiced to Death

Dying on the Vine

Death al Dente

A Healthy Place to Die

Eat, Drink, and Be Buried

Roux the Day

Peter King

Dine and Die
on the Danube Express

ST. MARTIN'S MINOTAUR 🐾 NEW YORK

www.minotaurbooks.com

Library of Congress Cataloging-in-Publication Data

King, Peter (Christopher Peter), 1922–
    Dine and die on the Danube Express : a gourmet detective mystery /
Peter King.—1st St. Martin's Minotaur ed.
        p.   cm.
    ISBN 0-312-28366-0
    1. Gourmet Detective (Fictitious character)—Fiction.   2. Cookery,
European—Fiction.   3. Europe, Central—Fiction.   4. Railroad travel—
Fiction.   5. Gourmets—Fiction.   6. Cookery—Fiction.   I. Title.

PS3561.I4822D56 2003
813'.54—dc21

                                                                2002191955

First Edition: June 2003

10   9   8   7   6   5   4   3   2   1

Dine and Die on the Danube Express

CHAPTER ONE

I walked away from Marienplatz square, past houses with leaded windows, flower boxes filled with red geraniums, and dormered, steeply gabled roofs. I walked by inns, antique shops, boutiques, and cafés—all with the lacy, gold signs that are so typically Bavarian. Along Munich's Dienerstrasse, the chic sidewalk cafés were filled with young people sipping *Milchkaffee*, beer, or wine.

I turned along Charlottenstrasse to my destination—the *Kempinski Hotel Vier Jahreszeiten*. One of the greatest hotels in Europe, its name can be translated as "The Four Seasons."

As always, the palatial lobby teemed with people, and I found my way to the Grand Ballroom, where the great event was to take place. An attendant in an eye-catching purple uniform with gold trim carefully checked my identity against his list and waved me through the entrance. The mellow wooden walls, festooned with bronze-and-scarlet tapestries, lent a venerable air to the huge room, filled now with a pattern of pristine white tablecloths, gleaming silver, and sparkling glass.

The sweeping, majestic strains of one of the greatest pieces of music ever written—Richard Wagner's *Die Meistersinger von Nurnberg*—was a fitting background to this historic occasion. A massive banner across one wall proclaimed the reason why I was here. It announced:

TWENTY-FIFTH ANNIVERSARY
THE DANUBE EXPRESS

Several dozen people were here, all to be passengers on the twenty-fifth-anniversary journey of the fabled Danube Express. One of the great trains of a bygone era, its tradition had been revived a quarter-century ago, and, since then, it had made its journey along the Danube Valley just once a month. The reason for such picayune service was that it was no longer a train of convenience—it was now a train of sybaritic luxury.

As it made its way through Bavaria, Austria, Serbia, Slovakia, and Hungary to Romania, it served the finest cuisines and wines, each according to the country it was passing through. No longer trying to fulfill the need for an "express train," it proceeded leisurely along the Danube Valley so that passengers could enjoy to the fullest, the magnificent panoramas of mountains, forests, lakes, and rivers. The ultimate in modern technology provided a smooth ride as it wound along the valley of the Danube River, so smooth that no feeling of motion was apparent.

It was a voyage for food lovers, wine lovers, and, well, lovers, including those of ancient trains and spectacular scenery. It was an experience for those who like to enjoy the indulgences of life and those who love to be pampered. The pictures in the brochure showed a massive green-and-gold monster with enormous wheels and a smokestack belching real smoke. It was a reincarnation of the legendary days of train travel when spies, counts, Queen's messengers, anarchists, and courtesans crisscrossed Europe on nefarious errands and mysterious missions.

Behind today's façade was a closed world of every luxury, comfort, and convenience modern ingenuity could devise. It was the kind of world that I always enjoyed though it was often beyond my reach. The times when it was within my reach, however, were when I was working—and I was working now.

This reception at the Four Seasons was hosted by the DS Bahn, the *Donau Schnellzug Bahn* or Danube Express Railway, before the dinner so that the passengers could get acquainted. Waiters in impossibly white uniforms carried around trays of *Sekt*, the German champagne, fizzing and sparkling.

Erich Brenner, president of the DS Bahn, greeted me after my ticket and credentials had been checked.

"Welcome, welcome, a thousand times welcome! I am delighted you can join us. This is a truly historic occasion and the DS Bahn is pleased that you can share it with us!"

He was big and beefy, as are so many Germans. I had learned that it is not fat that makes them that way but muscle. He had a large but aristocratic face and silvery hair. He squeezed my hand with a genuine sincerity.

"I'm very glad to be here," I told him. "I have been looking forward to this. I have always wanted to ride the Danube Express, but I didn't expect to be so lucky as to be present on its twenty-fifth anniversary."

"We have been preparing for this great day for some time. Now it is finally here. Tomorrow, we set off on our marvelous journey!" He caught sight of someone past me. "Let me introduce you. Herr Vollmer!" he called.

Gerhardt Vollmer was prematurely white-haired but had a skier's tan, a firm jaw, and the look of a businessman who would be tough in a negotiation. He smiled, showing good white teeth, and Brenner said, "Herr Vollmer made the decision to join us quite recently, did you not, Herr Vollmer?" To me, he said, "Herr Vollmer is with the *Nord Deutscher Energie.*"

I had heard the name. They were one of the leading suppliers of energy in Europe, with electrical power plants, oil refineries, and liquid natural gas tankers. Based in Germany near Hamburg, they had offices and operations in several other countries.

Herr Vollmer gave me a firm handshake. He addressed both of us as he said, "Yes, my decision was recent—that was because the need arose for me to attend a meeting in Costanza on the Black Sea. I require a couple of days of reviewing documents in order to prepare for the meeting, so when our travel department suggested the Danube Express, I agreed very quickly."

"And," interjected Brenner in his bluff, hearty manner, "an aux-
iliary reason came to mind, is that not so, Herr Vollmer?"

The German nodded. "We often transport heavy equipment used
in oil drilling, and we may soon conclude a contract with the Danube Express for that service. I can tie up a few loose ends on this
journey."

Erich Brenner nodded emphatically. "Yes, we are not only a luxury train service, we have routine transportation capabilities, too.
So," he went on, "this trip could turn out to have far-reaching
consequences, could it not?"

Vollmer gave a rueful laugh. "The word leaked out a few days
ago, yes, so now everyone knows." He must have caught the blank
look on my face, for he explained, "Exploration in the Black Sea of
the offshore potential for a high grade of oil has been bringing us
extraordinary results. The meeting I am to attend could—should it
have the success we all hope for—have the consequence of making
Germany independent of Middle East oil."

"I certainly wish you success in that case," I told him, and Herr
Brenner endorsed my sentiment wholeheartedly.

"We will be talking later," Vollmer said to Brenner. "We need to
establish your open capacity for the next three months." He shook
hands with me again. "A pleasure to meet you, and I am sure we
will have an opportunity to chat again."

"I certainly hope so," I said, and Vollmer left. Herr Brenner was
already waving to bring over another passerby.

"It is important you meet everyone on the train. This is Paolo
Conti, he is with the *European Wine Journal*. Reporter-at-Large—
isn't that your title, Paolo?"

Conti was tall, and, though the polite term was lean, he was
skinny. He had that haughty look that comes so naturally to many
Italians, inherited probably from Roman ancestors who had con-
quered Europe and part of Africa and Asia, looking down their noses
at unkempt and inferior races clad in animal skins and waving
wooden spears.

When he smiled, though, the haughtiness disappeared, and he

greeted me as if he really was glad to meet me. His proud, dark eyes were friendly and the high cheekbones suggested breeding and not arrogance. He was probably in his forties but with the touch of world-weariness that made him look older. His sleek black hair was abundant, and his smile showed strong white teeth.

"This journey will make a great story for the *Journal*," I told him.

"It will indeed. I did a story some years ago and described the vineyards we passed as we cruised by on the river. Since then, many of them have grown in significance and several fine vintages have been produced."

"And tomorrow's great journey will see the production of many more, no doubt," Erich Brenner said. A fleeting look was exchanged between the two of them, and I wondered what Brenner meant by the remark. Before I could ask, however, Conti was excusing himself to talk to a couple, and Brenner was introducing me to Dr. Richard Stolz.

"He will be our physician on this trip," Brenner said. "We always have an eminent physician accompany us—in a professional capacity, of course."

"An invitation which I, for one, am pleased to accept," said Dr. Stolz. "The twenty-fifth anniversary of the Danube Express is an opportunity few would refuse." He was gray-haired, and his face was gaunt and lined, but he might have been younger than his appearance suggested. He was sharp-eyed, though, and his manner was youthful.

"I took the journey on this train from Vienna to Bucharest many years ago," the doctor went on. "It was an experience I shall never forget."

"You may have to replace the memory with this journey." Erich Brenner smiled.

He went to bring to us an elderly American couple for introductions. Mr. and Mrs. Stanton Walburg from Cincinnati were inveterate travelers, we soon learned. They had "done" the Amazon, the Alps, Alice Springs, and Alaska, and, they went on to add, the Serengeti, the Middle East, and Madagascar. The list would have been longer, but Erich Brenner adroitly steered them to our impending journey, which he maintained would eclipse all others.

"Now this young lady—I don't know." He broke off to wave toward us a svelte young woman who was passing by with an empty glass she seemed eager to refill.

"Allow me, mademoiselle," he said gallantly, and, with a practiced gesture, beckoned a waiter with a bubbling bottle.

As he poured, Brenner introduced himself, then the Walburgs and me. "And you are—?" he invited the woman.

"Elisha Tabor. I am Hungarian. I am returning to Budapest."

"On the Danube Express?" questioned Mrs. Walburg. "I thought you young people preferred flying."

Elisha Tabor was just tall enough to avoid the description of "petite," but she had a slim, trim figure, black hair, and bright, alert eyes. "I fly a lot, but this is business—I am with a publishing house."

She had the autocratic air that so many East Europeans possess, and she tossed her hair back carelessly, regarding us with a raised chin.

"Now here is a man I know," said Erich Brenner, who was tireless in keeping track of almost everyone in the room. He beckoned the man passing to join us. The man was lean and spare and one of those individuals who project restless energy. He had long hair that he kept flicking back and a long face with a lugubrious expression.

"Herman Friedlander," said Erich Brenner, "the conductor of the Swabian State Symphony Orchestra."

The musician, who wore a slightly sad expression, acknowledged each of us in turn when Brenner did the introductions.

"We heard Ozawa last month in St. Petersburg, Russia," said Mrs. Walburg. "He was wonderful."

"His tonality," stated Friedlander in a grating voice, "is not consistent. I hope he didn't conduct Brahms."

Mrs. Walburg looked to her husband for support.

"He did Brahms," confirmed Mr. Walburg.

"A mistake," declared Friedlander. "He should never do Brahms."

The Walburgs looked nonplussed—surely a rare occasion for them. Friedlander warmed to his theme.

"I have told him many times—'Seiji,' I have said, 'don't play Brahms,' just as his teacher told Brahms, 'You could be a great pianist one day, Johannes, if you will only stop composing.' He didn't listen to his teacher, and Seiji doesn't listen to me."

The Walburgs nodded uncomfortably, but the diplomatic Karl Brenner rescued them. "Tell me, Herman," he asked the conductor, "have you talked to Herr Schaeffer?"

Friedlander brightened perceptibly. "No, is he on this journey?"

"He wanted to be," said Brenner, turning to the rest of us. "Herr Schaeffer is one of our directors and is considering having Herman here write a piece of music entitled *The Danube Express Symphony*."

"I must find him," said Friedlander, and promptly set off on his quest.

Brenner, the indefatigable friendship-broker, was about to detach the Walburgs and introduce them to a couple with unmistakable Australian accents, probably instigating a clash of travel reminiscences that could reach epic proportions. He was thwarted by waiters walking around striking wooden gongs with padded hammers and emitting three notes. This was presumably a Swabian way of announcing that dinner was about to be served.

I promptly approached Miss Tabor and asked her if I could have the pleasure of escorting her into the dining room. She gave me an imperious look that seemed about to tell me that she could find her own way there but she relented and actually accepted with a slight smile.

My gallantry was not rewarded, for the tables had place settings and name plates embossed in gold on a mahogany panel. She found her table at once, and I had to search further.

I was at a table with Helmut Lydecker, who described himself as a salesman; Irena Koslova, an attractive young Romanian woman who gave the reason for her presence as "something I have always wanted to do"; a small dapper Frenchman called Henri Larouge, who was associated with one of the organizations providing the train's food; and a Hungarian girl with reddish hair and a calm, serene air who introduced herself as Talia Svarovina.

The meal began with three "dollhouse dishes," as the Germans call them. A liver dumpling, the size of a marble, was accompanied by a few shreds of sauerkraut. A quail egg was larger, but only by about a millimeter. A teaspoon of mayonnaise with a distinct tang of lemon lay artistically over it although its cohort was another tea-spoon of potato salad. It was heated and was made in the German (South German) style, with brown cubes of bacon, olive oil, and vinegar.

The third item was a Wiener schnitzel, a miniscule sausage, half the size of a little finger (a very small female little finger) and it was flanked, as if by two guards, with a microscopic slice of fried potato on either side.

Each came on a separate segment of one large plate. Each was delicious in its own way, and each could be ingested in one mouth-ful, though I noticed that most guests made that mouthful last as long as possible.

"Dollhouse indeed," commented the lady on my left. She was the Hungarian girl, Talia Svarovina.

From then on, dishes were closer to normal size, although, as the ornately printed menu informed us, we were having six courses. In fact, the portions were small by German standards, but that managed to be balanced by an extremely high quality.

A clear asparagus soup came next. In it floated white truffle shav-ings, and I detected marjoram and chervil among the flavorings. Then came trout poached in champagne. Trout is very popular in Germany and the rainbow trout, introduced from America many years ago, is the most favored.

Everyone at the table approved heartily of this dish, and the Frenchman, Henri Larouge, said, "I must find out where they get their trout—this is really exceptional." The Romanian woman, Irena

Koslova, leaned across the table. "That woman at the next table—do you all recognize her?"

Helmut Lydecker, the self-described salesman, said, "I thought I did—but then I wasn't sure." He didn't look like a salesman. Was it because he was too well dressed? I wondered, but then I told myself that maybe he was a very successful one. He would have to be, traveling on this train.

We all studied the woman whom Irena had pointed out. She was stunning and certainly looked as if she must be somebody. She had an exotic appearance with high cheekbones, long almond eyes, and a pouting, irresistible mouth. She was dazzling the others at her table and was undoubtedly the center of attraction.

"She must be somebody prominent," said Henri Larouge. If he had had a mustache, he would have been preening it.

The woman was also attracting attention from other tables, and it was then that I noticed that the woman on my left, the Hungarian Talia Svarovina, was finishing her fish and not joining in the adulation.

"Don't you think she is very striking?" I asked her.

She dissected a piece of trout and put half of it in her mouth. She looked carelessly at the next table. After giving the woman there the briefest of glances, she returned to the enjoyment of her meal.

"I suppose she is," she said, then, aware that her disregard was about to promote argument, added, "Yes, she is striking." She continued to eat. Lydecker looked at her, then at me, and shrugged.

Talia disposed of the last of the trout, pursued a slice of potato across her plate, and dispatched it. She laid down her knife and fork.

"She's Magda Malescu," she said matter-of-factly.

"Really!" Henri Larouge had finished his course and was able to devote his full attention to ogling the woman.

"Of course!" Lydecker said.

"I've seen her on the stage many times!" said Irena.

"And in films," added Larouge. "She was in that wonderful one recently, *Forgotten Dreams*."

"I saw that," said Lydecker. "Her acting has not improved."

Braised lamb with rutabagas followed. The rutabaga is sometimes described as a Swede turnip and has lost popularity in many countries though it is still widely eaten in Germany.

The roast duck that came next had skin as crackly as phyllo, while the meat was juicy and flavorful. It came with timbales of Savoy cabbage, and these had leeks, carrots, onions, and celery streaked through them.

Throughout the meal, German wines had been served. First, there was a Rheingau from the Hattenheimer Mannberg vineyard. This is situated on a parallel with the middle of Canada, but this northern location does not pose the climatic problems one might suppose. Most Rheingau wines are descended from Riesling, and centuries of production and experience lay behind it—from as far back as the Romans. We had another Rheingau wine from the Rauenthaler vineyard, a delicate but mouth-filling white wine that lingered on the palate with a hint of fresh honey.

I was curious to see what wines would accompany the lamb and the duck, which I knew were coming up. The reason for this was that I had a friend who lived in the Black Forest area of Germany and every time I visited him, he would say, "I have a great new vineyard for you to visit." We would go there, and after a glass or two of white wine in the vineyard's tasting room, we would be served a glass of red.

The reason for this ritual was a more or less casual and possibly reckless remark I had once made to him to the effect that Germany does not produce a good red wine. We had many wonderful visits and drank many excellent wines, but never once had a really good red wine—and Eber, always determined to prove me wrong, reluctantly had to agree each time.

Here at the Four Seasons, they wisely avoided the problem and served Palatinate wines—that is, wines from the Pfalz region of Germany. The orchards there are full of southern fruit such as figs, peaches, and pears, and debate persists as to whether the soil influences the wines produced. Pfalz wines have more flavor and fuller body than other German wines and have long been the preferred accompaniment to the abundant game of the local forests. At least, I was relieved that a *Spatburgunder* had not been served. It is made from the Pinot Noir grape and, though it is drinkable, it is little more than that.

Two desserts were served. First came a poppy-seed ice cream. The trick to making it is to grind the poppy seeds, which must be absolutely fresh, to a fine and feathery texture. It was prepared to perfection. After it came small quince tarts with ginger sorbet.

As coffee was being served, Lydecker groaned audibly.

"Now comes the speech."

CHAPTER TWO

The advantage of speed as offered by jet aircraft was enjoyed by several decades of travelers before nostalgia set in, demanding a return to the alternates: of comfort and the sybaritic luxury and service offered by the train."

Erich Brenner, as president of the *Donau Schnellzug Bahn*, opened his after-dinner speech with these bold and challenging words.

"Numerous rail networks are enjoying great popularity throughout Europe. The Eurostar goes under the English Channel to link London and Paris and make it possible to live in one and visit the other in the same day. The TGV connects Paris with most major cities in France. Cisalpino links Milan with major cities in Germany and Switzerland. Talgo and Ave are Spain's high-speed trains, the X2000 links the bigger cities in Sweden, and ICE (Inter City Express) connects most German urban centers.

"Planners of transportation systems have found these to be a practical answer in linking city center to city center at almost two hundred miles an hour."

He paused, and his tone changed to one of reproof.

"So much for speed and convenience. They can be appreciated by the business traveler and by tourists with limited time at their disposal. But those with a less crowded schedule and those who love luxury and service can be accommodated, too.

"The famous Blue Train across South Africa, the Palace on Wheels that crosses the great plains of northern India and goes through the world of the Maharajahs, the Royal Scotsman that passes castle after castle as it puffs north through Scotland, and the Orient

Express, still thought of as filled with spies and revolutionaries while making its way from Paris to Istanbul—all of these great journeys of the past have been revived."

Erich Brenner paused again and surveyed his audience with an air that was prescient of a dramatic statement to follow.

"There is one other great journey—the greatest of them all—and it is the train that you are about to embark upon tomorrow.

"It is the legendary Danube Express.

"We offer you beautiful carriages, the ultimate in luxurious accommodation, delectable cuisine, superb wines, and Old World personalized service. The train is stabilized for your comfort twenty-four hours a day, and we make it possible for you to view the most historic sights along the Danube Valley.

"The most modern technology has been applied throughout the design of this train," Erich Brenner continued, "and you will find that you are hardly aware of motion. The very finest stabilizing and gyroscopic devices made by Hirschberg *und* Schneider of Stuttgart—the world leaders in this field—have been used. They were developed for the new generation of Zeppelins now being built in Germany. You will be as stable and secure when walking around as you are in your own home."

He beamed at his attentive audience. "You will not detect even the faintest ripple on the surface of your glass of wine. And now—please enjoy your coffee. Liqueurs are being brought around on the trolleys, and you will find the choice almost inexhaustible. So, ladies and gentlemen, I will see you all in the morning, and I shall accompany you on the most wondrous journey of your life."

The assembly applauded. Erich Brenner sat down, smiling. "I think I'll have an early night," said Irena Koslova. She finished her coffee and left. I saw the Walburgs rising to leave, too.

"I have to call our office in Tokyo," Lydecker said. "They'll be hard at work at this time—or should be." He left, and the red-haired Hungarian miss, Talia Svarovina said, "I've had a long day, too. See you all tomorrow."

Henri Larouge shrugged. "I have some discussions to make with the purchasing manager here at the Kempinski." That left me all alone. I looked over at the table where the glamorous stage star from Budapest, Magda Malescu, had been joined by people from other tables. Some apparently knew her, and others looked like theater fans. I made a mental note to make her acquaintance tomorrow on the train, when she would be more accessible.

A stroll after a meal like that was a measure of reparation that I always tried to make. I went out, through the lobby and out on to the *Charlottenstrasse*.

The Danube Express—what an experience it was going to be! Erich Brenner's description of the train had intrigued me. As a boy, I had always been fascinated by trains. They were such a powerful symbol of an earlier era and represented spectacular technical achievements in a time when technology was not as vigorous and rampant as today.

The lure was too strong. I turned in the direction of the *Hauptbahnhof*, the main railway station from which we were to depart the next day.

The thirty-minute walk was invigorating, the weather mild and pleasant, and Munich is a city that is friendly to pedestrians.

Bombing during World War II had destroyed the earlier station, and the present building had replaced it in the early 1950s. Railway stations throughout Europe are enormous structures, and those in Germany have always been among the most impressive. This rebuild had resulted in an edifice with a nondescript exterior that was, however, redeemed by its size.

The interior was entirely different, a temple dedicated to the ultimate in modern technology, with polished aluminum, stainless steel, glass, and marble everywhere.

Two stories of shops and restaurants make it an agreeable place to spend some time before your train is due to depart. Not that such time ever exceeded the schedule—German trains run on time to a degree that is equaled only by the Swiss. Large clocks on all the platforms tick away the minutes and the 10:30 train will leave for sure before the minute hand reaches 31.

The soaring, girdered roofs were so high they were almost out of sight. The clean and tidy platforms had colorful displays showing the makeup of every train with red, blue, and green indicating passenger coaches, freight cars, and postal wagons, and identifying coach and seat numbers. If you had a reservation, you could see at a glance exactly where you would be sitting.

I made my way to *Gleich 37*, the platform specially reserved for the Danube Express. A uniformed soldier with an automatic rifle stood on duty near the entrance, and a guard at the barrier stopped me.

"I have a ticket on the Danube Express tomorrow," I said. "I wondered if I could take a look at the train. I have never seen it."

"Do you have your ticket?" he asked. Fortunately, I did. He examined it carefully. "And identification?" I gave him my passport, which he read carefully, turning over page after page.

"*Alles im Ordnung*," he told me, an expression you hear widely in Germany. "Everything in order" it means, and it expresses German satisfaction that everything is, indeed, in order and that all is well; all is as mandated and nothing is being allowed to disturb the methodical and systematic way in which Germans like life to run.

He handed me my documents and waved me through. I walked onto the almost empty platform and there it stood—the Danube Express.

I felt as if I had stepped decades into the past. The green-and-gold monster brought back instant memories of a model train I once had. Some lights were on, and a greenish glow from low-voltage halogen floodlights made the Express look unreal. Brass glinted—rails, panels, fittings, and handles. I moved a few paces closer. A voice from behind me asked in German, "Can I help you?"

An elderly man in a one-piece working suit was there. He had a lined face, and, as he came toward me, I noticed a limp. He was probably one of the many who had survived the ordeal of the Russian Front and still bore the wounds.

I explained that I was to be a passenger on the train tomorrow and his face lit up. "Ah, the twenty-fifth anniversary! It will be a famous day!"

I told him of my boyhood fascination with trains, and he gestured to the metal creature as proudly as any father would indicate his child. "I have worked on her since she was built. She is a wonderful creation, is she not?"

I agreed and we strolled closer.

"The locomotive is based on the Laterus design."

"It's like the English Buddicomb, isn't it?"

His face widened in a smile. "Ah, you know trains! Yes, in those days, most trains were copies of either the Furst or the Buddicomb. This one is similar to both, but it resembles most closely the model that was selected for the maiden voyage of the original Danube Express in 1878."

"Those driving wheels," I said. "They are immense."

"Two meters in diameter," he said. The wheels stood well above my head. "The originals weighed twenty tons each. They have been redesigned and now use light alloys instead of cast iron, but they— like the rest of the train—resemble the original almost exactly. One of the outstanding features is the outside cylinders."

"I was just marveling at those; they're enormous, too."

"Yes, they're inclined at an angle, you'll notice. They reduce friction on the bearings, which was a common cause of failure in earlier trains—it caused fracture of the crank axles."

"I don't see any smoke," I complained. "Surely you've started to stoke up the boilers already?"

He grinned. "Oh, you'll see smoke sure enough. It will look real, too, but it won't bother your lungs. As for boilers, well"—he smiled—"they aren't necessary with electromagnetic motors."

"And I suppose they're silent?"

"Almost—but don't worry about that. We have a recording from one of the trains of 1935, and we play that at a low volume level."

"Including the steam whistle?"

"Oh, of course, wouldn't be authentic without it."

"Ingenious," I conceded. "Does the train run on a special track?" I asked.

"Special tracks are only necessary for the very-high-speed trains. That has been one of the factors which made high-speed train travel a long time in coming—it was necessary to lay all-new rails capable of handling the extremely high stresses placed on them."

"So the Danube Express can use existing railbeds?"

"Yes, and these are widely distributed all over Europe. The Danube Express does not exceed a hundred kilometers an hour"—that was about sixty-five miles an hour—"and even European railbeds that are nearly a hundred years old are adequate. We have laid new rails on these, and they conform to German Standard D-156, a special steel with superior properties."

I looked up and down the platform. It was deserted except for two indistinct figures down at the far end. The greenish glow of the halogen lights was almost subdued by the cavernous darkness that soared up to the roof.

"This will all look very different in the morning, I suppose?"

He nodded. "*Ja*, very different. The mechanical and electronic checks on the train and the track have just been completed. The food and drink supplies will arrive about 1:00 A.M." He pointed down to the end of the platform. "The cargoes will be loaded in a few minutes. We are told the guards will come with them and stay here until the train departs."

"Cargoes? Guards?"

"*Ja*," he said unhelpfully.

"Must be valuable cargoes—what are they?"

He shrugged. "I don't know. We have one coach—an armored vault—it is where the mail is carried."

"Can you compete with airmail?"

"We carry parcels and heavier freight. The Danube Express is a secure way to carry valuable items—much safer than a plane and far safer than road. Alas, hijackings on the Autobahn are not unknown."

He waved a hand. "Here comes the first cargo."

Two uniformed men carrying automatic rifles walked onto the platform, looking all around them with practiced movements. A small, hand-drawn truck came after them, and two more armed guards followed. The truck was operated by a cable and had on it what looked like a cubic steel box, about two feet on a side.

The man operating the control maneuvered the truck into position alongside a coach, which I now noticed was shorter than the others. He took out a key and unlocked first one door, then another inside it. The guards helped him place it inside the coach.

Two guards and the man handling the small truck left the platform while the other two guards stood, one on either side of the door. Within a minute, the truck and the guards reappeared. This time a larger cargo was on the truck. It was over six feet long and about two feet wide and two feet deep.

The man and I watched as they loaded that, too. The man with the truck carefully locked both doors, and one of the guards checked each to make sure it was secure.

"Whatever is in those boxes certainly must be valuable," I commented.

The other nodded. I gathered he knew nothing more than he had told me, and, even if he had, he was not going to divulge it.

I thanked him for the information he had given me, and he wished me a safe journey, concluding with the traditional Bavarian greeting and farewell, "*Gruss Gott.*"

As I walked off the platform, I was speculating over the nature of the cargoes we were taking with us tomorrow. The first box was cubic in shape and could contain anything.

It was the second box that caused me apprehension. Its size and its shape were associated with one type of container and one alone.

It looked exactly like a coffin.

CHAPTER THREE

I know that coffins are not lethal weapons and that their threat is merely symbolic. I suppose my superstitious fear of them arises from an incident a few years ago in Italy.

I was flying from Padua in the north of Italy to Palermo in Sicily, and found myself seated next to an Italian lady who spent the first part of the flight looking out the window and sniffing quietly into a handkerchief.

I did not want to intrude on her grief, but national volubility soon emerged, and she apologized for her tears and explained. She was one of a group of over thirty ladies of Palermo. They had been on a pleasure trip in the north, and one of their members had died suddenly. Her body was in a coffin that was now in the hold of this plane, as her friends insisted that she would want to be buried in Palermo.

When I extended her my sympathy on the loss of her friend, she explained that her grief was more than that. She, and all of her friends, firmly believed that they would never arrive in Palermo, as a coffin on board was bad luck.

Trying not to scoff, I assured her that her fears were unfounded— just as the captain announced that due to engine problems, we would have to land in Bologna. After some time on the ground, the plane was declared fit to continue. My companion shook her head. More was to come, she assured me.

Fifteen minutes after takeoff, we were told that Palermo was fogged in and not likely to clear. We would have to make an emergency landing in Perugia. We circled the Perugia airport for a seemingly endless time, and it was only when we landed that we saw the blazing wreckage of a previous aircraft being dragged off the runway. A near miss, my companion told me. Fate had intended that should have been us.

Our crew had now reached its duty hours limit and left. No other crews were there, and no other aircraft were available. We bussed to the Al Italia office in town, where we learned that the few hotels were full. I tried the two car rental offices, neither had any cars. Bed-and-breakfast places, youth hostels, even the Salvation Army were full. No more trains were scheduled for that evening. My path crossed that of other groups of passengers from our flight, all on similar quests. The ladies of Palermo were among them, and my companion was there, reminding me that she had told me so. Soon all the taxis in town were filled or gone off duty. All the restaurants were closed by then.

The rest of the night was a miserably uncomfortable one, but we left the next day on another aircraft, and it was that night that the headline news concerned the plane that had taken us to Perugia. It, too, had crashed, killing the entire crew. Perhaps it was not sufficient reason to be concerned about the coffin on board the Danube Express, but I could not dismiss the memory entirely.

The star herself was crossing the platform the next morning as I arrived. Magda Malescu looked glamorous in a light gray, pin-striped pantsuit. I saw her close-up for the first time and marveled at her high, Slavic cheekbones, big wide-set eyes, and flawless complexion. What was less apparent was how she managed to project that aura of stardom. It hung on her like a cloak.

It was more than the flashing eyes, the magnificent carriage, the opulent figure, and the dazzling smile—but the secret eluded me. It was far more than all of those, and, whatever it was—Magda Malescu had it in abundance.

I managed to be next in line to board, as it seemed we were both in the same coach. She flashed me a smile, and I introduced myself.

"I didn't have the opportunity to meet you last night," I added.

"You are going to Budapest?" she asked. Her voice was a little less sultry and inviting than it was on the screen, but only a little.

"I'm going on to Bucharest," I told her. "I hope to spend more time in Budapest on the way back. Budapest has always been one of my favorite cities."

"Ah, you know it then?"

"I have been there a few times. I find it to have all the charm that is expected of Vienna but that is sadly not there anymore. Budapest has not lost it yet."

She smiled in full agreement. I was speaking the truth although I knew that she was passionate about it as her home and birthplace.

"We must talk further on the train," she said, retrieving her passport and papers. I could understand that officials invariably found them in order.

We puffed out of the Munich *Hauptbahnhof* on time.

The entry into my compartment confirmed the most extravagant claims of the DS Bahn. The compartment walls and car doors were made of teak-and-mahogany paneling with inlaid marquetry. A deep armchair was covered in soft Spanish leather and embossed in silver patterning. The roller blinds were augmented by flowered-damask drapes held by silk cords and tassels of gold thread. En suite was the bathroom area with Italian marble tub and basin and gold knobs and fittings. Light fixtures were of Bohemian crystal, and the carpets appeared to be from Hyderabad.

My table companions from the evening before were either on the platform or boarding other coaches, and I saw several of those I had met during the reception. All of them, like me, were sufficiently concerned about getting established in the compartment that was to be their home for the next days that they had no time for fraternizing.

Once that was accomplished, however, several stood by the windows and watched the delightful rolling countryside of Bavaria stream by with its occasional slender church spire, its herds of fat brown cows, and its impossibly neat farms.

The design of the coaches was such that a corridor ran along one side and the compartments along the other side. One could view the passing scene through the windows in the compartment or go into the corridor and view the other side.

This truly was a train for the seasoned traveler, since reaching the destination was not the main reason for the journey—it was the journey itself.

After unpacking, I walked along the corridor. The lack of tilt was immediately noticeable, and it was clear that the claims made for the efficiency of the stabilizing system were not exaggerated. The electromagnetic engines were as silent as they were alleged to be— at least, I assumed that the faint swooshing noise was a sound track to allay the fears of passengers unaccustomed to silent travel.

I walked along the corridor. At the end, a glass door swung open at my approach, and I was able to go through into the next coach with none of the jerking and swaying that I recalled from early trains. Passage from one coach to the next had been a minor adventure in itself in those days, especially that glimpse beneath one's feet of the speeding ground beneath.

The next coach was the lounge. I had thoroughly digested the literature on the Danube Express and learned that this coach was originally called The Gentlemen's Smoking Room. In this modern era, ladies as well as gentlemen not only smoke but receive equal rights in all other areas. Still, the lounge looked much as it always had in its gentlemanly days, with leather fauteuils and footstools, bookcases with the day's newspapers, up-to-date magazines, and a section of travel literature describing the countries being traversed. It was all very much like a superior London club.

Helmut Lydecker greeted me with a nod. He was glancing through a magazine but also looking out the window at the countryside, which unraveled like a screen travelogue.

"First trip on this train?" I asked, wanting to break the ice.

"No," he said. "I have made it many times."

I thought he was going to dismiss me with that terse answer, but he continued, "It is a much more civilized way of going from capital to capital in this part of the world than flying."

"It's certainly a very comfortable way," I agreed. "You must travel a lot in your business."

"Yes, to the bigger cities, especially Munich, Prague, Vienna, Budapest . . ."

"Interesting," I said. "Your business is only in the bigger cities then?"

"Yes."

He was a big man, with a strong face beginning to develop jowls. His manner was authoritative, as if he were used to directing people. He would be a tough leader, I thought, not easy to work for, but he would get the job done.

"What kind of business?" I asked.

"Sales." He looked out of the window almost dismissively, but I kept looking at him, waiting for a fuller reply.

"I sell—" He paused. "I sell illusions."

Whatever reply I expected, that did not relate at all.

"Illusions," I repeated. "They must be difficult to sell."

He shook his head. "Not at all. People are gullible. They love to be deceived—they love fantasy and escape from reality."

"And how do you deceive them?"

He smiled, a thin smile that was not quite a sneer.

"Very easily—very easily indeed."

Well, at a certain point, you don't press any more. It was obvious that Lydecker had told me as much as he intended to tell me. He was not the kind of man to be coerced into explaining how and why he "sold illusions."

To emphasize his disinclination, he changed the subject by nodding to the scene outside the window. "I was born out there," he said.

"You are German?"

"Yes. I was born near Donauworth."

"North of Augsburg?"

"Yes." He sounded surprised. "You know it?"

"I visited Augsburg once, a very attractive town."

He grunted. "The village I was born in was not attractive."

"Most villages in the south of Germany have a rural charm. They look that way to a visitor anyway. Perhaps if you were born in one, you see it through different eyes."

"I have no pleasant memories of it. I left the village as soon as I could." He turned from his view of the passing countryside. "And you?"

"I'm in the food business. I'm a food-finder—I look for rare spices, unusual foods, substitutes for foods that become rare, and I advise on foods for banquets with certain themes."

"You can make a living by that?"

Germans have a direct way of asking questions that often sound rude or uncivil when translated into another language. It has always been my belief that this is merely a restriction imposed by the syntax of the German language and does not necessarily imply rudeness on the part of the user. I gave Lydecker the benefit of the doubt.

"Yes, I can. Most important though is that I enjoy it. I love food and the history of food."

"This train has a reputation for its cuisine," he said.

"So I believe, and I'm looking forward to it."

I expressed the hope of talking to him again and moved on. Maybe next time, I could dig a little deeper and find out just how Lydecker "sold illusions."

Erich Brenner was making his official rounds, earnest in his desire to ensure that everyone was comfortable and satisfied. I was telling him that I was as another man came along the corridor. "I must introduce you," Brenner said.

The other stopped at Brenner's raised hand. "This is Karl Kramer, our security chief on the DS Bahn."

Kramer was unmistakably German, with almost impossibly blond hair and Aryan features. His eyes were bright blue but cool and assessing. His build and bearing were stiff and military in manner. *He must make evildoers shiver in their boots,* I thought.

His handshake was cold and hard. His eyes bored into me as if he were reading my mind. "Ah, yes," he said in perfect English. "I have seen your name on the passenger list. You go to Bucharest, is that not so?"

I agreed that it was so.

"It will be a good journey," he said as if he were ordaining it to be that way. From the look of him, I had no doubt that it would take a person of exceptional powers to affect the journey any other way.

We went our opposite directions. I stopped to view the scenery. We were approaching Burgenland, a little border region between East and West. It had once been part of the Austro-Hungarian Empire and is the beginning of the *puszta*, the large flat steppe that reaches almost to Budapest. It is an area that has been bitterly contested over the centuries, in fact, ever since tribal days. Many battles have been fought there through the long years when it was part of the country known as Pannonia, through the times of the Ottoman Empire, and clear up to this century.

This is an agricultural region and is locally referred to as Vienna's vegetable garden. Fruit accounts for much of the produce, and it is a renowned grape region, with an ideal climate for wine making. The gently rolling countryside enabled one to see considerable distances, and, in many directions, vineyards covered the landscape.

I became aware of someone approaching. It was the Romanian girl, Irena Koslova. "So at last," I said to her, "you are doing something you have always wanted to do."

She gave me a look of surprise. "Last night," I reminded her, "you said this was something you had always wanted to do."

"Yes, I did." She had a delightful smile. In fact, she was very pretty, with those facial characteristics that are so typical of many Eastern European women—extremely feminine yet self-reliant and capable. She had a small but proud nose, soft gray eyes, a flawless complexion.

"You live in Bucharest?" I asked.

"Near it—but I was born in the city."

We rolled majestically through a station, and the locals were on hand to gawk and wave. MUHLDORF, the sign said, and flowers adorned the station buildings, while the flags of Germany and Austria fluttered in the breeze of our passing. Our steam whistle—or at least a very authentic recording of it—*beep-beeped* in salutation.

"So you're going home?" I asked her as the houses of the small town receded into the distance. On a road leading into Muhldorf, a truck piled with jugs of wine swayed under its load. Then we were out into the steppe again.

"I'm not sure I call it home," she said. "Not anymore."

I waited for elucidation of that cryptic remark but none was forthcoming. As I prepared another comment inviting explanation, she smiled. "I hope we can talk later," she said, and passed me.

"I hope so, too," I told her.

In the next coach, the corridor went past a sign that announced, COMMUNICATION CENTER. This was an area the size of three or four compartments and I tried the door. It was locked. A sign I hadn't noticed before proclaimed no admittance in three languages.

I recalled reading in the brochure on the Danube Express that it received information from a large number of sources, including satellites. Data on weather conditions, the track, the status of all the stations on the line ahead as well as readings on all of the electronic controls on the engine and the train came into the center. One could talk to anywhere in the world or receive messages, I remembered, but I supposed that such a vital center had to be secure.

We were traversing marshland, and, beyond, I could see the shimmer of a lake. I decided to retrace my steps and see what was at the other end of the train.

The Walburgs were on a similar reconnaissance, and we met in the corridor, exchanging greetings.

"We took the Glacier Express when we were in Switzerland in the spring," said Mrs. Walburg. "Have you ever been on it?"

I confessed that I had not.

"Some people take it and never see a thing," Mrs. Walburg stated.

"Why is that?" I felt obliged to ask.

"Fog," he said. "Can you imagine? A quarter of a million people take that train every year, and some of them see nothing because of the fog."

"We saw everything," his wife declared. "Rivers and lakes, waterfalls, castles, churches, forests—"

Her husband took up the account, "—gorges, high bridges, tunnels—"

"Ninety-one tunnels," Mrs. Walburg said. "I didn't like some of them. Too small."

"And the Matterhorn," her husband added. "We saw the Matterhorn. And just think, some poor people who took that train saw nothing because of the fog."

"I'm surprised," I told them. "The Swiss are very clever engineers. I would have thought they could figure a way around that problem."

"That's what I thought," Mr. Walburg said.

"We'd better get on," his wife said. "This counts as part of our walking for the day. We have to walk a mile every day," she told me, "three times up and down this train is nearly a mile."

Helmut Lydecker had gone when I walked through the lounge. A few passengers were absorbed in the scenery. We rolled along as smoothly as a billiard ball across a table. Not a tremor could be felt, and we climbed an incline with only a small decrease in speed. The engine appeared to have ample power in reserve.

Erich Brenner and the security chief, Karl Kramer, were coming toward me. They had evidently concluded their inspection tour.

"Everything under control?" I asked.

"Everything," Kramer said with a crisp nod.

There was a minor commotion behind me. Brenner and Kramer looked past me, and I turned. We all saw a man in the smart black uniform with red trim of the DS Bahn. The extraordinary thing about him was that he was running, running toward us.

Erich Brenner took a step forward. Karl Kramer was frowning

darkly, and it looked as if the unfortunate employee was to be strongly disciplined. Running was not an activity practiced by the highly trained staff of this august railroad.

He hurried to us. He was in his fifties and had probably been in the service of the railroad for many years, for I knew that most of the staff were longtime employees. His eyes were wide and alarmed. He was out of breath, part of which appeared to be due to his running but compounded more by excitement and stress.

"What is it, man?" snapped Kramer.

"She—she is dead!" the man gasped. He spluttered for more words, on the verge of hyperventilating.

"Who?" barked Erich Brenner. "Who are you talking about?"

"Fraulein Magda Malescu! She is dead! Murdered!"

CHAPTER FOUR

The moment of stunned silence that followed was the result of the thought that must be passing through the minds of Erich Brenner and Karl Kramer as it was through mine. The man with this astonishing news was coming from the rear of the train. Magda Malescu's compartment was in the forward part of the train. So how could he know?

Kramer recovered first. "How do you know this?" he snapped.

"I was passing the communication center when Thomas came out," stammered the man. "He told me this and said I was to tell you this personally—er, confidentially, he said. He did not wish to take a chance on a phone call."

He glanced at me as he said "confidentially," clearly aware that I ought not to be hearing this but just as clearly so shocked that rules had gone out of the window.

Kramer already had his phone out of his pocket. "I demanded a scrambled channel," he reminded Brenner icily, "but it was rejected."

Brenner's cool demeanor, shattered by the news concerning Malescu, was nonetheless resistant to Kramer's criticism. "We have customer relations to consider," he said, "and we cannot afford complaints that the Danube Express harbors spies and anarchists. First, there would be scrambled phones, next, we would have guards with automatic rifles, then they would insist on—no, no, this will not do!"

Kramer was already on the line. "Thomas? The news you gave to Ulbricht—no, no, don't tell me now, this line is not secure. I will be in your coach in a moment. Do not come out. Allow no one in. Speak to no one."

He banged the flap of the phone cover in place. "I will talk to him personally," he said, speaking to Brenner. "You should go to Malescu's compartment. Wait there for me." He strode off.

Brenner looked at me, uncertain. He didn't want me along, but neither did he want to send me away now that I had heard the news they were trying to conceal. He selected the lesser of two evils, setting off toward the front of the train, beckoning me to follow. He could keep an eye on me that way. I was as stunned and puzzled as either of them.

No one was in the corridor of the coach containing Malescu's and my compartments. We stopped at her door. I looked at it, but it gave away nothing. I looked at the window across the corridor from her door. I could see no cryptic message written with a finger on a steamy surface.

We did not have long to wait. Kramer appeared, approaching us rapidly with a long stride. He looked at Brenner, then rapped on the door.

No answer came, and he knocked again. Still no answer.

"You have a master key," Brenner said. Kramer gave him a look that said, "I know, I know." He took from his pocket a small wallet. He opened it, and a screen illuminated. On the number pad below the screen, he tapped in code numbers. He glanced at the number on Malescu's door, B-12, and entered it. From the wallet he pulled a cylindrical key no larger than a pencil and inserted it in the lock.

He turned the door handle and opened the door a few inches. "Fraulein Malescu!" he called. After waiting a moment, he pushed the door open slowly.

The layout of the compartment was essentially the same as mine but larger. We went into the "living room" first. It was decorated with vases of flowers, and the décor was notably more feminine. The actress was not in evidence.

Kramer led the way to the toilet and bathroom area. Nothing

there either. He turned to the bedroom. The door was closed. I thought he was going to knock again, but he turned the knob and opened the door wide.

The bed was not made, and a few female garments were strewn here and there. The closets were open and partly filled with clothes and shoes.

But a body? The compartment was empty.

Brenner grunted disbelief. Kramer went through the compartment again swiftly, but there were few places for a body to be hidden, and the search did not take him long.

The three of us stood and stared at each other.

"Where did this information come from?" Brenner asked.

"Thomas picked it up from the Budapest *Times*." Kramer was still searching the compartment with his eyes, trying to discern a hiding place.

"What did it say?" Brenner persisted.

"It said that Magda Malescu had been murdered in her compartment on the Danube Express. It also said that further details would follow later."

Brenner shook his head, bewildered. "Nothing seems unusual," he said.

"There is one thing . . ." I said.

Both looked at me.

"An aroma," I said. "I know that there is a smell of perfume in the air—that is what might be expected in the room of a famous actress. But there is also another aroma."

In my job as a food-finder, my senses of taste and smell have become developed well beyond normal levels. I didn't use this opportunity to mention that as it might trigger off second thoughts about my presence on the scene at all. It could come later. Right then, I had both men sniffing. It was Karl Kramer who was the first to nod.

"You are right. I smell it, too."

"I believe I do also," said Brenner, but I didn't know if he could smell it or if he didn't want to be left out.

Kramer and I moved around the room. Without any words, we had decided to trace the origin of the aroma. I was the first to pause by the table in the 'living' area of the compartment.

"It's strongest here."

Kramer came over, Brenner close behind. The sense of smell is the most ephemeral of man's senses. Aromas are difficult to put into words and almost impossible to communicate to others. A smell that is strong to one person may be undetectable to another. Different persons will rate them quite differently.

Kramer moved around the room, then came back. Brenner paused, not sure what he should do.

"Do you recognize it?" Kramer asked.

"Yes," I said. "Bitter almonds—prussic acid—cyanide."

Brenner exhaled loudly. Kramer said nothing, but his manner showed agreement.

After Brenner's initial expression of astonishment, he circled the table. "But where does it come from? We see no glasses, no bottles . . ."

The table was indeed empty. Kramer bent low, looking at the polished wood surface at an angle, searching for marks. He shook his head. He opened a cabinet built into the wall. It contained glasses of various kinds, but none showed signs of recent use. He went into the bathroom and came back.

"This is very puzzling."

He could say that again. I was about to make a further comment, but Brenner beat me to it.

"The door from the corridor was locked. You had to use your master key," he said to Kramer. "Where is the key that belongs to this compartment?"

A search revealed nothing.

———

Erich Brenner's instructions to me were absolute. "Do not say a word of this—not to anyone." The big, beefy president had wilted visibly under the strain, and it was understandable. A high-visibility crime such as this—whether it was murder or disappearance—could damage the reputation of the DS Bahn significantly.

Karl Kramer, on the other hand, grew in stature with every revelation. He became more determined, more resolute. His blondness seemed blonder and his Germanic attitude more pronounced. He was responding to the challenge.

"Act as if nothing has happened," he ordered. "We'll check the rest of the train manually, then we'll go through the compartment again."

The two of them stalked off, and, as I turned to go, too, another figure entered the corridor. It was Gerhardt Vollmer, the oil man. He looked at me, standing uncertainly in front of Magda Malescu's compartment door.

"What is it?" he asked. "What is wrong?"

"Why do you think something is wrong?"

He looked from me to the door. "I heard you and Kramer and Erich Brenner talking; you sounded alarmed."

I hesitated, not knowing what to say. I didn't doubt that Kramer would not want the word of either a death or a disappearance spread at this stage. Vollmer ended my indecision. He raised a fist to knock on Malescu's door.

I laid a restraining hand on his arm. "She's not in there," I said.

He lowered his fist. "Is that a cause for alarm?"

"We don't know yet," I said.

"You were in her compartment?"

"Yes, all three of us."

I wanted to make sure Vollmer knew I wasn't acting alone, but my words had the opposite effect. His eyes grew stern. "It must be serious for all three of you to go into her compartment."

"What did you want with her?" I asked, trying to reverse the initiative.

The question, surprisingly enough, disconcerted him although he covered it too late. I dived in with another question. "Do you know her?"

He could have told me to mind my own business, but I suppose he was associating me with Brenner and Kramer, so I appeared to have a modicum of authority.

"I did," he said in a lowered voice. "I did know her."

He looked again at the compartment door. "She's not in there, you say?"

"No, she is not."

"And you're looking for her?"

"That's right."

"Is that all?" He was getting accusatory again.

"As far as we know," I said, "until we find her."

He thought about that for a moment, then gave a brief nod and left me standing there.

It was lunchtime as we concluded yet another examination of the scene in the star's compartment. Before we began, I told Kramer and Brenner of my conversation with Gerhardt Vollmer.

"Vollmer says he knows her?" Kramer asked.

"He said so." The two of them digested that but made no further comment.

Our third search yielded no information that had not already become evident, and I headed for the restaurant coach looking as normal as I could.

I had been enchanted by my brief encounter with Magda Malescu and hoped desperately that she was safe, unlikely as that seemed. Yet how could she disappear on the Danube Express? Karl Kramer had selected two stewards and given them specific instructions to search the train without making it obvious. I had no doubt that it would be done with Teutonic thoroughness.

The restaurant car was sparkling and bright in the noonday sun that slanted in through the windows on the south side. The damask tablecloths were pristine white, the napkins were artistically folded in butterfly patterns, the cutlery glittered silver, and the glasses shone—they were made, I learned, from the finest Baccarat crystal.

I was a little early, and as I did not see anyone to join, I took a table alone. I did not mind on this occasion as I was still pondering the extraordinary event of the morning. I chose a green bean, leek, and red lettuce salad with warm onion and mustard dressing for the first course. It is a popular Bavarian starter. It was crisp and delicious and I followed that with *Kalbsleben Berliner Art,* calves' liver in the Berlin style. Berliners prepare the dish with onions and apples. It is simple in preparation and brings out the full taste of the liver.

Continuing to keep the meal light so as not to dull my mind, I finished the meal with mango slices in champagne. A half bottle of Piesporter from the Reinhold Haart vineyard in the Mosel-Saar-Ruwer region went very well with the liver, its barely discernible sweetness balancing its overall elegant dryness.

I was leaving the restaurant car as a waiter approached me and confirmed my identity. "Herr Kramer wishes to speak to you," he told me. "As soon as you complete your meal, he said. Coach Six, compartment J-4."

Was I the first passenger to be interrogated? I wondered. Was I under suspicion for being on the scene? The tough security chief was not wasting any time. I walked through several coaches on my way to Coach Six. Outside, the flat scenery persisted. Small farms with neat fences and old stone walls, vineyards covering acres, occasional vehicles, mainly farm trucks, tractors, and white-painted storage barns.

I wasn't looking forward to the grilling I was about to get from Karl Kramer. He looked as if he knew all the tricks of interrogation, although at least I had the satisfaction of knowing that he could hardly have a coach full of thumbscrews, dental forceps, and pointed tweezers—well, surely not on the Danube Express?

The swoosh of the train changed in tone, and I saw that we were traversing a bridge over a sizable river. No vessels were in sight, but a few fishermen sat immobile on the river bank, rods out over the water, which they obviously hoped teemed with fish.

I was stalling, pausing to note every detail. I walked on, though not rapidly. *Coach Seven, one more to go.* A couple passed me, smiling an acknowledgment as they went to lunch. A steward passed with a loaded tray—someone was not feeling companionable and was eating in the compartment.

I went on and knocked at J-4. A barked command told me to enter. The compartment was set up as an office. A large teak desk was the centerpiece, and Karl sat at it, studying a green folder. On the desk were two telephones, one black, one white, several other folders in various colors, a tray full of papers, and a beer stein filled with pens and pencils.

Two teak filing cabinets stood by the wall, and a fax machine and computer were on an adjacent desk. Two large document boxes were underneath it. The walls were unadorned, giving the compartment an austere look.

Kramer motioned to the only chair other than the one in which he was sitting. It faced him across the desk, and I took it. His attention returned to the open file before him.

"So you are a detective."

I groaned inwardly. This happens to me frequently. I am a food-finder, I seek out rare food ingredients, advise on the use of little-known food specialties, recommend menus for theme banquets, and suggest substitutes when delicacies become hard to get. But food and wine have become big businesses and it is inevitable that greed and avarice have crept in, sometimes to the extent of unlawful activities.

I have managed to get myself mixed up in some of these nefarious doings and have been lucky enough to work them out satisfactorily. I had been dubbed "The Gourmet Detective," and the sobriquet had stuck. Some in the official police departments of several countries had questioned my title, and I always start the rebuttal with the same disclaimer—"I'm not really a detective, the way it happens is that—"

My intention now was to trot out that same line but before I could do so, I looked again at the way Kramer was examining the file on the desk before him.

"Is that my dossier you have there?"

"A very interesting career. You have been present when crimes have been committed on previous occasions, is that not so?"

"Yes but—"

"Several occasions, in fact."

"Well, yes, I—"

"And several crimes."

"Not of my making—"

"How is that you are so often present when a crime is committed?"

It was time for a more vigorous defense. "Any multimillion-dollar enterprise attracts unscrupulous people. Food is such an enterprise, and it grows every year. Rare spices, for instance, are more valuable by weight than silver. The more important a business becomes, the more money is involved—and that brings in more unscrupulous people. I have never committed a crime, and I have no intention of ever doing so; but sometimes, when I am involved in such a case, I have to help in order to clear myself."

"You have to help," Kramer echoed, putting the green folder down at last.

"Yes. I have helped the police from time to time."

As soon as I had said that, I knew it was a mistake. It opened for him the opportunity to tell me to keep out of this affair and mind my own business or he'd have me behind bars as soon as the Danube Express reached a station. I hoped that at least he was too civilized actually to throw me off it before we reached one.

He pushed the folder away from him. His pale blue eyes searched my psyche—or so it seemed. He leaned back, his spine as straight as a ramrod.

"This is a very strange concern, *nicht wahr?*"

He was going to draw it out. In order to hammer home his message about noninterference, he was going to keep me on the rack a while longer. Well, two could play at that game.

"Very strange," I agreed.

"Mysterious, *ja?*"

His German was beginning to emerge here and there, but as he presumably knew I understood the language, it mattered less.

"Mysterious, too, yes."

It would come any minute now. He was just building me up before kicking my feet from under me and then opening up with both barrels . . .

"So you are a detective . . ."

I didn't answer that, it was an item we had already covered.

"I wish to ask you something." Finally he was getting to the point. I waited politely.

"I would like you to help me in this investigation. I would like you to be my assistant."

CHAPTER FIVE

I replayed that in my mind a couple of times, just making sure I had heard it right. I murmured an "Aha" as an invitation for him to continue.

"I have spoken with Herr Brenner, the president of the DS Bahn. He is in agreement with this request."

His manner relaxed—not much, but enough to notice.

"You see, this is my first assignment in the field. I have been the security chief for three years now, but in the DS Bahn office in Munich. I was given the opportunity of making this trip as it was such a special occasion—the twenty-fifth anniversary. It was never expected that we could have such a happening as this. As it is so unusual and, well, I think the English word is 'bizarre'—"

I nodded. It certainly was the word.

"Yes? Well, in the circumstances I felt I should have the assistance of someone who has had the experience of such crimes as this in the field, so to speak." He tapped the green folder. "You have worked with Scotland Yard, I see."

I nodded again, this time looking modest.

"So?" he asked. "You will accept?"

I was recovering from the surprise. "Yes, I will be glad to help."

He smiled. It was the first smile I had seen from him. It indicated satisfaction and though it fell short of 90 percent of smiles, it gave me a great sense of relief. I was spared not only Kramer's suspicions but also his interrogation, which I had been dreading. The puzzle he was facing was an intriguing one, too, and it would be a challenge to help him unravel it.

On the nearby desk, a machine began to buzz.

He ignored it. "I am very glad," he said. "We will work well together, you and I."

The machine ceased its buzz. A bell sounded, once then twice. Kramer rose promptly. "Twice means urgent," he said.

He ripped out the sheet, reading it as he came back to the desk. He sat and read it through again. He turned it around and pushed it across the desk to me.

It was translated from an on-line news service sponsored by the Budapest *Times*. The banner headline was eye-grabbing.

MALESCU MURDERED!

I read it aloud. "Fraulein Malescu was found murdered in her compartment on the Danube Express." I went on, "It tells of the twenty-fifth-anniversary journey, names many of the passengers— the best-known ones, at least—gives the itinerary, then the rest is an account of the life of Fraulein Malescu. Investigations are—it says— being conducted." He nodded agreement.

"Nothing we don't already know."

"True," he agreed. "You see to whom the piece is attributed?"

"No."

"Mikhel Czerny."

I looked blank.

"He is a well-known journalist, not perhaps known outside of Hungary, but he is a powerful force there. Everyone in the country reads his column. He often gets important news ahead of anyone else."

"Does this mean that someone on the train is feeding him information?"

"I have been going through the folder of everyone on this train to see if I could determine if one of the passengers is doing just that. So far, I have had no luck."

"How could they send the information to him?" I said.

"It would have to go by radio telephone."

"Would such a message go through your communication system on the train?"

Kramer permitted himself a slight smile.

"Messages do not go through our system, no. Passengers can use their own personal phones, but we have a record of every message that is transmitted or received by this train."

"Do you have a record of the message itself?"

"Unfortunately, no. We can identify the receiving party, though, but not the transmitter."

Invasion of privacy is a point of contention throughout the Western world. Increasing security was on the other end of the scale. The Danube Express went further than a lot of countries—Americans would be horrified. It did not go nearly as far as many others, especially in the Middle East. They would laugh at our concerns.

"I am having Thomas check now to see if a message has been transmitted to the Budapest *Times* since we left Munich," Kramer said. "I have also asked him to let me know what our security files can tell us about Mikhel Czerny."

It was a pretty sophisticated service that Kramer ran. Still, many of the most important people in Europe traveled on the train and their safety must justify such measures.

The fax began to buzz even as he finished speaking. He went to the machine and was reading it as it chattered away.

"It is Thomas. He says one phone call went out at 11:13. It went to the newsroom at the news service."

"It leaves little time for the dead body to be removed from her compartment though."

He handed me the message. "You can read the German, can you not?"

I could. The rest of the report gave a rundown on Mikhel Czerny. Halfway through it, I stopped and read again.

"I can see where you have stopped," Kramer said.

"Yes," I said. "This is very relevant, isn't it?"

"It is indeed."

After giving brief details of Czerny's career to date, the report told of some of his outstanding achievements. He had been the first to report the scandal that had forced the resignation of the finance minister, the first to expose an industrial espionage plot that had involved the biggest chemical company in Hungary, and—this is where I stopped . . .

Czerny had conducted what sounded like a vendetta against Magda Malescu. Instead of regarding her as one of Hungary's most valuable assets, he had criticized and condemned her at every opportunity. He had sneered at her performances, laughed on paper at her acting, and jeered at her lifestyle. He had exposed her affairs and scoffed at any who called themselves her friends.

I finished reading. "Thomas in our communication center is very thorough," said Kramer. "He will have more for us—I know him. Still, this is enough food for thought, is it not?"

"It certainly is. But if murder is concerned, it sounds like there's more reason for Malescu to kill this Czerny than the other way round."

"Yes, but was there a murder? We do not have a body."

"You say this Czerny is a powerful journalist in Hungary. He doesn't sound like the type to give out a false report."

Kramer shook his head. "That is so. This missing body is very perplexing."

"You are having the train searched, you said?"

"Our most trusted stewards are doing so. They are doing it in a manner that avoids alarming the passengers."

"One thing concerns me—"

"Yes?" he said eagerly.

"That smell of bitter almonds . . ."

"Cyanide."

"Well, yes—"

"What concerns you?" He was frowning. "You doubt the aroma now?"

"No, I am certain that I smelled it."

"You think it was something else?"

"No. My sense of smell is very accurate, and my memory of smells is reliable."

"So what concerns you?" he asked again.

"It's so—well, conventional."

The word bothered him. I tried to explain. "In nearly every mystery story that uses poison, cyanide is the choice."

"Of course. It is deadly and very fast."

"Yes, but in reality, it isn't the first choice of poisoners. I have been involved in a few murder cases, and other poisons were always preferred."

He was getting impatient. His pragmatic mind did not want to consider fiction as being of any help.

"What is it that you are trying to tell me?" In sentences like this, his delivery became more staccato, his accent, stronger.

"I'm not sure. I feel that something is wrong, but I can't put my finger on it."

He stared at me. I hoped he wasn't wondering if he'd picked the right man for an assistant. Feelings that cannot be substantiated were obviously not his choice as reliable clues.

"Don't worry." I needed to reassure him. "It will fall into place, I'm sure. One small clue will be all we need to explain it."

"*Ach, so.*" He was reassured for the time being, but aromas were not good clues to him—you couldn't put them on paper like words or numbers.

He tapped the pile of colored folders. "I must go through these once more, to see if I can find any useful facts."

"Good."

"However," he went on, and I could tell that he was reaching a point he particularly wanted to make, "in your own case, that reason is not altogether clear."

So that was it. If it had not been for the Scotland Yard backing, he might not have been so ready to ask for my assistance, but the matter of my reason for being aboard the train bothered him.

"I can explain that," I told him. "The concept of the luxury train is one that has been gaining popularity. In his introductory speech,

Herr Brenner referred to several of these—South Africa's Blue Train, the Palace on Wheels in India, the Royal Scotsman . . ."

I had his full attention. He waited for me to continue.

"I have been retained to advise on another such train. I am not the only advisor, of course: Others will be preparing data on routes, locomotives, coaches, and so on. I am to recommend on food and wine."

"This newcomer will be competitive with the Danube Express?" Kramer asked—as I had expected he would.

"Not in any way," I said firmly.

"You do not wish to tell me what railroad company this is? What route it will follow?"

"I have been asked not to do so." Then, before he could comment on that, I said, "However, if you should not be satisfied with that answer, I can contact them and—"

"It will not be necessary," he said.

"Good," I told him. "One point on which I am curious is this— what cargoes are being carried in the vault coach?"

He leaned back in his chair and smiled a thin-lipped smile. "That is supposed to be confidential"—he raised a hand to stop me—"no, no, I do not intend to keep it confidential from you. I tell you this because a number of people know about the cargoes already. They are no longer a secret at all."

"I am particularly curious about the coffin," I told him.

He stopped smiling and looked alarmed. "Coffin?"

"I walked onto the platform last night and saw some of the cargo being loaded. I was puzzled to see a coffin."

"Coffin?" he repeated, then relaxed. "*Ach*, of course! The coffin! It looks like one, yes, but it is not. It contains vines from Germany, to be delivered to Romania."

"So it's those vines!"

"Yes. You know about them in your business, naturally."

———

I knew a lot about those particular vines, but I had no idea that they were to be on this train. It was a fascinating story . . .

Like all agricultural crops, the vine is subject to pests and diseases. They come in the form of birds, insects, fungi, viruses, and weeds. One of the early fungi to be detected in the USA was the dreaded *Phylloxera vastratrix*. During the 1860s, this louselike aphid was imported into Europe. It splits and rots the grapes and, by the end of the century, most European vineyards had to be uprooted because of it.

The American grape varieties, however, were found to be resistant to *Phylloxera*, and, as it caused its worst damage to the roots, grafting was decided upon as the answer. Detached shoots containing buds were grafted onto the resistant American root stocks and European wine was saved.

The technique was employed on other occasions after that with equal success. A similar catastrophe, though on a smaller scale, had now threatened a portion of the Romanian wine crop. The German vineyards had sprung to the rescue, and a special hybrid strain had been grown.

Those vital vines were the contents of what I thought to be a coffin. Kramer explained to me why I had made that assumption. "The vines are in the central chamber in a controlled environment. On one side is a humidifier unit and on the other a temperature controller. No chances are being taken with such a precious shipment."

"I'm glad to hear it's not a coffin," I said.

"You are superstitious about such things?" Kramer asked, slightly amused.

"Oh, no," I said promptly.

"Then the vault contains another valuable cargo. You have heard of the missing Mozart?"

"Even our newspapers have been full of it," I said.

"Yes, it is a remarkable story, is it not? The manuscript, missing all these years, now finally come to light. It will be a great attraction at the Music Festival in Bucharest."

"You are carrying the usual cargo of parcels and freight that are too heavy for air freight?"

"Yes, a full load."

"So, two valuable cargoes," I said. "Both on the Danube Express."

He caught my meaning immediately. "We have an outstanding record. The vault coach is specially designed to be resistant to almost anything."

"In the meantime," I said, "we have a murder that we are not sure is a murder and also a disappearance."

"Yes, let us go to work . . ."

CHAPTER SIX

We were approaching Austria now. The border between Germany and Austria is no longer anything more than a line on the map, and the rails crossed it with a haughty disdain of the many centuries of historical division. Three-quarters of Austria's area is mountainous, but the border area where we crossed is covered with rolling hills. The train passed sunny slopes covered with the vines that are used to make the light, crisp, dry Austrian wines.

The city of Salzburg was the first major city we passed. It was once a Roman settlement, and its name comes from the salt mines in the region, a longtime source of revenue. It is known as "the city of Mozart," for he was born there, and it is there, too, that the land begins to rise to the south and become the Alps.

Then we were rolling majestically through the town, full of seventeenth- and eighteenth-century houses with frequent magnificent buildings, marble fountains, and large squares. On the main platform, a small crowd had gathered to take photographs and wave and cheer as we steamed slowly through—at least, we gave a great impersonation of steaming, billowing out puffy white clouds. A moment or two later, we came out into the Sudtiroler Platz and headed out of town to keep our rendezvous with the Danube. More vineyards stretched away, millions of beautiful grapes.

My thoughts went back to the problem at hand—what had happened to Magda Malescu? Was she dead or alive? Was it a kidnapping, a murder, or was it a voluntary disappearance?

Kramer and I had shared the thought that such a renowned personage must inevitably have made enemies along her road to stardom.

Which one of them hated her enough to kill her? And if she had
been killed, who had moved her body? Where and how and why?

So many questions, so few answers.

I had raised the obvious point concerning pushing a body out of
a train. After all, the train did have windows and doors, I said. Kramer had given me a look that had a large streak of pity for the
ignorant in it.

I had seen too many old train movies, he said. The only windows
on the Danube Express that could be opened manually were
mounted above the regular windows and were far too small to ac-
commodate a human body. The sophisticated technology on the train
included an electronic panel that illuminated a light indicating an
opened door or window when the train was in motion.

That meant that at least one answer was unavoidable—La Malescu must be on the train, dead or alive. The first search that Kramer
had instigated did not reveal her presence in either condition. His
barked command sent the stewards hurrying off to make the search
again.

I was sitting by one of the windows in the lounge. Talia Svarovina sat across the aisle watching the scenery move slowly past. She
seemed nervous, glancing up when anyone walked by, then relaxing
whenever she saw their faces. She had the features of many East
Europeans, as did Magda Malescu, with similar high cheekbones and
wide eyes. Her red hair gleamed sleekly and her smart light blue suit
had an Italian designer look. I smiled at her, but she gave me the
briefest of nods and resumed her alternate looks out of the window
and glances at passersby.

Henri Larouge sat a couple of seats behind her. He was at one
of the seats with a folding table, which he had covered with papers.
He was too busily engrossed in his work to pay attention either to
the scenery or other passengers. He frowned then scribbled franti-
cally.

Resume your journey as if nothing had happened, had been Kramer's
order, *but be doubly—triply—alert. Talk to everyone you can and listen
carefully to what they say. Some person—or persons—on this train have*

*information on these peculiar events and a word or two may give us a clue
we need.*

I was doing just that, but the other passengers were going to have
to be more forthcoming than Fraulein Svarovina, or I wouldn't be
able to learn a thing. I went across the aisle and sat opposite Henri
Larouge. He glanced up from his papers and didn't look particularly
pleased to be interrupted. I hoped this wasn't going to be two in a
row.

"Have you heard the rumors?" I asked.

"Yes," he said, and kept juggling numbers.

"I hope I'm not disturbing you—"

"I am reviewing the food shipments we will be taking on in
Vienna," he said.

"Yes, I suppose the train has to take on more food at intervals,"
I said, "sort of like in-flight refueling for planes."

He didn't appear to relish the comparison. "It would be foolish
to bring food for the entire journey from Munich. We take on food
in Vienna and in Budapest. We normally stop in Belgrade but the
present political unrest changes that." Despite his dislike of being
interrupted, he evidently enjoyed the responsibility of his job enough
to want to tell me about it.

"It is all planned by the DS Bahn. This way, we get food that is
really fresh and are able to serve the food of each different country
and know that it is authentic."

"I didn't realize that you worked for the DS Bahn."

"I do not. The company I work for us is contracted by the DS
Bahn."

"So you have heard the rumors?" I returned to my theme.

He could see he wasn't going to get rid of me that easily. He
pushed his papers away a couple of inches with a visible sign of
impatience. "I have heard that Fraulein Malescu has been murdered,
and I have heard that she has disappeared."

"That's what I've heard, too," I told him chattily. "I don't see
how she could do both."

"Nor do I. It may be some publicity stunt. She is a very flamboyant woman."

"Has she been in the news before in similar circumstances?" I asked.

"Several times. She loves the headlines."

"You have followed her career, have you?"

"No, not at all, but all the big newspapers and TV stations report her affairs, her movements, her appearances, her performances—she is news whatever she does."

"You sound disapproving," I said. It is a comment that I have found often useful.

"I do not disapprove," Larouge said. "Now Czerny—there is one who disapproves." He permitted himself a superior smile.

"Who is Czerny?" I had heard what Karl Kramer had to say about him, another viewpoint would be helpful.

"Mikhel Czerny, he is a journalist on the Budapest *Times*. He detests Malescu—he criticizes all her performances, makes fun of her escapades, twists her interview statements around . . ."

"Do you think he detests her enough to kill her?" I asked. "Or kidnap her?"

"Of course not," he said decisively, then he thought for a moment. "It sounds very improbable," he added.

Another thought struck me—could Czerny have a personal motive? Could a reason have arisen beyond his hate campaign in the media? Something personal? Maybe it was the other way around? Perhaps he had had a personal antipathy toward Malescu, and that had found a vehicle in his columns?

Larouge found my contemplation on these ideas an opportunity to return to his calculations. I decided to leave him alone and find another victim. A man in his late sixties with curly fair hair and twinkling eyes introduced himself. He was Henryk Sundvall, the Swedish historian and biographer of the Danube Express.

"We will be passing through Linz in a few moments," he told me. "It is one of the places where the Danube is at its widest."

"I am pleased to see that you look excited," I told him. "It is good to have a guide who is enthusiastic about his work."

He chuckled. "A guide? *Ja,* I suppose I am though I do not guide the train. I enjoy this job, though, and I love this part of Europe."

The countryside was getting more hilly, and the railroad descended gently into a beautiful valley with wooded hills on both sides.

"This is the Kirnbergerwald," Sundvall said. "It will be pines all the way to Linz." He pointed. "That is the pilgrimage church of Postlingberg, and coming up next—there it is—Mount Calvary or Kalvarienberg, also famous as a destination for pilgrims."

"Will we be able to see any landmarks in Linz?" I asked.

"The *Schloss,* the castle, stands high above the Danube and close to the south bank, so we will have a good view of it. It was built for the Emperor Friedrich III, who resided there with his court in the fifteenth century. It was burned down but rebuilt and is now a fine museum. We are approaching it now"—he pointed—"there!"

It was a square, solid-looking structure, more of a residence than a conventional castle. "And over there"—Sundvall pointed again— "is the old cathedral, the *Alter Dom.* It was built by the Jesuits."

He waved a hand. "Beyond it, just out of sight is the *Bruckner Haus.* Anton Bruckner, the composer, was born there. The building is now a concert hall, one of the most acoustically perfect in Europe. Many famous composers have lived in Linz—Beethoven, Mozart, Schubert composed some of their finest work here."

"What a pity the Danube is never blue," I commented. The dirty brown color belied its soubriquet completely as it slid out of sight behind us.

"Oh, but it is always blue!" Sundvall protested. He smiled at my questioning look. "Yes, it is always blue to Austrians!"

The train was picking up a little speed as we left the city. "We will be passing through Melk very shortly," said Sundvall. "It is famous, too. Melk Abbey is one of the finest Baroque buildings in the world."

"It's mentioned in the *Niebelungenlied,* isn't it?"

"That's right. I believe its fame in present times is due to its use in Umberto Eco's excellent novel, *The Name of the Rose*. It stands overlooking the Danube and has done so since before the year nine hundred."

"Three hundred years before the *Niebelungenlied* was written," I commented. Every German knows the epic poem that tells of Siegfried and Brunhilde and the attempt to steal the vast treasure of the *Niebelungen*, a tribe of dwarfs. People of the other Western nations know the music of Wagner that illustrates the same story.

"Unfortunately," said Sundvall, "we will not be able to see another famous sight just past Melk Abbey—and that is *Durnstein* Castle."

"Ah, yes, where King Richard the Lionheart was imprisoned on his way back from the Crusades."

"Exactly—when, from outside the walls came the sounds of the lute played by his troubadour, Blondel, who was searching for his master."

"A wonderful story," I said. "Why can't we see the castle though?"

"It is north of the Danube. We use the track that follows the Danube Valley."

"What are those large birds?" I asked.

"They are herons. The men who operate boats on the Danube call them 'water makers' and observe them closely."

"Why is that?"

"If the heron is seen to be standing in the shallows with its beak pointing upstream, then it means that high water is approaching. If it is pointing downstream, then a stretch of low water is approaching. That used to be very important in earlier days when the depths of the Danube had not been measured and mapped. Heavily laden vessels could easily run ashore without the guidance from the herons."

The Danube was twisting and turning as we rolled on, but the railbed smoothed it out, using bridges, some old and stone and some newer, steel and ugly.

"We come now to the *Strudel*," said Sundvall. "It is a series of white-water rapids. Many vessels have been wrecked here. There are whirlpools, too."

A tall, sharp rock rose on the far bank, a ruined castle on its tip, and just beyond it, on the near bank, was another castle, much larger and in better condition.

"Tales of hauntings are common here." Sundvall smiled. "Ghostly orchestras, armed knights, the clash of swords, and the neighing of warhorses—all have been heard or seen. We are approaching another ruined castle—there, it is coming in sight. It is known as the Devil's Tower and is said to be inhabited by the Black Monk, who shows false lights that lure ships onto the rocks."

"Lucky we're on a train," I said.

"Indeed it is. Ah, I am sorry, I must go. My wife awaits me."

"Thanks for all the information. I look forward to talking to you again."

At the other end of the coach, Herman Friedlander, the orchestra conductor, appeared. I approached him and asked if he was enjoying the journey.

He brushed back his long hair with a flick of the fingers that was obviously an oft-repeated gesture. The long face that I had initially considered doleful was the same, clearly normal for him.

"*Ja.*" He nodded. "I thought this was going to be an enjoyable trip, but there are stories. You have heard them?"

He was making it easy for me. I lowered my voice to a suitably conspiratorial level. "I have heard that Magda Malescu has disappeared. I have also heard that she has been murdered. Both sound ridiculous—but I have not seen her on the train. What have you heard?"

"I have heard those, too—but then the woman is such a demon for publicity, one must take the stories with a large amount of salt."

"I understand that not everyone in Hungary is a fan of hers," I said. "There's that journalist—"

"Mikhel Czerny, yes. He tears her apart in print at every opportunity."

"That's what I've heard. Does he treat any other prominent persons that way?"

"No, none."

"It sounds as if he has some personal hatred for her, doesn't it?"

Friedlander shrugged. "I suppose so." He pointed out of the window. "We are now in Austria." The landscape that was rolling by did not look very different, but I didn't doubt that he was right. I presumed that he did not find the Malescu mystery absorbing so I tried another tack.

"You are going to Bucharest?"

"Yes."

"Are you conducting there?"

"Yes, I am guest conductor of the Bucharest Symphony."

"Are you conducting the missing Mozart?"

For a moment, he didn't answer. It was as if he had not heard. He kept watching the rural scenery sweeping past the window. His voice was cold when he said, "Certainly not." I wondered if he was going to say more, and I waited.

Finally, he said, "Evidently, you do not know. Most people who follow European music are aware that I am a descendant of Antonio Salieri."

"Ah," I said, "the famous rivalry between Mozart and Salieri. I thought that had been dismissed by musical historians as largely fictitious and promoted by Peter Schaffer's play?"

"Not at all. There is such a faction, of course, but the rivalry— well, it was much more than that. Pushkin had already written of it in very strong terms."

"The missing manuscript is on this train, I believe."

Friedlander dismissed my comment with another shrug. "So I have heard."

"Our newspapers haven't reported much about it. I suppose it has been reliably authenticated?"

"I have heard that, too."

"It must be very valuable," I went on, determined not to be put off by Friedlander's personal prejudices.

"Not to me," he said icily.

"You must agree that Mozart is a musical genius though?"

A third shrug was inevitable—and it came. Here was a man who carried a grudge a long way.

"So this missing manuscript could be one of his greatest works?"

"Will no one rid me of this pestilent fellow?" was written all over Friedlander's face, but I was determined to learn all I could about as many passengers as possible, and I wasn't going to let go of my victim of the moment. After a pause, he said, "It could be, but I doubt it."

"Why do you say that?"

"It was written while the foolish boy was still in love with both his cousin, Maria Anna Tekla, and the singer, Aloysia Weber. It was a productive period in his life, certainly, but he was smitten by both these girls and was not able to concentrate on being musically creative."

"The love of a woman can be stimulative to an artist, can it not?"

"Not in Mozart's case. He was an adolescent all his life. His idea of love was to write obscene and suggestive letters, and his language when with women he 'loved' was on the same vulgar level."

"We have instances of many artists who could completely separate their personal lives from their careers. Maybe he was one such example."

"No!" Friedlander's answer was almost explosive. His heavy face took on a flush—the first sign of emotion I had seen from him. "He was a child who never grew up. His humor was that of the toilet. He did not know what love was."

"What will happen to the manuscript when it reaches Bucharest? Is the work going to be performed?"

"It will be on display at the Music Festival." His lip curled. I have read about people doing that—now I saw a perfect example.

He was watching the fields and streams as they passed, but his mind was still on our conversation. "What will happen to it when it arrives in Bucharest, you ask?"

He turned from the panorama unfolding outside to face me. "Better to ask—*if* it arrives," he said slowly.

CHAPTER SEVEN

A steward approached me. "*Entschuldigen Sie, Meinherr*, but Herr Kramer would like to speak with you."

I was curious to know why Friedlander had doubts that the manuscript would arrive in Bucharest but at the steward's interruption, Friedlander said quickly, "We must talk again later," and walked away down the corridor.

I went to Coach Six, compartment J-4, Kramer's "office." He was deep into the contents of a colored folder as I entered, but he looked up. "Ah, come in," he called. "You too, Hirsch," he added to the steward who had brought me.

"Please sit," he invited me, and when I was seated, he said to the steward, "Now, Hirsch, tell us again your story."

Hirsch was white-haired, a capable-looking man in his smart uniform. He had just the right balance for a responsible job as steward on the prestigious Danube Express—competent but not presumptuous. He stood at what was the nonmilitary equivalent of attention. In Germany, the difference between the military and the nonmilitary versions is minute.

He told his story, looking at Kramer but with an occasional glance in my direction.

"When I was seeing passengers onto the train and helping them to their compartments, one of the station staff brought me what he said was an urgent message for Fraulein Malescu. I delivered it to her just as she was going into her compartment."

"Describe the message," rapped Kramer.

"It was in an ordinary white envelope. There was nothing written on it except, 'Fraulein Malescu,' and in the corner in large letters 'URGENT.' I waited to see if there was an answer she would wish sent at once. She opened the envelope, took out a single sheet of paper, and read it."

"Go on."

"Well, she stared at me for a moment—as if she was looking right through me. Her face turned pale. I mean, her makeup showed clearly—underneath it, her face went white as if she had seen a ghost."

"Did she say anything?"

"No."

"Then what happened?"

"I asked the *Fräulein* if there was any answer. After a moment, she shook her head. I asked her if she was all right. She asked me what I had said, and I repeated it. She said, 'Yes' in a low voice. I asked if there was anything I could do, and she shook her head. She said I could go."

"What did she do with the letter and the envelope?"

"I don't know—she still held them as I left."

"Any conclusions, Hirsch?"

"She was terrified, *Meinherr*—I assumed that whatever was in that note terrified her."

"Anything else, Hirsch?"

"No, *Meinherr.*"

"Thank you, Hirsch. You can go. You will not, of course, speak of this to anyone."

Hirsch bowed obediently and left.

Kramer looked at me expectantly.

"It sounds like a threat of some kind," I said.

He nodded.

"The compartment has been searched for the note?"

"Yes," he said. "There is no trace of it or the envelope."

"And I'm sure you tried to track its origin on Munich station?"

"Yes, but it had passed through too many hands."

"Any indication of where the smell of bitter almonds in the compartment came from?"

"No," Kramer said. "It is still noticeable, though it is now faint. But there is nothing to suggest where the odor came from. Nor did we find anything else unusual."

"I was talking to Larouge," I told him, "when a thought occurred to me. That journalist, Czerny, seems to have concentrated much of his venom on Malescu. Apparently, he didn't write about anyone else as critically as he did about her. Is it possible that there was something personal between them? Perhaps from an earlier time?"

"A motive for him, you mean?"

"Yes."

He looked thoughtful. "I have Thomas digging deeper. I will suggest this to him. Anything else?"

"I was talking to Friedlander also. I asked him what will happen to the Mozart manuscript when it arrives in Bucharest—he said, the question was *if* it arrives in Bucharest."

"That is strange. Friedlander is conductor of the Swabian State Symphony Orchestra. Such a man should be considered as above suspicion."

I recalled a line from a Charlie Chan movie. " 'No one on the train can be considered as above suspicion,' " I said sternly.

"You are right. I must read his file again."

Not for the first time, I wondered exactly what was in my own file, but I was not going to rock the boat by asking. Kramer had accepted me as his trusted assistant, and I wanted to keep it that way.

While I was cogitating along those lines, Kramer was rubbing his chin. I had noticed that he did that when he was thinking more intensely. "There have been rumors . . ."

"What kind of rumors?" I asked.

"We have many informants. A large number of persons are associated with the railroad in one way or another. Persons who pass along to us any whispers that they hear that affect—or could affect—the railroad. Much of what they tell us is useless but, now and then, fragments may fit together, and what emerges may be a clue."

"And you have heard some fragments concerning the Mozart manuscript?"

"Yes, but that is what they are—just fragments, not substantial enough to act upon. Still, such rumblings may indicate that something is—what is the English expression—afoot?"

"That is the expression," I admitted.

"You should also know that we have picked up similar fragments about a threat to the vines. Not as many, but some."

"I'm surprised at that," I told him. "The vines are invaluable to the future of the Romanian wine industry, but they can't be of much interest to anyone else."

"Yes," said Kramer, "but what about the reverse?"

"Reverse?"

"Yes," Kramer said. "Could someone want to stop Romania getting the vines?"

I thought for a moment

"Hungary, the nations of the former Yugoslavia, Bulgaria? They all compete for the same export market in white wines. But that's too far-fetched."

He frowned. "Far-fetched?"

"Improbable, unreasonable, unlikely."

"Because they are governments, you mean?"

"Well, yes. You sound skeptical—I suppose in your job, you run into a lot of international intrigue along such lines?"

He nodded. "More than you would imagine."

"Have you had attempts on cargoes previously?"

"Yes," he said. "Just a few. We have prevented them occurring in most cases. One or two have come close to an actual theft and those we stopped. We have an excellent record."

"It sounds as if you are going to have a busy trip on this occasion. The vines, the Mozart manuscript, and the Malescu mystery."

He nodded glumly. "It appears so."

"One other thought—doesn't a famous actress like Malescu usually travel with a maid? Someone to set out her clothes and attend to details for her? It seems odd that Malescu should be alone."

Kramer looked pleased with himself. "I can see I picked the right man as my assistant. That is a very good point. Yes, I thought of that myself, and asked Thomas to check previous reports of Fraulein Malescu's travels. She does, indeed, have a personal maid who is always with her."

"Always?"

"Yes, always—except on this occasion."

"Do you know where the maid is now?"

"The Budapest police made inquiries for me at the National Theatre, where Malescu appears often. The maid is flying to Bucharest to meet Malescu there."

"Is the maid afraid of trains?"

Kramer's sense of humor didn't extend that far, or perhaps he was too caught up in this aspect of the investigation. "No," he answered seriously. "The theatre said she had some personal matter to attend to before leaving Munich."

"Interesting," I said. "You're having the maid checked out, too, I'm sure."

"Of course."

"We are dining in Vienna tonight, I believe?" I said.

"Yes, although there was almost a change of plans. Because of the Malescu mystery, the police in Vienna wanted to take control of the investigation. That would have meant holding the train there."

"But that is not going to happen now?" I asked.

"No. Herr Brenner believes that if we stop there, the Austrian police may not let us leave until the mystery is solved."

He paused, evidently weighing if he should say more. He decided. "I will tell you. The franchise under which the Danube Express is allowed to use the railroad lines of various countries states that delay in arrival in Bucharest may be cause for cancellation of the contract."

"Herr Brenner must have a lot of pull to override the Austrian police."

Kramer was enjoying learning these slang English expressions. "Pull! *Ja!* I like that!"

He rubbed his chin again. "Herr Brenner expects us—that is, you and me, to solve this quickly." He gave a small smile of satisfaction at the thought of Brenner overriding the Vienna police. "He has friends in Berlin—influential friends—and Germany still has power to influence Austrian decisions."

"So we just attend the banquet, then we return to the train. Is everyone attending?"

"We have arranged it thus. That will give us the opportunity to search the train once more—very thoroughly."

"Good thinking," I told him. "That will be important in knowing how to proceed with the investigation—if we know for sure that Malescu is or is not on the train."

"Just so." He rose from the desk. "Now I must go and talk further with Thomas in the communication center."

"And I'll spend the time before dinner in the lounge coach. Maybe I can pick up some more gossip."

We both left, Kramer going in one direction and I in the other. I stood in the corridor watching the Austrian scenery unfold and thinking over what I had recently learned.

What I was looking for were clues although this was made more difficult by having three possible events to consider: the theft of the vines, the theft of the Mozart manuscript, and the death or disappearance of Magda Malescu. Could there be any connection?

I was still pondering these various puzzles when I heard the soft booming of the gong that announced meals. "Cocktails are now being served in the lounge car," came the announcement in several languages. "We will be arriving in Vienna in two hours."

I bathed, changed, and went to the lounge coach. The Walburgs were there, so was Elisha Tabor, the Hungarian editor with, I was surprised to note, Paolo Conti. The two of them were deep in conversation.

Irena Koslova, the Romanian girl who was doing something she had *always wanted to do*, was drinking a glass of clear liquid. It could have been anything from Alpine springwater to straight vodka. She was alone. Henri Larouge was chattering away in French with a woman I hadn't seen before, a blonde in a severe evening dress.

Erich Brenner came into the coach with the Sundvalls.

"Professor Sundvall and Mrs. Sundvall," said Brenner. "The professor is with Upsala University in Sweden. He is the DS Bahn official historian."

"We have met," I told Brenner, but I shook hands with the Swedish couple anyway. "I enjoyed talking to you, Professor," I said. "I look forward to learning more."

"As I enjoy this assignment," he assured me. "Continually, I am finding new information on the early days of the railway." He had the slightly singsong intonation of Swedes but, like most of them, his mastery of English was excellent.

"And now that he has retired from the university," said his wife, "I am able to travel with him. We were very fortunate that this allowed us to be here on the twenty-fifth anniversary of the DS Bahn."

"And my next assignment will be to tell you a short history of Vienna," said the professor. "I may consider having a fortifying drink first however."

"We will take care of that immediately," said Erich Brenner, and signaled imperiously to a waiter.

I looked for Friedlander, the conductor, anxious to know why he had used "if" instead of "when" in referring to the manuscript arriving in Bucharest but he was not present. I didn't see Lydecker either, so I took the opportunity to sit at the small window table opposite Irena Koslova, who sat pensive, a glass of clear liquid in front of her.

"I'll join you in one of those," I said, "providing it's not water."

"It's Bulgarian vodka," she said. "Have you ever drunk it?"

"No. But I will now."

The service was, as expected from the superbly operated Danube

Express, prompt, and a glass of the clear liquid appeared in front of me. I tasted it.

"It is the belief in my country that any alcoholic drink that is clear and without color cannot cause a hangover," she said.

"I wouldn't have thought that hangovers were your problem."

"They are not," she said.

"It's a very pleasant drink. I'm not surprised you like it. Powerful but not overwhelming."

"I like the Zubrowka vodka, too, although it has a yellow color."

"That's the buffalo grass that is added to it," I told her.

"Really? I didn't know that."

She was a very attractive girl. She had a flawless complexion that almost glowed, it was so smooth. Her features were delicate, and her soft brown eyes were demure at the moment, though they could probably become resolute very quickly. Her hair was a light chestnut shade and shiny as silk.

Her face was heart-shaped making it more gentle. Her two-piece outfit was light brown with wooden buttons, and it fitted snugly— but not tightly—to a slender but curvy body.

"There's a new vodka out now—it's flavored with Arctic cranberries," I commented.

"I haven't tried that. Is vodka a hobby of yours?" she asked.

"More of a business," I said.

"Oh? Do you make vodka or sell it?"

I had my mouth half-open to describe my food-finder role and explain just what I did, but I paused in time.

"Neither, I just drink it."

"So how is it part of your business?"

The brown eyes were astute, assessing me over the rim of the glass, now frosting with moisture.

"I conduct investigations in the food and drink businesses," I said carefully.

"Are you conducting an investigation now?" she wanted to know.

I decided to confide in her to a limited extent. My role would have to become known soon, and if I was going to investigate, I wanted to do it with the full cooperation of the people on the train.

"Herr Kramer, the head of security on the Danube Express, has asked me to assist him."

"So you are a detective?" Her eyes were wide.

"Herr Kramer asked me because I work with Scotland Yard."

Her eyes widened still more.

"Scotland Yard!"

"Yes."

"So you are looking into this strange matter involving Magda Malescu?"

"You know about it?"

"Everyone on the train knows about it," she said scornfully.

"What do you know?"

"It is said that she has disappeared. It is also said that she has been murdered."

"What do you think has happened?" I asked.

"Me?"

"Yes, you. I am interested in the viewpoint of every person on the train. Someone may have noticed some tiny clue that does not seem important to them but may have meaning to a trained investigator."

I was exaggerating a bit, but it was in a good cause.

She remembered her vodka and took another sip, a large one. "One of her lovers probably murdered her in a fit of jealousy. She has so many, though, it will probably be impossible for you to find out which one."

No vote of confidence here. I would have to work on changing that.

"It is not certain that she has been murdered," I said. "She has disappeared also. Maybe one of her lovers has kidnapped her so that he can keep her for himself."

"H'm." She thought about that then said, a little wistfully, "It must be nice to be loved that much."

"I would appreciate it if you would say nothing of what I have told you." I squeezed a strain of officialdom into the words. The unfortunate citizens of the East European countries, grasped by the yoke of Communism for so long, have become inculcated with the power of the official. I didn't want to intimidate her, but I believed that I could count on her discretion. To help make my statement more palatable, I added, "I may ask for your viewpoint—as a woman, I mean—on this investigation. Fraulein Malescu is not a woman who is easy to understand."

She smiled tantalizingly. "I'm sure that many men have reached that conclusion. Do you personally find many women easy to understand?"

"I suppose not. Perhaps the next will be the first."

"I'll drink to that," she said, and held out her glass to touch against mine.

"I hope you'll be at my table for dinner tonight in Vienna," I said.

She pouted, shrugged, smiled. I took her reactions as a yes, or at least as a maybe.

CHAPTER EIGHT

Long, gleaming black limousines flying the flags of Germany, Austria, Hungary, Croatia, Serbia, and Romania whisked us from Vienna's *Westbahnhof* through the busy downtown area of the city to the Hotel Imperial. It wasn't exactly a sight-seeing tour, but Henryk Sundvall was in the same limousine with me and pointed out several landmarks on the way, including the age-blackened labyrinth of mansions, palaces, and public buildings known as the *Hofburg*.

From that complex, we drove through the covered tunnel and into the large square called the Michaelerplatz and past acres of beautiful gardens. We curled on to the famous Ringstrasse or, as the Viennese call it, simply "the Ring." We cruised past red Viennese trolley cars and the professor kept up his running commentary on buildings and historical sights so enthusiastically that he looked positively dismayed when we reached our destination.

The Hotel Imperial evokes immediate thoughts of the Austro-Hungarian Empire and Strauss waltzes. It is two blocks from the *Staatsoper*, the State Opera House, and one block from the *Musikverein*, the music association building, and has a long history of visits from famous names. Wagner stayed there, writing much of *Tannhauser* and *Lohengrin* during that time. The names of Domingo, Caballe, Carreras, Fonteyn, Furtwängler, and von Karajan are intertwined with that of the Imperial, said Sundvall.

The Swede also reminded us that the hotel was built in 1869 and was already renowned when the Nazis commandeered it as their headquarters in World War II and the Russian Army followed suit in 1945. The restoration of Austria's independence returned it to its former glory.

It looked the part without a doubt. On the staircase leading up from the glittering salons are archways supported by statues of gods and goddesses along with two magnificent portraits of Emperor Franz Josef and his wife Elizabeth. Polished red, black, and yellow marble make a startling background to the crystal chandeliers, the Gobelin tapestries, and the Persian rugs.

Our banquet room was not the largest but an intimate chamber with murals of mythical heroes and unicorns, oval mirrors and gilt everywhere. The chairs had red satin upholstery and white-and-gold paint.

I found Irena's name plate at the same table as mine, but it was located three chairs away and my attempt to correct that and put us side by side was thwarted by other guests moving in swiftly—all evidently anxious for the all-Austrian meal we were promised.

The meal began with a cheese-and-spinach strudel, and the creamed cottage cheese that is customarily used in such a dish was enlivened by the addition of feta cheese. Salmon mousse on very thin pumpernickel toast followed.

Next to me was an effervescent woman who introduced herself as Eva Zilinsky. "Viennese?" I guessed, but she shook an expertly coiffured head. "I know Vienna well," she told me, "but I am not from there." I waited, but she did not enlighten me. Her accent was vaguely Central European, but half a dozen languages stirred together and permutated by a score of dialects in each one and blended further made any guess a futile conjecture.

Spargelkremsuppe followed. The Germans and the Austrians both love asparagus, and its preparation in this cream soup was kept simple, with no frills. All at the table approved heartily. My companion told me that Bavaria made the best *Spargelkremsuppe*. "You recall it from your childhood?" I hazarded.

"I have never lived there," she said, "except for short periods."

"Where have you lived?" I asked.

"Almost everywhere in Europe—oh, and some other places, too."

She was probably in her forties, but she had clearly spent a lot of time and money avoiding getting beyond the forties. Face-lifts and other surgical cosmetic operations had kept her face young and attractive though some features were a little hard. She was tall and slim though her breast development was admirable and surely the result of surgical augmentation. Her silver-and-crimson gown was probably one of the most expensive Milan could offer.

She must have sensed that I was going to continue asking questions until I got some satisfaction. She leaned toward me—bringing a small cloud of 'Pure Passion' with her—and said, "My father was in the Diplomatic Corps. I traveled extensively with him."

Stuffed Breast of Veal with Buttered Chestnuts was served with Braised Fennel and small boiled potatoes with watercress and tarragon. Brandy and Gruyère cheese were just discernible in the stuffing, and the veal was succulent.

"This is the way I like food," commented Eva, and others agreed.

"Avoiding frills and fancies is the way to enjoy Austrian food at its best," said Friedlander, who had not hitherto appeared to be anything of a food critic.

A *Wachau Gruner Veltliner* wine was served. It is one of the best white wines to come out of the Austrian vineyards although it is not well-known because it is best when consumed young. It is seldom exported and does not travel well, so we all agreed that this was *Veltliner* at its best. It was delicate but with a pronounced flavor and aroma and although not considered a sparkling wine, it nonetheless causes a faint prickling on the tongue. Some wine connoisseurs turn away from such young wines, but when served with uncomplicated food, they are extremely enjoyable.

In keeping with the rest of the meal, a dessert was served that could be declared prosaic but was far from ordinary. It was also as typically Austrian as a Strauss waltz. It was the world famous *Salzburger Knockerl*.

Eva sighed dramatically. "I suppose it had to be. Oh, I know it's famous, but isn't it a little too touristy?"

"The most renowned dishes of every country have come in danger of being called 'touristy,' " I said. "It's the price we pay for making travel accessible to so many people."

"What a shame!" Eva said. She leaned back, looking just like a character in a Noel Coward play.

"A few decades ago, you would have been traveling on the Orient Express," I told her.

"I would," she agreed immediately. "Now why do you think I would have been doing so? Carrying diplomatic secrets in my handbag? On my way to a rendezvous in Istanbul?"

"More likely you would be on the train to cajole secrets out of a helpless courier," I suggested.

"Cajole? H'm," she said contemptuously. "I would like to think that I could do better than that."

"Seduction, you mean? Well, the Orient Express certainly had a reputation for that."

"It did. Mata Hari was a frequent traveler on it, you know."

This promising line of conversation was unfortunately interrupted by the arrival of waiters with dishes lined up on both arms . . .

A soufflé must always be treated as something special. The success of the dish depends largely on the egg whites being beaten to exactly the right stiffness. Folding the yolks into the beaten whites is also tricky. The milk needs to be just the right temperature, and the dish must be removed from the oven after a carefully measured baking time—and as if all these precautions were not enough—*Salzburger Knockerl* must be served immediately. Banquets, obviously, challenge the kitchen on this last point.

This *Knockerl* was perfection. The first two mouthfuls asserted that. I am sure that succeeding mouthfuls would have confirmed it but I was never to know . . .

A waiter bent close to my ear. "Pardon me, sir, but Herr Kramer wishes to speak with you. The matter is urgent."

He led me to the security chief, who was standing by the curtained doorway. "I am sorry to disturb you during such an excellent meal," he said, "but we must return to the train immediately. Come!"

At the entrance two commissionaires, attired as commodores in the Ruritanian Navy and heavy with gilt and braid, had cordoned off a parking space by the curb, and, at a signal from one of them, a police car swept deftly into position, and we climbed in.

We were promptly whirled into the maelstrom of Vienna evening traffic. "What's the emergency?" I asked Kramer.

"As soon as all the passengers were off the train, we commenced a thorough search of all the public areas. We found no sign of Fraulein Malescu, and I came on here alone, leaving the stewards to check the compartments. I just received a call saying that a woman's body has been discovered in one of them."

"Oh, no!" I said involuntarily. The sudden image of that vibrant star as a dead body was as much of a shock as if I had known her well. A dozen memories of her films flashed through my mind. "How did she die?" I asked.

"As soon as I heard this, I told the head steward to do nothing, touch nothing until we arrived there."

We were both silent, each with his own thoughts, as the police driver wove swiftly and expertly through the dense traffic. In minutes, we stopped and were crossing the platform where the Austrian railroad police had several men on duty. The door of the nearest coach was open, and Kramer hurried in while I was close behind.

"Ah, Heinlein," Kramer called out as a steward approached us. He had an extra strip of gold braid on the epaulets of his uniform, and Kramer confirmed my guess. "Heinlein is our head steward. He has been with the DS Bahn for—how long is it now, Heinlein? Forty years?"

"Forty-three, *Meinherr*." He was a stalwart-looking man, with a steady gaze, a spare frame, and a resolute chin. Like most of the other stewards, he had the bearing of a former military man, and it was likely that the railroad chose such men on the basis of their records.

He took us along the corridor and produced a key. He stopped before a compartment door. Kramer asked the question a fraction of a second before I did, both of us still staring at the gilded number on the door.

"*This* compartment?"

It was the compartment of Magda Malescu.

"Yes, *Meinherr,*" said Heinlein.

Kramer made a helpless gesture but turned it into a wave to Heinlein to unlock the door.

"No one has been in or touched anything, as you instructed, Herr Kramer." He stepped aside, and Kramer and I entered.

Female clothing was strewn around. A black skirt, a shoe, and a stocking were on the couch; the other shoe was across the room near the entrance to the bedroom. Kramer led the way, and we both paused at the bedroom door.

The body lay sprawled across the bed, arms and legs outstretched. A silvery gray blouse and another stocking were on the carpeted floor, and a black brassiere was on a chair.

Kramer and I went to the bed. The body showed no sign of life. She lay on her back, but her head was nowhere near the elaborate pillow. She wore a flimsy, almost transparent robe of a light silvery color, and on her feet was a pair of fluffy slippers.

"She looks different," I said, and I heard my own voice, hushed in the presence of death.

"It is true," said Kramer. "She does."

Magda Malescu looked younger and totally vulnerable. She wore no makeup, and her face was smooth and unblemished. She looked, somehow, more feminine. No visual evidence of the cause of death could be seen, and though we both looked carefully around the bedroom, nothing appeared out of place, and there was nothing that should not have been there. Kramer prowled around. "We left everything as it was when we found Fraulein Malescu missing," he said. "Nothing seems to have been changed."

"Do you notice an aroma?" I asked Kramer.

He sniffed. "Perfume."

The bathroom was untidy. A score of cosmetic items were in front of the ornate mirror, bottles of various colors and sizes, most of them opened. She was evidently a big user of towels—one was over the shower door, another half in the bathtub, another on the bathroom floor, and yet another by the sink. She was also a user of hair dyes, several opened bottles of brown, black, red, and various shades in between stood there. I looked in the waste basket—often a source of valuable information—but I could see nothing that looked like a clue.

Kramer prowled like a tiger, determined to find some hint or trace of significance. Finally, he paused. We were both back in the living area. "Well?" he demanded.

I shook my head. "I don't see anything that suggests who was here with her. Nor anything to indicate where she was between being killed, disappearing, and getting back here."

Kramer opened the door to the corridor. Heinlein, the head steward, was outside, and Kramer beckoned him. "Call Herr Brenner. Tell him to send Dr. Stolz here immediately. The police car that we came in is waiting here at the station. Tell the driver to pick up Dr. Stolz and bring him here."

Heinlein nodded and left. Kramer looked at me. "We don't want any more people to know about this than is necessary," he said.

"Dr. Stolz may be helpful," I said optimistically.

"Yes," Kramer said, musing. He straightened, the man of action again. "Let us make one more search."

We did so, but nothing fresh emerged. We were exchanging frustrated looks when Dr. Stolz arrived.

He went through the customary checks. He tested her pulse at both wrist and carotid artery and raised an eyelid. He opened his bag and took out his stethoscope. He listened for a heartbeat in various locations but showed no reactions as to what he was finding. Kramer was watching him impatiently, but the doctor went on with his examination and paid Kramer no attention.

Finally, the doctor folded his stethoscope and carefully tucked it back into his bag.

"Well?" Kramer demanded.

"She is dead," the doctor said. "Positively no signs of life."

"Cause of death, Doctor?"

"Kindly assist me in turning her over," said Stolz. "Be very careful."

I didn't think it required three relatively stalwart men to turn one slim female body, so I stayed back while Kramer and the doctor gently lifted her into a sitting position. "Now turn her to one side," ordered Stolz.

"Poison," said the doctor. "I cannot be positive but all signs point to Farfalia, a fungus that is lethally poisonous."

"How long has she been dead?" Kramer asked harshly.

"I would say"—the doctor stopped, went to the air-conditioning control and read it—"at least three hours, less than six."

Kramer frowned. "That means she died before the limousines left for the Hotel Imperial."

"So that anyone on the train could have done it," I completed the thought.

"You think she was murdered?" asked the doctor thoughtfully.

"There is nothing to suggest suicide, and accident seems unlikely," I pointed out.

Kramer nodded reluctantly. "It looks that way. So," said Kramer with a heavy sigh, "Magda Malescu, the famous actress, is dead, after all."

Dr. Stolz turned his head sharply at the words.

"She is?" His tone was full of surprise.

Kramer gave him a contemptuous look. "You said she was!"

Stolz shook his head. "I said nothing of the kind."

Kramer took a step forward as if he were going to grab the doctor by the throat. "What is wrong with you, Doctor! You just told us she was dead." He looked at the body, and the doctor, apparently baffled, followed his look.

"Oh, no," he protested. "I did not say Magda Malescu was dead." He moved a hand slowly to indicate the body on the bed.

"This woman is not Magda Malescu."

CHAPTER NINE

The doctor looked from one to the other of us as if we were a couple of mentally challenged medical aides.

"Did you think it had to be Malescu just because this is her compartment?"

"We were of that opinion," I said. I wanted to deflect some of the doctor's sarcasm, as Kramer looked ready to fire a verbal salvo that would have been less amiable.

Kramer composed himself to a degree. "Then perhaps you will tell us who this woman is?" he suggested.

"Yes," said the doctor. "She is Talia Svarovina."

"But she's a redhead." The words were out of my mouth even as I recalled the bottles of hair dye in the bathroom.

Kramer had noted them, too, I was sure. "She probably changes her hair coloring frequently."

"She does? Or Magda Malescu does?" I asked.

The doctor wasn't finished yet. "Surely you can see the differences between the two women?" He was scornful of detectives who didn't have his power of observation. "Malescu has high cheekbones, Svarovina's are much less pronounced. Malescu has bigger breasts, wider hips, and is an inch taller. Also, the two—"

"Thank you, Doctor. You may wish to put these comments in your report."

The doctor shrugged, unperturbed by Kramer's acid tone. I was thinking though that I had noticed the high cheekbones of both women, but now that the doctor brought it up, I could see that he was right. He was right, too, in pointing out that Malescu was much more generously endowed although women have ways of at least partly transforming such dimensions.

"They do look very much alike though," I was obliged to say.

"Of course they do," Dr. Stolz said, as one stating the obvious. "That's one of the reasons why Svarovina is Malescu's understudy."

To give us our due, neither Kramer nor I repeated the bombshell contained in the doctor's last word. I could see that Kramer wasn't inclined to give him an inch more credit than he was obliged. He had had enough examples of the doctor's superior knowledge already.

"In films," said the doctor, "the double is supposed to look like the star, but in the theatre, an understudy only needs to resemble the star." The doctor gave us an amused smile. "Didn't you know that Svarovina was Malescu's understudy?"

"No," said Kramer tightly, "but it would have emerged very soon anyway." He looked at the doctor more closely. "You must be an enthusiastic theatre fan, Doctor."

The doctor suddenly seemed a little flustered. "No, I wouldn't say that, I—"

Kramer seized on the reply, switching from defense to offense in a second.

"You knew both of these women, did you, Doctor?"

"I was Malescu's doctor for some time."

"Were you more than her doctor?"

Stolz didn't reply.

"She had many lovers, I understand," Kramer went on, relentless now. "Were you one of them?"

"I don't believe that is relevant to—"

"Everything is relevant in a murder case," Kramer said, and I wondered which German detective in fiction had repeated that, for it was a Charlie Chan-ism if ever I heard one.

The doctor considered his reply for a moment. Then he said, "I consoled her during a difficult time in her career."

"I shall take the answer to my question as positive." Kramer was really on a high. "And Fraulein Svarovina? What was your relationship with her?"

"I encountered her once or twice when she was understudying Malescu in a role—that was when I was visiting Malescu at the theatre regularly. I had to prescribe medication for Magda—"

"You—encountered—Svarovina, you say, doctor?"

"Yes."

"Two or three times, you say?"

"It—it might have been more—"

"And your relationship with her?"

"I exchanged a few words with her in the theatre."

"And you say that was when you were visiting Malescu—at the theatre?"

"Yes."

"And since then?"

Dr. Stolz raised his chin. "I don't believe I will answer any more of your questions at this time."

Kramer was a tiger when he was on the attack, but he was clever enough to know when to withdraw and regroup. "Very well, Doctor, we will talk later."

"What do you intend to do with the body?" Stolz wanted to know.

"As Fraulein Svarovina is a Hungarian citizen, we must take her body on to Budapest," Kramer said. "The laws have been carefully delineated in such matters for the DS Bahn which travels through several countries."

There was silence for a moment.

"You may go if you wish, Doctor," Kramer said.

Stolz paused, then walked out.

Kramer was looking through the compartment. "Do you see the key?" he asked.

We searched but couldn't find it.

"The passengers will be returning on board very soon," Kramer said. "I will arrange for the body to be transferred to the vault coach."

He prowled still, peering, poking, his eyes roaming everywhere. At last, he stopped. "So—we have more questions now."

"We do," I agreed. "How did Svarovina get into Malescu's compartment? Why did she go there? Who else went there? Was it someone she knew or someone who knew she would be there?"

"Was it someone who had reason to think that Malescu would be there?" Kramer took up the line of questions. "Who was the intended victim? Malescu or Svarovina?" He sighed. "This is very complicated. It is difficult to consider motives when we are not sure of the victim's identity."

"It would help if we could learn the precise relationship between these two women," I pointed out. "We know now that Svarovina was Malescu's understudy, but did they like each other? Hate each other? Have merely a working association?"

"I will have inquiries made at the theatre," Kramer said.

"Traditionally, the understudy is jealous of the star she would like to replace."

Kramer grunted. "Yet it is not the star who is murdered, it is the understudy."

"Unless there is another factor here that we haven't uncovered yet," I said, "it is unlikely that the star is the killer."

"We don't even know that the star is still alive," Kramer complained with a sour look.

"If Svarovina was in Malescu's compartment," I said slowly, trying to work it out as I talked, "I wonder who was in Svarovina's place at the banquet?"

"Or was anyone? Well, that will be easy to establish," said Kramer. He brightened once there appeared courses of action to be followed.

"Then there's Svarovina's attire—" I added.

"Underwear and a sexy robe." Kramer nodded. "That suggests a rendezvous with a man."

"H'm," I said, and he glanced at me sharply. "That was my first thought, too, but these are liberated times. We can't eliminate all the women on the train from suspicion."

Kramer was getting a dejected look, but he rallied. "We must search her compartment," he said. "Let us do it now."

A steward stood on guard outside as we did so. Svarovina's compartment was smaller than Malescu's, and she did not have nearly as many possessions in it. We worked our way around separately. This kind of searching had the advantage that there could be no secret drawers or built-in hiding places, so the search did not take long. I heard a grunt from Kramer at one point, but he did not elaborate on it until we had both finished.

"Find anything useful?" he asked.

"Not a thing. How about you?"

"This was in her makeup case." He held out a typed half sheet. It was in German, and I read—

'You will receive this on departure of the Danube Express. Make no attempt whatever to contact me—I will contact you and give you the details.'

It was not signed.

" 'Details,' " I repeated. "This suggests that Svarovina was an accomplice in some plot—to steal either the vines or the manuscript, I wonder?"

"We would not reach that conclusion quite so immediately," said Kramer, "if she had not been murdered. But it does look that way. So who killed her and why?"

"Someone who knew her well enough to be drinking with her—and whom she did not suspect of poisoning her," I suggested.

We discussed it further but made no progress. "We must return to Malescu's compartment," Kramer said, "take one more look, and arrange for disposal of the body."

Heinlein, the steward, was still on duty there, guarding the door but not being obvious about it to anyone passing. Kramer gave him a nod, and we went in. We were making a final survey of the compartment when there came a knock at the door. Kramer went to answer it. Heinlein was looking agitated. "I am sorry, *Meinherr*, but someone is here who insists—"

Voices came from behind the head steward. One was a female voice, sharp and strident, "*Meinherr,*" Heinlein went on, "I do not understand it but—"

He staggered sideways, evidently pushed from behind. "Please, I cannot—"

Through the doorway surged Magda Malescu, irresistible as a storm across the steppes.

She was wearing a dark pantsuit that was surprisingly subdued for her, and her hair was red. Her makeup was demure, it minimized the shape of her cheeks and diminished the power of those magnetic eyes. Her mouth was reduced in size, the full lips carrying only a line of lipstick. My immediate thought was that she looked like Talia Svarovina, and I recalled Dr. Stolz's comments about Malescu's more impressive physical measurements. The pantsuit was surely a size or two too small . . .

It took only a few seconds for all these impressions to register, and, as they did, she pushed past both of us, her eyes on the open door to the bedroom.

She saw the body on the bed, and there was little doubt, even to a layperson, that she was dead.

Malescu's hand flew to her mouth. "Oh, no!" she sobbed, and tears welled in her eyes.

"We need to talk to you, Fraulein," Kramer said, and his voice was hard.

More tears came, and she tried unsuccessfully to wipe them away. Her face was wet, and her lips quivered. If it was acting, it was an incredible performance.

Fifteen minutes later, we were in Kramer's office. Malescu had recovered her composure, but her bearing had the right touch of tragedy. She was calm but stiff.

Kramer showed no hint of softening his approach. Nor did he appear to be acquiescing to the status of one of Europe's greatest dramatic stars. He plunged into his questioning.

"Please tell us, Fraulein Malescu, what you know of this crime."

"Nothing, nothing at all." Her voice was low and controlled. "I cannot believe it."

"That is not enough, Fraulein. Talia Svarovina was your understudy. Why was she in your room?"

"I—I don't know."

"This interrogation will continue until you tell us the truth. A woman has been murdered. You will tell us why."

"I cannot, I don't know."

Kramer edged his voice with menace.

"Did you murder her?"

"Of course not!" Some of the dominating actress came through, but Kramer continued.

"Then you know who did."

"No, I have no idea."

Kramer glanced at me. We were beginning to develop the initial stages of a partnership, each knowing when to make use of the other.

"Why are you dressed as each other?" I shot out the question.

"We are not! She—"

"You are wearing one of her pantsuits, are you not?"

"No, it's mine."

"We can quickly determine if that is the truth," Kramer cut in. "Do you wish to change that statement?"

"I—" She stopped whatever she was about to say.

"Go on," snapped Kramer, not wanting to give her time to think.

"We sometimes wear each other's clothing—"

"This is more than exchanging clothing. You exchanged identities. Why?" Kramer was uncompromising, and she looked at us, from one to the other.

"All right, I'll tell you." She sounded humble, and I had the thought that it was uncharacteristic of the star.

"I—I have had these letters—"

"What sort of letters?" Kramer sounded as if he were not going to believe a word of it, whatever she had to say.

"Threatening letters. I had another one of them delivered to me on the train just before we left Munich."

I recalled the steward, Hirsch, telling us of delivering a message to Malescu that had terrified her.

"These threats, how many have you had?"

"Four, I think, yes, four."

"Have you reported them to the police?"

"No."

"Why not?"

"They threatened my life if I told the police."

"Do you have any of these letters?"

"No, I don't—"

"What about the letter that was delivered to you on this train?"

"I don't know. It may still be in my compartment."

Throughout this interchange, Malescu was dry-eyed, and her voice was steady. It was easy to believe that she was still shocked by her understudy's death. She was controlled, though, and Kramer's uncompromising method of interrogation did not upset her.

"These letters," Kramer continued. "Do they merely threaten to take your life? Don't they give any reason, do they say anything else at all?"

"Oh, yes," Malescu said. "They are very clear."

Kramer must have been surprised at that, but he didn't show it. "Tell us, Fraulein, what do they say?"

"Well," she said, "they all concern Rakoczi's daughter."

CHAPTER TEN

To his credit, Kramer didn't turn a hair at the reply. He was remarkably calm as he asked the predictable question.

"Who is Rakoczi?"

Malescu looked surprised. "You don't know Rakoczi? Well, I suppose he is not well-known outside Hungary."

"And his daughter? Is she better known?"

Germans are not noted for their ability to be sarcastic. Sarcasm is not a weapon in their verbal vocabulary. Perhaps that wasn't derision in Kramer's tone—perhaps it was merely probing.

Whatever it was, it was wasted on Malescu. "I will have to tell you the whole story," she said, and proceeded to do so.

"Ferenc Rakoczi is one of Hungary's heroes. He was the son and grandson of famous rebels. His family was wealthy and powerful, but they detested the terrible acts of the Emperor and his troops. The Rakoczi family led rebel armies against them for generation after generation. When Ferenc came of age, he was a prince of Transylvania, but he was determined to free the people from their oppression."

As she paused for breath, Kramer said, "Fraulein, I hope you are going to tell us—"

"Of course," said Malescu, and her imperious manner was returning with each breath. "Ferenc Rakoczi spent time at the court of the Emperor Leopold because of the high position of his family, and the emperor even sent Rakoczi to make a deal with the rebels. Instead, though, Rakoczi found himself supporting the rebels more and more, and soon he became their leader. They gained control of all of Transylvania and most of Hungary.

"Rakoczi fought on. He was captured but escaped before he could be executed. Poland wanted to join his struggle and offered to make him king, but he refused. Still he fought on, but the imperial army was too strong. His rebellion crumbled.

"Rakoczi went to France for support but could get none. He went to Turkey and died there. His two sons died soon after . . ."

"The history of your country is fascinating, Fraulein," Kramer commented, "but I fail to see what this has—"

"I am about to tell you," said Malescu firmly. "A legend arose that he had a daughter. There is no proof of this, but it became a rallying point for the rebels. A woman leader appeared who may have been Rakoczi's daughter. She was executed, and another appeared immediately.

"Now, we come to today. A Hungarian playwright has written a play called *Rakoczi's Daughter*, and I have been asked to star in it. It is a wonderful role"—her eyes took on an anticipatory gleam—"and I would do anything to play it."

"But," said Kramer, who had been commendably restrained throughout this recital, "you are now going to tell us what this has to with the threats against your life."

"Yes, I am. You have heard of the IMG surely?"

Kramer nodded. "Hungary's independence movement for the northern states." He looked at me. "It is akin to the IRA in Ireland, the ETA in the Basque area, the Quebec separatists . . ."

"That is right," said Malescu. "The IMG are the ones making these threats. They believe that making a heroine out of Rakoczi's daughter will harm their movement."

"Sounds as if it should help," I said. "Make more people aware, bring up more support."

"The IMG don't believe that. They believe that fictionalizing Rakoczi's daughter glamorizes her and turns her into a star of operetta—a sort of Merry Widow of the Resistance."

"So they don't want you to play the role," Kramer summarized.

"Exactly." Malescu turned the full candlepower of her magnificent eyes on the security chief.

"You take these threats on your life that seriously?" I asked.

"The IMG shot and killed the assistant public prosecutor a year ago in Szeged," Malescu said indignantly. I took her answer as a definite affirmative.

"Are you suggesting that the IMG murdered Fraulein Svarovina in mistake for you?" Kramer asked.

The question bothered Malescu. She thought, looked away, thought more before she answered, "I am not sure . . ."

"Have you definitely turned down the role?" Kramer went on.

"No."

"You told me earlier that you haven't told the police of the IMG threats."

"That was true."

Kramer tried another approach. "So you persuaded your understudy to change places with you."

Malescu nodded again.

"If you suspected an attempt on your life, wasn't it cold-blooded of you to expose your understudy to murder?"

"She has replaced me on many occasions," said Malescu loftily. "She never considered it as being a risk."

"Unfortunately, we can't ask her that," commented Kramer.

"It is an understudy's job to take the star's place whenever it is necessary, both on the stage and off. It is not at all unusual in the theatrical world."

"So while your understudy replaced you in your compartment, you went to the banquet in the city? Wasn't that exposing yourself to danger?"

Malescu gave him a scornful look. "Of course not. I was not Magda Malescu, I was Talia Svarovina. I was safe."

"You were certain no one would recognize you?"

"I am an actress," she said simply.

"Fraulein Svarovina was wearing only underwear and a revealing robe. Does that not suggest to you that she was expecting a man?"

I noted that Kramer's question did not include the possibility of the visitor being a woman. He was leaving it to Malescu to bring up that alternative.

She did not bring it up though. She gave a careless shrug. "No, it does not. She liked to wear my clothes. Naturally they were better and much more expensive than she could afford."

"She has done so before?"

"Many times."

Kramer looked away, then turned back to her with an assault on a different front. "Are you aware that a report appeared in the Budapest *Times* to the effect that you had been murdered?"

Her lips curved in a slight smile. "That reporter has been telling lies about me for some time. This was another one of them."

"A lie or a mistake?"

"I don't know."

"You know about the story then?"

"Certainly. Everyone at my table in the Hotel Imperial wanted to know what I thought of my mistress—the star—having been described as murdered."

"Then," said Kramer, "when we went to your compartment to check on this story, we found it empty. Where was your dead body?"

"I wasn't dead," Malescu said contemptuously.

"So where was Svarovina's body?"

"She wasn't dead either. She was obviously somewhere on the train."

"This reporter on the Budapest *Times*—"

"Mikhel Czerny."

"Is that his name?" Kramer said. "You know him?"

"No, and I don't wish to."

"Why does he harbor such a grudge against you?"

I saw a definite hesitation in Malescu's reply. Kramer must have, too.

"I don't know," she said.

"Would you say he hates you?"

Malescu raised her head in a gesture that must have come from a role in one of her plays. "Many people think so. He is a hateful person."

"Hates you enough to want to kill you?"

"I—I don't know enough about him to say that."

"It sounds unlikely though, doesn't it?"

"I don't know, I suppose so." Malescu sounded unwilling to debate the issue, and it led Kramer to continue more intensely.

"Surely reporters don't kill people they hate? Even if their business is persecuting personalities on paper, they don't pursue them in real life and kill them, do they?"

"As you say, it is unlikely."

"But not impossible. Is that what you are saying?"

She shook her head in a meaningless gesture.

Kramer pursued the investigation with questions about the number of years Svarovina had been Malescu's understudy, where she had been and what she had done before that, what kind of a person she was, who were her friends, and so on. She replied to them all in a matter-of-fact way, but I could not detect anything of real value in her responses.

Finally, Kramer let her go.

She is not telling the truth," was Kramer's first comment after she had left.

"In the most confusing way," I said. "Truth is here and there among her statements, the trouble is that so are nontruths."

Kramer picked up a paper from his in-tray. "Thomas has been busy collecting information for me." He read through it quickly. "The maid seems to be quite legitimate. She stayed in Munich because her mother was ill. The Munich police have confirmed that the mother is in hospital but will be able to leave next week."

He read the next item. "Now, this is interesting. I asked Thomas to see what he could find out about this Mikhel Czerny. It seems that his column in the Budapest *Times* became so popular that the Hungarian television service invited him to appear on a nightly news program. He declined."

"Unusual," I agreed. "Any apparent reason?"

"None given," Kramer said, reading on. "Thomas also contacted a person he knows on the rival newspaper, the *Daily Journal*. It seems no one knows what this Czerny looks like."

"So ugly he didn't want to appear on television?" I queried. "He can't be on this train then, even under another name. I haven't seen anyone that ugly on it."

"H'm," Kramer murmured, rubbing his chin, "an intriguing thought nevertheless."

"Worth following up. I had a friend with the London *Daily Telegraph*, one of Britain's most prestigious newspapers. It had a gossip columnist for many years, and no one knew what he looked like. Perhaps the same reason as Czerny, he didn't want to risk some aggrieved victim of his tittle-tattle taking a shot at him."

" 'Tittle-tattle,' " Kramer said, "I do not know the expression, yet I can see what it means. Yes, as you say, it is worth following up. Herr Brenner is well-known in Budapest and has good connections there. I will see if he has one at the Budapest *Times*. Someone at the newspaper must know this Czerny."

"I'd like to meet this Thomas—he sounds like a valuable man."

"Valuable indeed. And so you shall—but not at the moment. I have schedules to check."

I rose. "I'll see what I can learn from some of the passengers."

Kramer looked at his watch. "The train will be leaving any moment now. We continue our journey. From now on, we will be seeing a lot of the Danube as we progress along its valley. I say progress, but it will be slow. Not only does this so-called Express cover only about seventy kilometers each hour—about forty miles— but we weave along the banks of the river, crossing bridges frequently so as to provide the best views and utilize tracks that are accessible to us."

Several people were in the corridors and in the lounge and observation coaches. It was dark outside but they presumably wanted to watch the brightly lit city of Vienna by night as we pulled out of the station and "steamed" out through the suburbs.

The strains of that eternal waltz, *The Blue Danube,* filtered softly out of the invisible speakers, setting the mood. Then a voice announced our imminent departure. From down the platform came the thumps of coach doors closing—an unmistakable sound to any train traveler, and inexplicably unique to trains, quite unlike the sounds of any other doors. A finality was in them and perhaps a sad farewell.

The steam whistle added a final note to that farewell and, without a jerk or jolt, the Danube Express moved from stationary to motion, smoothly as a panther.

The lights of the station faded and were promptly replaced by the city lights, but then they were lost as the track dipped underground to pass beneath the Stubenring, one of the ring roads that comprise the Ringstrasse, a string of roads that run along the old city walls and enclose the inner city.

We exchanged the darkness of the tunnel for the darkness of the night as we emerged to climb onto the bridge crossing the Vienna River, a waterway completely eclipsed by its world-famous companion river. We rolled along, silent except for the muted sound track that reminded us of simpler times, on through the eastern part of the city.

We swooped underground again, under the Danube River, and picked up a little speed—but no more noise—as we headed for Bratislava on the Slovak border.

CHAPTER ELEVEN

We had had some new passengers join us on the train in Vienna. One of them came through the observation coach, introducing himself. He seemed to be a gregarious individual, smiling, chatting to everyone. He was young to middle-aged, with a round, happy face and a habit of bending forward to talk to people. He seemed genuinely friendly, and the smile never left his face.

"Franz Reingold," he said with that jerky motion that many Germans have. It has always been my opinion that it is all that is left of that heel-clicking motion so common in the Germany of the past, an affectation abandoned because of its association with excessive militarism.

I reciprocated—but without that particular mannerism—and gave him my story about being a food-finder. It was my watered-down version, the one that contains no suggestion of a detective. He listened with interest. *"Ach, gut,* then I shall call on you when I am in doubt what to order for dinner!"

He looked more than capable of making up his own mind on that subject, and I asked him if he was traveling on business. "I presume you are not a tourist," I said.

His smile did not waver. "I am not on business and I am not a tourist. I am a Swiss—I live near Bern, the German-speaking part of Switzerland. I am very fortunate that my family has money— quite a lot of money, in fact. You see, my grandfather was clever enough to invent one of the early ski lifts. Of course, they have been changed and improved several times since then, but each improvement just makes them more in demand and brings us in more money!" He beamed with pleasure, and I reflected that he had good reason to do so.

"To answer your question," he went on, "the one about being on the Danube Express . . . You see, I am an idle fellow and spend my life indulging in my hobbies. One of those is trains. I have what is possibly the finest collection of model trains in Europe, but I also like the real ones. The twenty-fifth anniversary of the famous *Donau Schnellzug* is an occasion that I simply could not miss."

He had the Swiss-German accent that can be difficult for foreigners to understand, even foreigners who are proficient in German. His accent had been refined and smoothed out, though, probably by frequent travel, so I could follow him without difficulty.

We chatted a little longer. He wanted to meet everyone on the train, he said finally, and wandered off, glowing with bonhomie and shaking more hands than a politician.

Farther along in the observation coach, Elisha Tabor, the Hungarian woman in the publishing business, was sitting alone, and I joined her. She gave me a charming smile and wished me a good evening. "Did you enjoy the banquet?" she asked.

"It was excellent. Like everyone else on the train, I wished we could have spent more time in Vienna, but I know this is not that type of trip. At least, it serves as a reminder to us all that we should return soon."

"I like Vienna, too," she said. "Naturally, my first love is Budapest, but Vienna is second."

"And third?"

"Paris, without a doubt."

"You were born in Budapest?" I asked.

"Yes. I have left it several times but always returned. I have lived there now for some years."

"You must know it well," I said, steering the conversation.

"Very well."

"Tell me something about Budapest—"

"Of course." She turned large brown eyes toward me. She was a good-looking woman with a complexion like cream. Her features were regular and might have been ordinary, but the nose was just Roman enough and the chin just strong enough to give her real character. She looked as if she might be a formidable figure in the publishing business and more than able to hold down a responsible position.

"Tell me about Mikhel Czerny."

Her eyes searched my face. It was a moment or two before she answered. "I'm surprised you know the name. He is famous in Hungary, of course, but not known well in other countries."

"I've heard about him a few times since I have been on the Danube Express."

"Ah, yes, the story on Magda Malescu."

"Yes. What's the opinion in Budapest? Does he have some reason to hate her?"

"Hungarians are a very volatile people. When they love, they love more than any other people. When they hate, they hate more than any other. The blood of Attila the Hun and Genghis Khan courses through their veins. They are a very passionate people."

"So it is nothing personal?"

She shrugged. "If it is, the public doesn't know about it. You know the story about Leo Szilard, the Hungarian-born atomic scientist?"

"No, I don't think so."

"Szilard was talking to Enrico Fermi, another scientist, and they were having a discussion about extraterrestrial life. Szilard said he thought it was a distinct possibility. 'In that case,' Fermi said, 'they should have been here by now. So where are they?' Szilard said, 'They are among us—only they call themselves Hungarians.' "

I laughed. "But that still doesn't explain Czerny's attitude toward Malescu—or if it does, why doesn't Czerny treat every one of his victims that way?"

"He does. His style is always caustic, critical, biting, but Malescu is such a vulnerable target, so easy to attack. She almost makes it easy for him. She hardly makes a move that is not reason for him to write at least a paragraph on her."

She glanced at her watch. "Well, I think I'll retire. It has a been a long and exhausting evening."

"There's still a lot of it left," I told her.

"Maybe, but it will have to get along without me."

I couldn't see any other good-looking women either to interview or to chat with but some minutes later Helmut Lydecker came through the coach, and I invited him to sit in the seat vacated by Elisha Tabor.

"How is the illusion business?" I asked by way of openers.

"I'll know better when we reach Bucharest," he said.

"The Romanians are big on illusions, are they?"

"I'm hoping so."

Well, that didn't advance my knowledge of either his business or him. I tried another approach. "At least you can't have much competition."

"I am well-known now, so I don't."

Perhaps another topic would draw him out. "This Malescu affair is mysterious, isn't it?"

"All her affairs are mysterious."

"First, she's dead, then she disappears, now she's back with us."

"What have you heard?" he asked.

I could hardly give the pompous response of *I'm the one asking the questions* so I decided to go along. "I understand there have been threats against her life, so she decided to become invisible for a while," I said.

"Threats?" he said.

"Yes, haven't you heard that? She wants to star in a play called *Rakoczi's Daughter* but the IMG doesn't want her to do so. They have been threatening her."

"Ah, I see."

"You have heard of the play?" At last I had reversed the process. Now our relationship was as it should be, and I was asking the questions.

"The papers and the TV have been full of stories about that play," he said. "It would be just like her to build up a big publicity campaign like this. Wonderful advertising."

He didn't sound sympathetic to the star. "You think that's what it is? Publicity?"

"She's done this sort of thing before."

"Makes a practice of it, does she?" I asked.

"When she was a teenager, she faked a disappearance. She's been doing it ever since. In recent years, it's become a more elaborate story."

"You know a lot about her."

"I should," he said. "I gave her her first job."

"Really?" This had to be a breakthrough, I had to keep him talking. "I thought she had always been in the theatre."

"She has."

"Were you in the theatre at that time?"

"In a way."

"A producer?"

"No," he said simply. It didn't seem to matter to him whether I made sense of his answers or not. I persevered anyway. "You were in publicity yourself—public relations?"

"No," he said, and I thought he was going to say no more when he added, "I was then—and still am—a magician."

So that was what he meant by saying he was a seller of illusions. "And you hired Malescu?"

"Yes, as an assistant."

"On the stage?"

"Yes, I was perfecting an illusion at that time."

"What was it?"

"The Vanishing Lady."

He didn't acknowledge the irony of that; perhaps he didn't realize it.

"She said she was eighteen, but she was probably sixteen, I learned later," he said. "She was exceptionally lovely, a little gawky and untutored, but that made her all the more attractive. She didn't stay with me long, she matured rapidly, got into the chorus of a show, then got a singing part in another. She didn't have much of a voice, but with her looks and figure, that didn't matter. She was a fast learner and exceptionally ambitious. She would do anything to progress in the theatre, and at an early age she was clearly a star in the making."

He smiled, clearly reminiscing. "I had two assistants at that time, Magda and another girl—I don't remember her name, I have had so many. An accident during rehearsal almost killed Magda and another, similar, occurred shortly after. Both might have been the fault of the other girl. I dismissed her though she swore she was not responsible."

"Did you ever learn if she was?"

He shook his head slowly. "I was never sure, but I heard later that Magda bragged of getting rid of the other girl. Soon after, Magda left me to further her ambitions."

"Did you see her after she left your act?"

"Oh, yes. Now and then, the shows we were both in would be running in the same city."

"Have you talked to her on the Danube Express—this trip, I mean?"

"No." He looked out of the window, but only blackness was out there. "The last time we met was a few years ago in Copenhagen. It was—well, acrimonious. We haven't talked since."

I was thinking how quickly Lydecker had gone from a clam to a nightingale. What had caused the change?

"You can tell all of this to the security chief, Kramer," he said.

"Why should I do that?" was the best I could come up with at short notice.

"You are working as an assistant to him, are you not?"

Before I could answer, he said, "I saw you go into Malescu's compartment with Kramer and Brenner."

That was ironic. He had reached the right conclusion for the wrong reason. At that time, I had not been asked by Kramer to work with him, but from Lydecker's point of view, it was a fair assumption.

"I—er, helped Scotland Yard on one or two occasions, and Kramer has asked me for my opinions," I conceded.

He yawned and stood. "You can tell him that I had nothing to do with Malescu disappearing," he said. "My 'Vanishing Lady' illusion is confined to the stage."

He wished me a good night and walked off down the coach, leaving me with several points to ponder. First, if I was supposed to be operating undercover, I was doing a terrible job. *Damage control?* I asked myself. The best answer seemed to be to turn it to my advantage by utilizing the prestige of Scotland Yard and continuing to aid Kramer to investigate. As long as Scotland Yard didn't hear how I was shamelessly using their name, I was safe.

Lydecker's earlier association with Malescu raised a few possibilities, especially as it sounded as if he might have had liaisons with her since then. Had they parted on terms that could lead to murder? If so, could Lydecker have mistaken Talia Svarovina for Malescu and killed her in error? Pretty fanciful, I thought. Hercule Poirot would have sneered at it as a conclusion.

I followed the example being set and retired for the night.

W hen I awoke the next morning, it looked as if we had not made much headway. We were doing little more than thirty miles an hour, and the railroad track zigzagged its way along the Danube River valley in a series of corkscrews, steep climbs, and spiraling descents. Its erratic progress had clearly been determined in an earlier day when railroad engineering was cautious and limited. Old stone bridges carried us from one bank of the Danube to the other, affording fine views of one of the world's great rivers.

The scenery was highly rural, with tiny hamlets, inns with porches, and balconies covered with red, white, and yellow flowers, and farms with fat cattle grazing under the windows. This, I thought, was the way to see a country and a vivid contrast to flying over it in a jet plane at near the speed of sound.

The dining coach was not yet half-full, and I was able to reflect on breakfast habits. There is the fast American breakfast of bagels and coffee or the more extensive one of bacon and eggs with hash browns. In contrast is the Italian breakfast of sweet, cream-filled buns, a small glass of brandy, and hot, thick black coffee. The English are perhaps the only people that eat fish for breakfast, and kippers are an acquired habit. The French stick to their flaky croissants, while Germans and the Dutch like various cheeses with cold salami, ham, and tongue. In Morocco, workers will stop at a hole-in-the-wall street-corner café for a dish of stewed fava beans and a glass of hot mint tea.

The Danube Express, with supreme nonchalance, offered all of those plus the Austrian variation—small finger sausages. I knew there was a bakery on board, so that all the bread served was literally fresh from the oven. Austrian bread is among the best in the world—it comes in all shapes, sizes, and colors and is made with a wide variety of flours and grains. I chose a flat, saffron-colored bread, moist and succulent and filled with poppy seeds.

Franz Reingold, one of our most recently arrived passengers, came in and wished me a jovial "Good morning." I chose a boiled egg and a slice of ham to go with my poppy seed bread. Then came the choice of coffee. With most European countries offering their finest and all being different, this was a problem. I said to the waiter, "I suppose I should ask for Viennese coffee. I know the city's coffeehouses are famous."

"You may know this, *Meinherr*," he said, bending forward a little so that his voice should not spread his heresy too far, "but Turkey really established that tradition for the Viennese."

"You are not Viennese," I guessed.

"I am not, I am from Estonia."

"Your Viennese colleagues in the kitchen will disagree with you."

He smiled. "They do. But history books say that when the Turks besieged Vienna in 1683, they were losing too many troops and ordered a retreat. They did so, leaving bags of coffee behind, which the Viennese seized and thus became coffee-drinkers."

"Addicts, even?" I asked.

"Yes, indeed."

"So if I ask you for Viennese coffee now, what will you bring me?"

"First, I will ask if you would like *verkehrt,* which is one part coffee to four parts milk—or *mocha,* that is ebony black in a demi-tasse—or *mit schlagobers*—you may know that—"

"That's with whipped cream—there's also *doppelschlag,* which is double cream."

"You are correct. Of course, Turkish coffee is still popular in Vienna, too."

"Much less so elsewhere," I said.

"That is true. Mainly because the Turkish method of making coffee is to brew it at least three times."

I settled for *verkehrt.*

Friedlander, the conductor, entered, looking grouchy, and growled something that I took for a greeting. The dining coach did not fill up any further. Presumably many passengers were taking breakfast in their compartments, not a simple matter logistically but accomplished in a polished and unobtrusive manner on the Danube Express.

I was leaving the dining coach when a steward came alongside me. He didn't speak out of the side of his mouth, but he was politely discreet as he said, "Herr Kramer would like you to join him in his office."

The security chief was studying a document from among a pile on his desk, but he put it aside when I entered.

"Come in, my friend," he invited. "I believe we have news for each other."

How did he know I had something to tell him?

"One of the stewards tells me you have been chatting to various people," he said. "That is good. I have the feeling that answers to many of our questions may exist among the passengers—if we can extract them."

So he had the stewards reporting on my movements. Well, he was being thorough, I had to admit that.

"My talk with Herr Lydecker was illuminating," I began. "His relationships with Magda Malescu have been both intimate and tempestuous. It is possible that one of them has led to this murder, but it is by no means certain." I filled him in on the details, and he made notes, nodding as I talked. When I told Kramer that Lydecker had concluded—albeit from the wrong evidence—that I was helping the police, Kramer nodded.

"He is a shrewd man, that much I have gathered from brief talks with him. Still, it is of little consequence if a few people learn that you are helping the police under these circumstances."

I told him, too, of Elisha Tabor's belief that Mikhel Czerny was not pursuing any personal vendetta against Magda Malescu. "It may be a typical Hungarian viewpoint," I suggested.

"Aggressive." He nodded. "Controversial, argumentative, belligerent even."

"You are a student of national behavior," I told him.

"Hungarians are the New Yorkers of Europe," Kramer said. "Very well. Now for my news—information coming in on the Italian wine fellow, Paolo Conti, indicates that he may not be what he purports to be. Some of the answers he gave me are not corroborated. The dossier we have on him is sparse to say the least. All of this makes him suspect, to my way of thinking. Have you talked to him?"

"No, I haven't."

"Do so at the first opportunity. Let us see if he tells you different stories."

"I will."

"The excellent Thomas has been diligent—you say that, diligent?"

"It's the right word," I assured him.

"Good. Thomas learned that a radio-telephone message went out from a device on this train almost exactly fifteen minutes before the limousines left for the Hotel Imperial."

"Do you know what it said?"

"No. Unfortunately, the law does not allow the recording of personal calls by passengers. But Thomas did succeed in determining who received that call."

He sat back, spine rigid as always. His blond hair almost gleamed with triumph. His light blue eyes certainly did.

"I can't wait," I told him.

"That call went to the offices of the Budapest *Times* on-line news service." He continued.

"One other point—as I told you, Herr Brenner has some powerful connections throughout Europe. At my request, he called a friend of his who is on the board of directors of the Budapest *Times*. He asked this friend what he knew of this Mikhel Czerny. Herr Brenner learned that although Czerny uses many people as sources of information, the paper only prints what Czerny personally tells the news editor."

I thought about that for a moment. "That suggests that it was not a contact of Czerny who called in with this story—it says that Czerny himself phoned it in to the editor."

"That is so."

"That in turn means that Czerny is on this train."

Kramer banged a fist on the table. "That is the conclusion we must reach. Herr Brenner's friend at the Budapest *Times* was reluctant to say much about Czerny. Of course, with more evidence, we could get a court order and force him to tell us more. Meanwhile, though, Herr Brenner says that his friend tells him that Czerny is fond of adopting various roles in order to get his information. Informants do not always know who they are talking to—and he pays out generous bribes where necessary."

"This is really reaching," I said, "but have you considered the possibility that Czerny himself could have killed Malescu?"

"Surely Malescu had more reason to kill Czerny than the other way around—but what you say needs to be included in our thinking. Then, that consideration assumes that Czerny wanted to kill

Malescu—but perhaps he didn't? Perhaps he knew that Talia Svarovina was not Malescu—perhaps he knew whom he was killing?"

"Possible," I conceded. "About Czerny—you say he adopts various roles. Does that mean disguises?"

"I suppose so, yes."

"So he could be any man on the train?"

"That must be so," Kramer said. "Not I, of course."

"Nor I," I added quickly.

"Certainly not," he agreed.

He did so promptly. I hoped it wasn't too promptly.

CHAPTER TWELVE

In the lounge coach, Professor Sundvall was talking to an attentive group on the subject of Wolfgang Amadeus Mozart. Someone had apparently asked him a question concerning the musical genius, prompted, no doubt by the presence on board of the "lost" folio.

"Mozart was born in Salzburg," the professor was saying. "His father had wanted to be a lawyer but gave up the idea and joined an orchestra there. He started to teach his son to play the clavier when Wolfgang was only three, and the boy made such extraordinary progress that within a year he was composing music for it."

Sighs of awe arose at that statement.

"From then on, Wolfgang was oblivious to everything else in life. Music completely absorbed him—so much that even when obliged to play children's games with his older sister, he would only do so to the accompaniment of music.

"His father took Wolfgang and Wolfgang's sister, Nannerl, to the Imperial Palace in Vienna to play as a trio at a concert. The seven-year-old Wolfgang climbed on to the Empress's lap to kiss her then ran over to a royal guest from France who was present—Marie Antoinette—and proposed to her."

Chuckles of amusement at such precocity greeted that comment. "Wolfgang's prodigious talent continued to expand. Before he was eight, he could play any piece of music set in front of him—and play it equally well on the harpsichord, the organ, or the violin. Proud of his own ability—which amazingly enough, he recognized in himself—he would throw a cloak over the clavier keyboard and prove that he could play just as easily when he could not see the keys."

"A true genius," commented someone.

"Unquestionably. By the time he was ten years old, he had composed masses, arias, symphonies, sonatas, serenades, and even two operas. One of the operas was in typical Italian style and the other in the German style.

"When Wolfgang's father took him to Rome, they went to a recital of Allegri's famous *Miserere* in the Sistine Chapel. After they had sat through the performance, which was in eight parts, Wolfgang wanted his father to get him the music so that he could play it. His father told him that written music was forbidden by the Pope so Wolfgang went back to their rooms and wrote the piece out in its entirety from memory. To satisfy himself that it was accurate, he went back to the Sistine and listened to it again, comparing it note by note to his own version. There was not one significant variation."

"Did he become a recluse as he grew older?" a voice asked.

"Not at all. One of his closest friends was the son of Johann Sebastian Bach and later, he became a good friend of Haydn. Wolfgang had a friendly nature and made friends easily—"

"You are omitting something, Professor," a new voice broke in. Heads turned. It was Herman Friedlander, the conductor who had told me of his relationship to Antonio Salieri. The hush that followed promised a lively exchange.

The genial Swedish professor did not look at all perturbed. He had probably had experience of being heckled and contradicted before. "Please join us, Herr Friedlander," he invited. "An alternative view of Wolfgang will give balance to our little discussion here."

Friedlander came farther into the group. "Mozart was always ready to criticize others, frequently for their inability to demonstrate a talent equal to his. He made enemies far more easily than he made friends. He had a complete lack of tact, he was a braggart with no thought for the feelings of others."

"Genius is often intolerant," said Sundvall. "It must be difficult for it to descend to the level of us ordinary mortals."

"Is it true that you are related to Salieri?" came a question to the conductor.

"Yes, it is," was Friedlander's vigorous response. "A man viciously mistreated by historians, unfairly condemned of a crime of which he was completely innocent—"

"What crime is that?" asked someone, obviously not afraid to voice their ignorance.

Friedlander turned a malignant stare in that direction. "He was said to have poisoned Mozart. It is a vile calumny, a wicked slander. On the contrary, he often praised Mozart, and it was Antonio Salieri who recommended him to the Elector Karl Theodor when that official was seeking a composer to write an opera. That was to become Mozart's first great dramatic work—it was called *Idomeneo*, and many critics declare it to be his finest composition."

The questioner declined to pursue the point, but another took up a different line. "This manuscript that's on this train—is it really outstanding, as some say? Or is it just because Mozart composed it?"

"I doubt its quality," said Friedlander.

"Although there are some who believe it may rank among his best work," said Henryk Sundvall, determined not to be elbowed aside.

"How valuable is the manuscript?" asked a Philistine member of the group, and the query hung in the air for a moment.

"Possibly priceless," said Sundvall.

"Is it true that a Japanese buyer has offered ten million dollars for it?"

"I doubt it very much," said Friedlander dismissively.

"A Japanese man paid 31 million for a van Gogh painting, didn't he?" The questioner was persistent.

"I believe so, but that sale has no influence on this so-called lost folio."

"Mozart died very young, didn't he?" someone else asked.

"He was thirty-five," replied Sundvall.

"That's very young, even for those times. What did he die from?"

"He had repeated attacks of vomiting." Friedlander was quick to reply. "He had a very high fever, his body was swollen, and he was probably suffering from kidney failure. The accusations of poisoning are preposterous."

"Do you agree with that, Professor?" was the question to Sundvall from someone anxious to provoke an argument between the two.

"There is no evidence of any poisoning," Sundvall said equably. "That is true. Salieri's jealousy of Mozart is not well substantiated although Salieri certainly had occasion to feel eclipsed by the younger man's genius. But he praised him frequently—he spoke very highly of *Die Zauberflöte, The Magic Flute.*"

"Wasn't Mozart autopsied?" asked a member of the group who presumably had a medical background gained from television drama.

"No. Techniques for determining the presence of poison in a dead body were not well developed at that time." Sundvall's answer terminated that line of inquiry.

Someone called out to thank the professor for his presentation, and Friedlander departed with a curt nod to no one in particular. I noted that Paolo Conti had joined the group late, and, as people drifted off, I stayed around so that I could talk to him. Before he could leave, too, I had moved toward him.

"Fascinating, wasn't it?" I said. "Considering Mozart is such a genius, we don't know enough about him. At least, I learned a lot I didn't know previously."

"I came in late," he confessed. "Missed the early part. Sounded interesting though."

" 'The Wine Preferences of the Great Composers.' " I said. "Now there's a title for one of your columns."

Conti smiled his world-weary smile. "I'll keep it in mind."

"For the time being, I suppose you are busy preparing a column on the wines aboard the Danube Express?"

"Yes. We're having a rare Slovakian wine tonight with dinner, did you know that?"

"No, I didn't. That will be an unusual occasion."

"It will. Slovakia does not produce much wine—even Switzerland has twice their production. We'll be going through Bratislava today and it's located where Austria, Slovakia, and Hungary meet. On the slopes of the Carpathian Mountains and to the north of the city are some fine vineyards—a pity that their wines are not better known."

"Light and dry, a touch of fruit, fragrant but assertive—is that what your column will say?"

"Something like that. You know wines?"

"No, but I'm supposing that they are similar to the wine from the countries around them—Austria, Bulgaria, Romania. The soil and the climate are similar, so it's likely the wines are of the same general types."

"That's right, and with more aggressive marketing, the wines from all of those countries could be more widely appreciated."

"Unfortunately," I said, "it may take a little while to develop fully the capitalistic spirit to that extent. Half a century of Communism needs a lot of overcoming."

"I suppose so." He leaned against the window where a view of the Danube was sweeping past. The water was still muddy brown, but a long barge with a line of washing prominent along its deck brought a new element to the scene.

"Now how about you?" he asked. "Why are you on board the Danube Express?"

It was a direct approach, and I tried to sound equally direct with my answer, which necessarily had to be evasive.

"A European consortium is interested in the luxury railroad concept," I said, trying to sound as if I had nothing to hide. "I'm contributing some viewpoints."

"Railroad espionage, eh?"

"Far from it. Before opening a new restaurant, any sensible chef-owner eats at other similar restaurants. This is the same approach—what do the existing railroads offer and what else might be offered?"

I like to keep as close to the truth as possible even if my work does sometimes require some—well, let's call it—ambiguity. I wasn't sure whether the answer satisfied him or not. His face didn't show outright doubt, though he asked, "Does the Danube Express fall short in its offerings?"

"They do a wonderful job," I said, thankful to be shown a sidetrack to develop. "It's hard to fault the way they run this operation."

He glanced out of the window at the Danube curling slowly away from its parallel course to the line. "One way they are failing is surely in their security," he commented, and turned back to look at me.

"That criticism is leveled more often at the airlines," I said.

"This Malescu business is bizarre, though, isn't it?"

"I didn't know much about her before this trip, but it seems that she has a flamboyant existence. She's often in the news, usually in the headlines. Maybe she maintains her eminence in the theatre partly by keeping her name in the public eye."

He didn't look convinced. "I heard that another woman was found dead in Malescu's compartment. Who was she, do you know?"

"I think the railroad security people are working on that."

He made a contemptuous sound that expressed a negative opinion of Herr Kramer and his operation. "Maybe they're more worried about somebody stealing that Mozart manuscript."

"Ah, you arrived in time to hear that, did you? You must have heard the question about a Japanese investor offering ten million dollars for it."

"Sounds crazy to me, and, anyway, I didn't know that the Japanese were such music lovers."

"Maybe one of them wants to buy it as an investment," I said.

"Maybe," he conceded. He looked at his watch. "I might go for an early lunch."

"Yes," I said, "I think I might—"

I was interrupted by the opening of the door at the end of the lounge coach. Two figures came through, and conversation in the coach died away. Eyes were all on the couple who came in. It was the glamorous star of the stage and Hungary's one and only, Magda Malescu, and she was on the arm of Dr. Stolz.

CHAPTER THIRTEEN

The "Queen of the Hungarian Theatre" was how the press often referred to her. She looked like a queen now. She wore a rust red suit with a leopard print blouse, calfskin boots, and chunky gold jewelry. Her hair and makeup were impeccable. She walked as if everyone was looking at her and, of course, they were.

Dr. Stolz should have looked as proud as Punch but he had only his habitual gaunt and tired look. His eyes were still lively, though, and he took in the passengers in the lounge car with a sweeping glance. The two of them came walking through the coach like a queen and her consort.

Malescu had that half-smile that many celebrities have perfected. When bestowed on an individual, it gives the impression that the bestower is personally greeting the bestowee but then the look moves on, and the next person becomes the delighted beneficiary.

To my astonishment, they stopped before me. I didn't think I was expected to kiss the hem of her gown, so I didn't do so. Stolz said, "This is the young man from Scotland Yard," and she gave me a charming smile as she held out her hand. This was better than the hem of a gown so I obliged. That introduction, though . . . If Kramer heard about it, I could make the rest of the journey in the locked coach with the Mozart folio and some vine roots.

I shot a look at Stolz, unclear whether he knew better or not. His face told me nothing. I had to mend the fence somehow, and I started to say, "I'm not actually with—"

But the star of stage, screen, and television said, "You were not here on duty, I suspect, but the DS Bahn's resourceful security service asked you to help."

"Yes, that's——" was all I could get out before La Malescu asked, "Would you join us for lunch? We would so love to have you, wouldn't we, Richard?"

"Certainly," the doctor purred, given little choice.

As we took a table in the dining coach, I received a few stares, jealousy probably. A waiter appeared magically, like a genie out of a bottle, and placed a single red rose in a tall, cut-glass vase in the middle of the table. Malescu gave him that smile, and perfect service was assured for the rest of the meal.

"Would you care for an aperitif?" the waiter asked.

"Panna for me," said Malescu. It is a popular bottled water from Italy and believed to be extra pure because of the layers of rock, gravel, and geological sand that the melted snow and the rainwater have to pass through. These are supposed to filter out all the chemical and microbial impurities and add a few parts per million of minerals. The producers of Panna allege that the water spends several years being cleansed and improved that way so it must be the best.

I asked for a glass of Kloster Und as we were still passing through Austria. Kloster Und is another of the light white wines from the southern wine area of Austria. It is little seen outside the country as such wines are best drunk young and thus seldom exported. Estate-bottled wines are still not common here and I relied on the waiter to bring me one of the better examples of Kloster Und.

Dr. Stolz ordered a scotch and soda. As a medical man, I presumed he was prescribing for himself a stimulant. Before the waiter left to fill the order, he handed us menus, elaborate affairs on heavy shiny white cardboard with the words in computer-simulated handwriting in gold.

Malescu ignored hers. She turned the full candlepower of her gaze on me. "I know you are doing all you can to find out who killed poor Talia, but please tell me what you have learned so far."

It was a tough question to answer, but I tried to satisfy her that we were making progress. "Numerous inquiries have been sent to people who knew her, in and out of the theatre," I said. "Some of these are expected to yield clues that will advance us further. You could perhaps help us as far as her presence on the train is concerned."

"Of course," she murmured. "What can I tell you?"

I had the distinct impression that Dr. Stolz was listening to our conversation a little nervously. Was he worried about what she might say, I wondered? Did she know something he didn't want divulged or at least, did he think that?

"Did your understudy always travel with you?" I asked.

"Sometimes, not always. We were close, you understand. She has been my understudy for many years, so I knew her well."

"Then perhaps you knew who might want to kill her?"

She shuddered delightfully. "Certainly not. She was a likable girl, I can't believe that anyone would want to do that."

"Someone did."

She shook her head. "I still can't believe it."

"The theory that the IMG wanted to kill you, but they killed her instead, believing she was you—what do you think of that?"

I was treading close to the edge, I knew that. She might pull a temper tantrum and yell at me for blaming her. She didn't though. It looked as if tears might well from her eyes but, if they did, she controlled them. She was either genuinely sorry for Talia Svarovina, or she was the world's greatest actress.

"I—I suppose it's possible," she admitted.

The waiter came with the drinks and asked if we were ready to order. We obediently looked at the menus and after some questions and answers, the latter being authoritatively provided, we all placed our orders.

Malescu said she would have the Fillets of Sole with Mussels. I ordered the Carp, Danube Style, and the doctor decided upon the

Spinach Roll with a Chicken Filling. The waiter looked pleased that we had all ordered Austrian dishes.

As we sipped our drinks, I asked Malescu about Talia Svarovina's private life.

"She didn't have a lot of it," said Malescu. "We have to travel a lot. Plays in Hungary, Austria, and Germany do not have long runs like plays in New York or London. That means going to medium- and even smaller-sized cities and runs of one or two months only." Her voice was musical and a pleasure to listen to, and certainly she was good to look at—I was glad, after all, that I was from Scotland Yard.

Dr. Stolz was relaxing, it seemed. He no longer had that anxious look, and I wondered what topic he had been worried that we might develop. "Then, too," he said, "much of the time, even when Magda is on the road, the troupe is rehearsing a new play. That leaves little time for social contacts."

Malescu agreed with this promptly. "Our audiences do not have the same acceptance of re-runs that American and British audiences have. They like new and different plays."

"Good for playwrights," I said.

"Unfortunately, no," said Dr. Stolz. "They receive little recompense for their labors. Theatre seats are much cheaper, too—that brings in good audiences but most of the auditoriums and theatres are not large."

"Under Communism," said Malescu, "they received some state support, but now they can no longer rely on that."

"So Talia had little opportunity for making friends," I said, trying to get back to the investigating.

"I suppose she made her friends mostly from the troupe as you traveled around," suggested Stolz to Malescu.

"Yes, she was a friendly girl and had no problem getting along."

"And you and she had no friction?"

Malescu pouted. "I am a woman," she said, and I didn't doubt it for a second. "I am temperamental sometimes," she added, and although I hadn't seen any real evidence of it, I didn't doubt that either. "If we had any disagreements, they were purely professional."

That sounded good, but I didn't buy it. I would bet that they had had a few blowups but I wouldn't expect her to admit it about a person who had just been murdered.

"Did she have any particular friends in the troupe?" I asked.

I thought Malescu hesitated over that, but she may have just been savoring the tiny bubbles in the Panna. "She had a brief affair with a young man who was with us during the run of *A Woman of the Night*."

"Did you star in that?" I asked.

"Of course," she said, sounding surprised. Perhaps she thought it an obvious connection from the title, or maybe she thought the "star" designation made it obvious that it referred to her. "I starred in it, and Talia was my understudy."

"Did she get to play your role?"

"No. I played every performance, including matinees."

"Magda has not missed a performance in—how long is it now, Magda?" asked Dr. Stolz, as if proud of a protégé.

She shrugged. "A long time, I do not know."

I thought she probably did know and didn't want to make it clear that Talia Svarovina rarely got a chance to take the starring role. Still, what did that tell me? Only that Talia had a theoretical reason to want Malescu out of the way.

The faces of the two women, one dead, the other very much alive, merged before my eyes. Their similarity was—or could be when either chose—remarkable. That might be meaningful, but I couldn't take it to any firm conclusion.

"This young man you mentioned—is he still with the troupe?"

"Oh, no, he was with us only for a run of one play, it lasted about four months."

"Did the two of them part on friendly terms?"

"Yes—well, as friendly as the breakup of an affair can be," she said.

"Did they see each other afterward?"

"I wouldn't know." She shrugged.

The food arrived, the plates hot and sending up delicious aromas. I was familiar with the cooking method of Magda's fillets of sole. They are first poached in white wine with butter and shallots, then the liquid is reduced. Bechamel sauce is added, meanwhile the mussels are cooked in water and mushrooms are sautéed separately in butter and lemon. Whipped cream is folded into the sauce, which is then glazed before serving. Cream is widely used in both Austrian and Hungarian dishes. They were served with a tiny mound of haricots verts.

Carp is a very popular fish in this area, too. The Danube style of preparing it spreads carrots, onions, and peppercorns on a little water in a baking pan, then the carp is laid over them. It is baked until the fish is flaky, with basting done continually. Hard-boiled eggs are chopped fine and mixed with butter, lemon juice, and salt and pepper, then simmered. This is poured over the fish, and it is served. It is a simple dish and derives from true country-style cooking, but the quality of a plump and fresh carp makes it excellent. Potato dumplings would be the normal Austrian choice with it, but the decidedly up-market Danube Express served a small quantity of Duchesse potatoes.

Dr. Stolz replied to my query about his Spinach Roll with a Chicken Filling with a grunted acquiescence that it was "all right." The chicken filling was probably minced chicken mixed with cream, beaten eggs, dill, parsley, scallions, and salt and pepper, then blended and croutons added.

Eating quelled the conversation and slowed my investigation. It gave the opportunity to view the scenery, too, although Magda and the doctor had evidently seen it so many times that it no longer held great attraction for them.

I took the opportunity to ask, "Don't the Spitz vineyards spread over the banks of the Danube somewhere near here?"

The doctor paused in his devouring his spinach roll long enough to tell me, "So closely do they cover every available square meter of ground here that there is a local saying that the town is the only one in Austria where grapes grow in the market place."

Soon, the vineyards came into sight, narrow terraces coming right down to the water's edge in serried ranks. I could see orchards, too, with fruit trees, and I asked what they were. "Peaches," said Stolz.

The Spitz castle stands in ruins on top of a grim black rock, and Magda saw me looking at it. "It is very picturesque, is it not?" she asked. "There used to be a castle like that on almost every peak, and the ruins of many of them still remain but are covered with vegetation so they are no longer visible."

"Every robber baron built one," said Stolz. "Many of them strung rope barriers across the Danube and charged a toll from every vessel wanting to pass. It was a lucrative business in those days."

The sky was clouded in shades of gray, but a golden sun persisted in thrusting shafts through them, illuminating an occasional village as if with a giant spotlight.

We finished the meal, and the three of us decided on coffee for the finale. Once more came the choice of all the various blends, but we all ordered black. I returned to my questions of Magda Malescu.

"I presume that you are no longer worried about the threats from the IMG," I said. "Has something happened to cause you to make the decision to be visible to the public once more? Don't you fear danger still?"

Dr. Stolz answered for her before she could speak.

"The receipt of the threatening letter just before we left Munich was a shock to Magda, of course. Her reaction was naturally one of fear. She has now had time to reach a more balanced point of view. She is still afraid, but she is a strong—"

The actress broke in. "Fear is something which is always a shock at first. It is true, as Richard says, that I am still afraid, and my immediate response to the letter was to hide, to disappear from public view. But I cannot do this forever—I am a public figure, people expect to see me, and I will not let them down."

It was a good story, and she told it well. How much was behind it that she wasn't telling me though? I pondered that question as we sipped coffee while the Danube Express swept majestically between the cliff tops, along rocky ledges, and made periodic sorties down almost to the waters of the mighty river.

CHAPTER FOURTEEN

Magda and the doctor left me immediately after the meal. They gave me no hint of their destination, though on a moving train there are not many places to go. As I left the dining coach, I met Karl Kramer.

"You have had lunch?" he asked.

"Yes, with Magda Malescu and Dr. Stolz."

"There is a smile behind those words," he said. "That of a cat that has just had a tasty canary."

Several innuendos were embedded in his statement, but I chose not to acknowledge them. I merely said, "Let me tell you about it."

"Very well. I am just going to talk to Thomas. I know you would like to see where he operates. Why don't you come with me?"

"I'd like to do that," I told him, and we walked through the train, stopping before the door marked COMMUNICATION CENTER and announcing "no admittance" in three languages.

A small bell push was mounted in the doorframe, and Kramer squeezed it several times in a way that clearly made a coded sequence. It was not audible here on the outside, though, making it impossible for anyone to reproduce it.

An unseen speaker demanded identification, and Kramer gave his name and a string of numbers. A tiny lens was set in the middle of the door so that Kramer could be scanned, and, after a pause, a lock clicked, then another. The door swung open, and we entered.

The room was in semidarkness and it took a moment for my eyes to adjust. Kramer introduced me before this had fully occurred, but I was able to make out a small figure. He had white hair and wore a black suit with a neckline like a clergyman's collar. As we went farther into the room, my eyes made a full adjustment to the gloom. I could see that Thomas was younger than I expected. He was almost an albino, and I wondered whether living in semidarkness had made him this way or if he had already possessed the attributes and they had made it easier for him to adapt.

The room was illuminated by a dim green glow, which I realized came from the screens. There were dozens of them—on walls in rows, some mounted on stands, others on tables and desks. Many were multicolored with graphs and bar charts, while others were flickering with lines of rapidly appearing type.

"Perhaps you will explain briefly the purpose of some of your equipment," said Kramer, and Thomas's pale eyes showed the enthusiasm of a scientist more than ready to impress the visitor.

"On this wall here, we have all the data referring to the Danube Express," he said in a high voice. "The speed, temperature, voltage, amperage, and other characteristics of the engines as well as the condition of the bearings, the brake linings, the track, the gyroscopic controls for maintaining stability, and many other such factors. Here, we have the atmospheric conditions inside the train, such as temperature, humidity, barometric pressure, and equipment analyzing for noxious or poisonous compounds. Should any of these be detected, an automatic air replacement system comes into operation.

"Over here"—he motioned to another portion of the same wall—"we have the conditions all along the line ahead of us. If there were a snowfall, we would know of it; if there was ice formation, we would know of that, too."

"What are those moving red squares telling you on that screen?" I asked.

"They show the location of every train within a hundred-kilometer range, so that a collision is virtually impossible. However, should two trains approach within ten kilometers of each other, propulsion power would immediately be disconnected."

"Does that mean," I asked, "that other trains are using this track at the same time as the Danube Express?"

"No, they are not. That is strictly forbidden, but it is theoretically possible for a train to take a wrong track, and that could potentially cause a collision."

He led the way to the adjacent wall. "This is our communication panel. We are in touch with Munich, where our journey originated, and all the stations through which we pass. Vienna, Budapest, and Bucharest are the main stations, but we are also in constant touch with the smaller ones along the way."

He moved to the third wall. "This is the outside world. We receive news from all over the globe. We can communicate by satellite with anyplace on the globe."

"Very impressive," I said. "I'm quite overcome by all this technology."

Thomas beamed. His pale eyes took on a glint of satisfaction. "We are very proud of the Danube Express. Even the Concorde does not have more instrumentation."

"Tell me, Thomas," said Kramer, "have you received any word from the theatres?"

"Yes," Thomas said. "It just came in." He kept looking at Kramer. He was well trained to be discreet.

"You can speak freely in the presence of our friend here from Scotland Yard," Kramer said. To me, he went on, "Thomas has been in touch with the theatres where Malescu has appeared."

"Ah, yes, you told me you were going to check on these and see what opinions said about Malescu, about Svarovina, and the situation between them."

"Unfortunately," said Thomas, "it is not especially helpful. The relationship between Fraulein Malescu and her understudy shows no motive for murder. Certainly, the understudy was a little envious of her mistress but that seems to be not unusual in the theatre. None of the persons interviewed mentioned any violent disagreement between them."

Kramer nodded. "Anything else?"

"Svarovina had an affair with a German. Werner Klimt is his name. It was while they were touring—"

"Was there any reference to a rivalry between Malescu and Svarovina? Over this Klimt?"

"No, none."

"So where has Klimt been recently?"

"After one tour with the Malescu company, he joined a theatre in Dresden and has been making a minor name for himself."

"He is still there?"

"Yes, he lives there now."

"So . . ." Kramer let out his breath. "That does not appear to be a promising lead."

I took advantage of a pause in the conversation to ask, "I presume you have reports on the passengers who joined us in Vienna?"

Kramer looked at Thomas. "Yes," Thomas said. "The Swiss, Franz Reingold, appears to be without blemish. He has a great deal of family money and spends it on his hobbies and on traveling. No associations with disreputable people are evident, and he is not known by the Swiss police as an offender."

"The other passengers?" asked Kramer.

"Two Austrians and a Lebanese," Thomas said. "No records on any of them other than routine."

Kramer nodded and turned to me. "What did you learn from your lunch with Malescu?"

"You had lunch with Malescu?" Thomas's eyes reflected green but perhaps it was the glow from the screens.

"Yes, I did. She was anxious to know how the investigation was going, so I used that to ask her about her relationship with Svarovina."

"She was forthcoming?"

"Oh, yes. She mentioned this German actor though she did not do so by name."

"A pity Dr. Stolz was there," Kramer said. "You could have asked her about the doctor's relationship with Svarovina."

"I'll keep that in mind," I told him. "As for her disappearance, she sounded convincing about the threats from the IMG—what does that stand for, by the way?"

"It means Organization for Magyar Independence," said Thomas promptly. "The word 'Magyar' is used to mean ethnic Hungarians."

"Thomas is a fund of information on all topics," said Kramer. "In addition to all the outputs from his electronic devices."

"He sounds like an extremely valuable man," I agreed, and though Thomas didn't preen at the compliment, the faintest smile appeared on the smooth pale face.

"I'm still not satisfied though," I said. "I know I said Malescu sounded convincing about receiving the threats, but there's something there I don't understand. I'm sure there's more than she's saying."

Kramer turned to Thomas. "What do we know of the IMG?"

"We have a file on them," Thomas said, "as we do on all revolutionary and terrorist organizations. Their activities have been more prevalent in Hungary than in surrounding countries. Several assassinations of public personages have been attributed to them. Outbursts in the Hungarian Parliament have been initiated by them, and sometimes they get a newspaper to print one of their—shall I say—complaints?"

"Is the Budapest *Times* one of them?" I asked.

"Yes, it is," Thomas said.

"The sweep," said Kramer. "Is it providing anything useful?"

"Herr Kramer asked me to run another check on everyone on the passenger list," Thomas explained. "I have printouts here for you on those that have come in so far. Only one is interesting . . ."

He picked up several sheets from the tray of a printer that was still silently churning out page after page. He sifted through the stack and pulled out one of them.

Kramer turned to catch some light from a nearby screen. He read it through, grunted, and handed it to me. "This is an inquiry agency we use from time to time," he said.

The report was brief, and the name of the person investigated was Paolo Conti. Essentially, it said that information on him was sketchy—to a degree that was suspicious. Large blocks of time were unaccounted for, and no address could be located for those periods.

A village near Venice in Italy was given as his residence but locals knew nothing of him. Postal services and Internet providers had no listings of his name.

"Very peculiar," I said. "Erich Brenner introduced him to me. I wonder if he has any knowledge of Conti?"

"He does not," Kramer said. "I already talked to him."

I read through the final paragraph again. "He contributes to the *European Wine Journal* sure enough according to this. He told me that—and it is what he had told Herr Brenner."

Thomas was listening to all this. He raised a tentative finger. "Yes, Thomas?" Kramer prompted.

"I took the liberty of asking the *European Wine Journal* for an account of his association with them."

"Very good, Thomas. Have you had a reply?"

"Yes. He is strictly freelance. His contributions come in to the magazine on an irregular basis."

"Did they say where they get them from?"

"Always by e-mail—so they could come from anywhere."

Kramer and I exchanged glances.

"He is *ein Irrlicht*," I suggested.

Thomas nodded, a gentle smile on his lips. Kramer gave me a sharp look. "Ah, you know our German word?" he said. "In English, it is 'will-o'-the-wisp,' I believe."

"Correct," I told him.

"That he may be," said Kramer grimly, "but we shall 'nail him down.' That is correct, too, is it not?"

"It is."

"We will do this separately, I think. I will interrogate him further on an official basis; you should do so on a more personal level. You are both authorities on wine, you have some common ground there."

"You evidently have a further file on me, too," I said.

"The wine, you mean? Yes, I do have another file on you. But then, you would think me inefficient if I did not, is that not so?"

"I can't believe you are ever inefficient, Herr Kramer," I told him, and he gave me a curt nod of acknowledgment. "It won't be difficult to develop another discussion with Conti on wine. He and I have already had one discussion on the subject, he was telling me about Czech wines. Incidentally, he was very direct in asking me why I was on the Danube Express. I gave him my cover story— well, it's the truth really."

"Does he suspect that you are helping me?"

"He gave no indication of it."

I thanked Thomas for the "tour" of his facility just as a beeper sounded from somewhere in the equipment-crowded room. "That is Budapest calling," he said, adding, "Each area has a different tone. Excuse me."

He hurried across the room, and Kramer pointed to a flickering screen. "This shows our progress. We are about to pass through Heldenberg. I would like to have this crime solved before we reach Budapest." He gave me a hard look. "We may have to adopt unusual measures."

"I'll do anything I can do to help," I said.

"We will talk again very soon," he promised. Outside, he checked the door carefully to make sure it was locked and strode off down the corridor. I headed for the lounge car, and the Stanton Walburgs were my first encounter. "All these castles!" said Mrs. Walburg. "Never saw so many in my whole life."

"Almost one on every peak," I said. "Did you see Aggstein Castle?"

"We certainly did," said her husband, "that white-colored one. It's very unusual. Did you hear about Hadmar the Hound?"

"No, who is he?"

Mrs. Walburg shuddered. "A terrible man. He was the Lord of Aggstein. He and his brother plundered this entire territory and all vessels that tried to pass on the river. The two of them were known as 'the Hounds.' Finally, some merchants banded together and hired several dozen knights, who hid in a boat. The merchants made sure that word of this boat reached the castle—and the word was that it was filled with treasure. When Hadmar stopped the boat to rob it, the knights sprang out and overcame the brothers and their men."

"Making that stretch of the Danube safe for passage once again," her husband said, "at least, until the next tyrant came along."

We chatted a few minutes longer before they left and I watched the Danube slide by, still brown but moving sluggishly. A steep-roofed church nestled amid a stand of poplars, and a tiny village had figures moving around in what looked like traditional costumes. Entering the village was a plodding ox pulling a cart with a heavy load.

Then the track climbed up the riverbank, giving fine views of the extraordinary rock formations on the other side. Rock edges had been worn away over the centuries giving the appearance of a rough wall consisting of irregular slabs of stone. It made it look impregnable, and I could only hope that our problem would be less formidable.

CHAPTER FIFTEEN

Irena Koslova was staring wistfully out of a window in the corridor. She looked lovely in profile, and I stopped beside her.

"I hope the journey is continuing to be all you hoped for," I said.

She shrugged enigmatically, then said, "Yes," but it was not entirely convincing. I turned to the view she was watching.

The train was climbing effortlessly up a steep slope, the track clinging to a hillside. Oak trees grew in profusion, many of them gnarled and twisted as they struggled to survive on the inclines, some of them precipitous. Their branches reached out like grasping arms, seeking for something to hold on to for stability.

"The lounge coach is next," I said. "Shall we sit?"

She nodded, and we walked on into the lounge coach, which was almost empty. We sat opposite each other across a small folding table. She produced a wan smile, then took a deep breath.

"I was having 'some gray moments,' " she said. "Do you say that in English?"

"No, but I know what you mean," I told her.

"We have a number of sayings like that in Romanian. I suppose you would call us a melancholy people?"

"The English are considered a stiff, unfeeling people," I said. "Unemotional, ungiving, and a lot of other 'uns'—so I suppose all nationalities look different to others."

"You didn't look unemotional when you were having lunch with Magda Malescu," she said, looking out the window.

I laughed. "You saw that, did you? Well, I don't think any man could be unemotional sitting opposite her."

"Yes, I saw you enjoying yourself." She was relaxing now and spoke more easily. "You described her to me when we last talked as a woman not easy to understand. Do you understand her better now?"

"It would need a lot more than a lunch to do that. But then I'm not sure I find any woman easy to understand."

"You surely don't include me?" she asked, turning away from the outside view. "I think I am very transparent."

"A woman who travels alone on the Danube Express because it is something she has always wanted to do? No, I wouldn't describe that as transparent. Unusual—certainly. Mysterious—very possibly."

"Ah." She nodded and was silent for a few seconds.

Then she said, "Perhaps I should explain that to you. You see, I was engaged to be married, and we had planned to spend our honeymoon on the Danube Express. We went for a short boat trip on the Black Sea. The steamer rammed a pier and we hit another boat. My husband-to-be was drowned. I was rescued."

"What a terrible tragedy. I'm so sorry." I couldn't think of anything else to say.

"That was more than a year ago. When I heard about this twenty-fifth anniversary trip, I decided to take it. My decision was late, but there was a cancellation. Maybe it was not such a good idea—I have had a few of these 'gray moments.' Still, I'm trying to enjoy the journey, and it really is a rare occasion."

"I hope you will enjoy it," I told her, "and anytime you feel a 'gray moment' coming on, and you want someone to talk to—well, I'm here, I'm on the train."

She smiled charmingly, and her mood seemed to have passed. "So what progress are you making in the investigation?"

"Not enough. I'm still puzzled about Malescu's disappearance although it doesn't seem likely that she is responsible in any way for the murder of her understudy."

Her expression didn't change.

"You've heard that that's who was murdered?" I asked.

"Of course. It's all over the train."

"Have you heard any suspicions?"

She hesitated. "It's all right," I said, "you can tell me. I'm only collecting opinions."

"Well, it's probably only gossip, but one or two fingers are pointing at Herr Lydecker. Did you know he was a magician?"

"That's what I heard. Is there anything between him and Malescu?"

So much for collecting opinions. I was collecting gossip now. The investigation was indeed in a bad way.

"They worked together on the stage—" She stopped and looked at me accusingly. "But you must know that."

"I heard that she was an assistant in his magic act and that it was her first stage appearance," I hastened to say, "but I haven't heard any word to suggest that they have had any contact recently. That first stage appearance was a long time ago."

She smiled. "La Malescu wouldn't want to hear you say that—a long time ago indeed!"

I returned the smile. "Promise not to tell her," I said.

"Not much likelihood of that," she said, "but in any case, even if it was recent, it would have to mean that Lydecker had mistaken her understudy for Malescu, and that doesn't sound reasonable. Surely he knew Malescu too well?"

"The two look very much alike," I pointed out.

"Actually, they don't," Irena said, "but they can do so. There is a basic similarity, and both women look like they are makeup experts and, of course, both are actresses."

"If they want to look alike, they could, yes, that's true. Now, when we talked before, you suggested that one of her many lovers killed Malescu—that was when she had disappeared and everybody thought she had been murdered. Who else beside Lydecker might fit into that category?"

"That doctor—Dr. Stolz—isn't he a possibility? The way she clings to his arm when they parade through the train—"

Was there a touch of envy there, I wondered? From a woman who had lost her man not that long ago? If so, it was understandable. "It's hard to see what motive he might have," I said.

"M'm, I haven't heard any motives being suggested," she admitted, and she looked especially pretty when she was pensive. She brightened. "Then there's the Italian, Paolo Conti—"

"Have you heard anything about him?" I asked casually. Perhaps I could learn something about the mystery man with gigantic holes in his dossier, I thought, but she shook her head.

"Not really, but he's very—what do you say in English?"

"Dishy?" I suggested.

She repeated the word doubtfully. "What association does he have with a dish?"

"I don't know. Some English slang words have strange origins."

"Well, I'll use it," she decided, with a brief nod of her head. "He's dishy."

"And—?"

"Well, he's a man, isn't he? And Malescu's an eater of men."

"She is? Oh, you mean a man-eater. Yes, I suppose so."

"There are only so many men on this train," Irena said. "One of them must be guilty of Svarovina's murder."

"Couldn't the murderer be a woman?"

"No. Certainly not." She was unhesitating in her answer, and I held back a comment about female intuition.

"There's another puzzle on this train," I told her.

"Really?" Her eyes lit up. "I don't like people being murdered when I'm on holiday, but this is exciting, isn't it! What's the other puzzle?"

"This is beginning to sound like a Mystery Train Tour," I began. "They are popular in many countries now. Actors and actresses put on a murder play, and the audience has to guess who did it."

"This is a little too much like that," she said with a delightful shudder, "but go on—what's the other puzzle?"

"When Malescu disappeared, someone on the train gave out the story that she had been murdered. The story seems to have come from a journalist called Mikhel Czerny."

She nodded. "He is very well known. He gets a lot of sensational stories."

"He also seems to have a vendetta against Magda Malescu."

Irena smiled. "He certainly does!"

"So," I persisted, "nobody seems to be sure what he looks like, but if the story came from somebody on the train, who is he?"

She was quiet. Then she murmured, "Another puzzle, yes, I see." She turned her gaze to the window where the Danube was almost on a level with the track. It looked very wide, and we passed a white cruise boat. It had several decks, and passengers by the rails waved. White smoke came from a large funnel, and I wondered if it was as synthetic as our smoke on the Danube Express. We surged past it and soon left it behind.

"Conti is a journalist, too, they say." Irena's comment was in a thoughtful tone of voice.

"Yes. He writes for the *European Wine Journal* among other magazines. Do you know anything about him?"

"No, but couldn't he be Czerny?"

I considered that. "Possible, I suppose." I decided not to say anything about Kramer's information concerning Czerny's shadow-like existence, but here was a thought that hadn't occurred to me. If he didn't have much of a profile as a wine journalist, was it because he spent his time reporting for the Budapest *Times*?

I looked at Irena in a new light. "It's an idea," I told her, and she smiled with satisfaction.

"Would I make a good detective?" she asked.

"No," I said, "you're too attractive."

"Wouldn't that make me a better detective?" she purred.

"Do you know anything else about Czerny?" I asked.

"No, and no one seems to know anything." She moved in her

seat. "I must go. I have a lot of work to do on myself to get ready for dinner."

"You look great to me," I said gallantly.

"Ha! Wait till you see me tonight!" She rose and was gone before I could ask her what her plans were.

It would not take me as long to get ready for dinner as Irena said she needed. I meant it when I said she looked great and, by my estimate, fifteen minutes would be ample to get her looking terrific, but my experience of women was that they always thought they required six times as long to get ready as they really did. Maybe that is because they have to try out the image in the mirror with six different pairs of shoes or six different combinations of a blouse and a skirt.

Regardless of such speculation, fascinating as it might be, I didn't need to start getting ready yet, so I had plenty of time to carry out a task I had been thinking about for some time. It was a task of which I had reminded myself by talking about Malescu's double mystery—being allegedly murdered and being definitely missing.

I went in the direction of the restaurant coach, which was being prepared for dinner. Glasses were being carefully examined before being placed on the snowy white tablecloths, knives, forks, and spoons were being given an extra shine, and vases of flowers were being strategically located.

I went on through and into the first kitchen coach. This was something I would have wanted to do anyway. I always like to look at kitchens, and I was curious as to how one that was expected to provide outstanding meals could do so in the limited space of two coaches, even coaches on the renowned Danube Express.

The head chef was an Austrian, Heinz Hofstatter. He was big, bearded, and jovial—almost an archetypal chef, but then I knew that such a responsible position required a person with good PR skills in addition to his talents in the kitchen.

I mentioned Erich Brenner's name after telling Hofstatter who I was, and cooperation was immediately assured. "Herr Brenner told me that you would wish to see our railroad kitchens." Hofstatter beamed. "Let me show them to you—it will be a pleasure." He hesitated momentarily. "I hope you will not be disappointed that we do not have any Scottish dishes in preparation."

"Not at all," I said. "I am English, I'm not—"

"But you are from Scotland Yard—"

"Ah, I see—but Scotland Yard is not actually in Scotland."

"No?" He was surprised.

"No. I am not here on official business in any case. It's just professional interest."

He beamed again and led the way. Stainless steel glittered everywhere in the halogen-lamp-illuminated coach—ovens, workbench surfaces, storage cabinets, exhaust hoods, all were made of it, and the reflection doubled the lighting intensity. Pans simmered softly, and enticing aromas were already beginning to fill the air. A young woman came in with a box heaped with fat, pink shrimp.

Another woman with fair hair braided in traditional Austrian fashion was pressing aspic into elaborate shapes, while a small Latin-featured man with dark circles under his eyes and burns on his hands was tasting the contents of a large, steaming pan.

The train's air-conditioning system had to work overtime here, I guessed, and it was doing a fine job, keeping the working temperature at a level much lower than most kitchens I knew. It was doing it despite all the ovens, infrared heaters, and the high-induction surface burners.

"I had thought you might have to serve fixed meals because of lack of space," I told Heinz Hofstatter. "I am amazed that you can offer a menu with such a wide choice of dishes as you do."

"We don't do the impossible," Hofstatter said jovially, "but we come close."

A door opened at the far end of the coach, and a young fair-haired man came in with a large basket on his shoulder. I inhaled. "That must be marvelous bread," I said.

"Olive bread, pepper bread, mushroom bread, sun-dried-tomato bread—we even have anchovy bread," Chef Hofstatter said. "We bake and serve them all. Then we have focaccias, garlic twists, brioches, and Sicilian breadsticks—Bertrand, come here a moment!"

The young man approached. He had a smile on his face that I was glad to see—work in a kitchen should be satisfying and enjoyable. "Bertrand is one of our bakers," Hofstatter said. "He is from Alsace—Bertrand, give our honored guest a taste of one of your offerings for today. What do you recommend?"

Bertrand looked dubious. "They are all good—"

Hofstatter laughed. "That I am sure of. For a taste though—what do you suggest?"

After a moment's thought, Bertrand reached into the basket and unwrapped the top of a stack of small rolls. Each was the shape and size of a large egg.

"Please take one," Bertrand invited, and I did so. It was deliciously browned and hot from the oven. I bit into it and chewed. Crispy on the outside, it was soft and delicious on the inside. "Magnificent!" I said.

"Tell the *Ehrenmann,*" Hofstatter said, using the flattering but seldom-used German name for a gentleman, "about it."

"In Alsace, we have a large number still of Benedictine monasteries," Bertrand said. "Alsace also has the finest charcuteries in all of France—"

"Bertrand is prejudiced"—Hofstatter smiled—"but in that statement, he is correct."

Bertrand went on, "Well, there are none better in Europe. Naturally, we make the most use of these, and a popular bread has become this one." Bertrand paused, watching me eat the rest of the roll, daring me to guess its ingredients.

Hofstatter watched me, too, still jovial but not above putting me on the spot. "I'm not familiar with the taste—which is superb," I said. "You gave me a clue by referring to charcuteries, so there is obviously a pork product included in the baking. The pork, the bacon, the sausages from your Alsace charcuteries are the finest."

Both smiled, waiting. I went on, no stopping and no turning back now. "The ingredient that gives it such an unusual flavor might be chopped sausage, but it is richer than that, firmer and fuller. I think that it is what is called 'blood sausage' in England, 'blood pudding' in the USA, and known as *'boudin noir'* in France.

"Traditionally, it consists of pigs' blood and suet—suet is not seen much anymore as it is considered too fatty. It comes from the fatty tissues around the liver of cattle and sheep. Consuming blood is not well accepted today either—"

"Not even in Transylvania." Hofstatter and Bertrand chuckled, and I acknowledged that riposte with a grin.

"—but it is still used in some parts of Alsace, especially in the Strasbourg region," I continued. "Finally, I think *'boudin noir'* is *'Blutwurst'* in German, is it not?"

Hofstatter burst into raucous laughter. Bertrand looked from me to him, then set down the basket with a wide grin.

"Yes, *Meinherr, Blutwurst* is the correct word," he admitted.

"You are a chef?" Hofstatter asked, still amused.

"No, not anymore," I said, "but I used to be."

"You can identify the ingredients in all foods?" asked Hofstatter.

"No, not all. Some, though."

"You know *Steinmetzbrot*?" Hofstatter asked. He pointed to a dark loaf in the basket. "Rye or wheat can be used. It is a little spicy, and it has to be baked long and very slowly in order to caramelize the starches. It has a very unusual flavor."

He indicated another loaf, smaller in size, and Bertrand picked it up with a napkin, handling it as tenderly as a kitten. It emitted an aroma that was discernible above the other breads. "*Schluterbrot,*" Hofstatter said. "It is made with rye and oats. Then we have linseed bread and—" He broke off with a laugh. "You must excuse me. Bertrand and I get enthusiastic about our breads."

"It's good to see enthusiasm," I told him, "about any food."

Bertrand picked up his basket and went on his way, giving me a cheery wave. Hofstatter said, "Shall we continue the tour of our tiny establishment?"

"Certainly," I agreed.

"Fraulein Malescu wanted to see everything—I think you should see everything also."

My pulse quickened. Aside from my professional interest in seeing the kitchens, that was why I had wanted to take this tour.

I particularly wanted to know if Magda Malescu had been there.

CHAPTER SIXTEEN

Through the next coach, we went past the bakery, where the ovens sat quietly but hard at work as the dials on the panels indicated. Dough- and pasta-making machines spun and turned softly, and next to them was a battery of shining machines ejecting various shapes of pasta.

I said to Herr Hofstatter, "No doubt you would have preferred to have the shapes made manually," and he nodded. "*Ja,* but owing to space limitations, it is not possible. These machines can provide every shape at the twist of a knob."

In the storage rooms, we stopped. Rows of boxes, crates, jars, and bottles filled the shelves, and next to them were the freezers, some of them glass-fronted. I could see ducks, quail, pheasants, sides of beef, joints of veal, and saddles of venison. A separate unit contained fish and shellfish.

"I am amazed," I told him. "You have an incredible array of food. You must be able to produce almost any dish that a normal restaurant can offer."

Herr Hofstatter patted his stomach with both hands in a self-satisfied gesture. "I believe we can." He led the way down the corridor. This section of the train had no windows, and the absence of a passing view emphasized the extraordinarily sensitive leveling mechanism of the Danube Express. There was none of the swaying and rocking usually associated with a moving train. It was almost as stable as if it was not moving at all.

At this end of the coach were the spices and the herbs, the flavorings and the condiments, some in temperature-controlled cabinets. I stopped and looked at some labels. Once again, the range of products was remarkably comprehensive.

I examined several. I said casually, "I am surprised to hear that Magda Malescu showed an interest in your very efficient operation. She enjoys food, I know; I just had lunch with her. But I didn't realize that she was concerned with anything beyond eating it."

"Ah, but she is," Herr Hofstatter assured me. "She asked me many questions."

"About what?" I asked, still examining labels.

"She asked about bread, she wanted to know all the ingredients, and she asked about baking times, too. Then she asked about herbs— she wanted to know if we used fresh ones, and I told her that we did. She asked how often we replaced them, and I told her that we carry sufficient stock only for three weeks, so they are always fresh."

"Nice to know that your passengers are curious about such matters," I said. "Did she ask anything else?"

Herr Hofstatter didn't express surprise at my continued inquisition, but to allay any possible suspicion, I said lightly, "She sounds as if she knows more about food than a lot of famous actresses. Most of them would say they had no time for such things."

"That is so," Hofstatter said. "She asked too about our fruit and nuts. She said she thought it would be difficult to have fresh ones on board at all times."

I nodded. This was what I had been hoping for.

Hofstatter continued. "I told her that we replenish supplies every trip. Of course, we do not make trips all the time. This is a special train."

"She didn't eat any fruit or nuts during the lunch we had together," I said. "It sounds as if she must be particularly fond of both."

"She did not talk about them any further," said Hofstatter. A kitchen helper came along at that moment and sought Herr Hofstatter's help in locating the olives. When that quest was satisfied, we walked back to the kitchens.

I thanked the head chef for the tour of his domain and congratulated him on an extraordinarily competent operation under very difficult circumstances and restrictive space. I strolled back through the train, thinking over what I had just learned.

When I walked back through the train after dressing for dinner, the view out of the left-side windows was of Slovakia and the view out of the windows to the right was of Hungary.

The Alfold, the great Hungarian plain, offers a contrast to the hills and mountains visible during the earlier part of the journey. There can be great fascination in flat country, though, even if a river is not the best vantage point. Still, the cruise boats suffer from that disadvantage more than a train, and the Danube Express followed the track that frequently climbed up to the edge of the Danube Valley.

The Alfold is nearly four hundred feet above sea level and is the most extensive plain in Europe. It did not require a great stretch of the imagination to picture the massed hordes of the Mongols sweeping across the Alfold—the Mongols, those wild warriors who lived, fought, slept, and ate on their horses. Their vast numbers would stretch to the horizon and strike terror into the hearts of all who saw them.

They attacked, massacring men, women, children, and beasts with equal savagery. Their faces covered with long whiskers, their dress of rough animal skins, the crooked sabers and their fierce yells as they butchered entire populations earned them the deserved name of "Barbarians." Now, with a gorgeous crimson sunset behind us, it was all too easy to see why contemporary historians said, "The land ran red with blood."

They took no satisfaction in conquest and occupation. They were not farmers or traders or empire-builders—they lived only for war. Battle was their only satisfaction. Many writers have spoken of the facility with which they poured across the plains, unimpeded by mountains and unhampered by forests or difficult terrain. The Alfold was a feature of geography that facilitated the satisfaction of their ambitions.

Groves of birch trees and pines were dotted here and there, and orchards could be seen, a ghostly blue in the evening light. In places, the banks of the Danube were willow-grown, while, at the limit of vision, vineyards lay over the land like great blankets.

The Danube Express wove a slow but steady route along the rim of the river valley, the automatic leveling mechanism of the coaches canceling out the sporadic tilt of the track. Darkness was falling fast, and lights twinkled on in villages, tiny chips of light in the darkness.

In the dining coach, one table was occupied and caught my immediate attention. Paolo Conti was there, and his companion was none other than Irena Koslova. She looked charming in a dress of soft green with puffy sleeves. She gave me a smile and Conti disbursed a condescending nod. Concealing my disappointment commendably, I smiled back and took a table farther down the coach. I had planned on talking more with Conti myself, but maybe Irena could do it better.

I ordered a gin and tonic for fortification and devoted my attention to reading the menu. While I was doing so, Helmut Lydecker and Herman Friedlander came in, engrossed in conversation, and sat down at a table together. A magician and a music conductor—not such a strange pair, I supposed, both entertainers though in different spheres.

I was still studying the menu when my drink arrived. Erich Brenner came in, speaking to those at every table in an apparent goodwill gesture.

"Everything going well?" he asked me jovially, and with equal bonhomie I said that it was. He lowered his voice and leaned a little closer. He avoided looking conspiratorial and managed to make it appear nothing more than friendly. "The investigation is making progress?" he asked. A tinge of hope was discernible in his tone.

"Yes," I said, "it is making progress."

"We will be in Budapest soon," he said. "We need to be able to convince the authorities there that there is no reason to impede our journey onward."

"I am sure we will be able to do that," I said, and hoped he couldn't see the tongue in my cheek.

"Good man," he said. He gave me his best company smile and moved on down the coach.

Elisha Tabor came in wearing a tailored suit that looked a little severe. She looked around imperiously and chose a table. She had no sooner sat than Henri Larouge entered, saw her, and made his way over to her table. The two of them had a short conversation. He was looking persuasive, and she was seeming unreceptive. Their voices did not carry and lipreading is a skill that I ought to acquire, but I have not yet done so. Consequently, I was not certain what was happening, but Larouge tightened his lips, said something quickly, and went off to another table. It looked like a brush-off from where I sat.

I devoted myself to the menu. I chose a smoked mackerel pâté to start, to be followed by *Rollmopse*. These brine-pickled herrings are a German specialty, but many neighboring countries have adopted them, and their popularity has spread enough that we eat them in America and England, and the restaurateurs are sufficiently unoriginal as to call them by the same name, "rollmops."

In France, rollmops are put into a marinade that is based on white wine, but the Germans prefer the herrings much more acidic in taste. They use vinegar instead of the wine and add dill pickles and onions.

The main course required a lengthier decision. The Escallopes of Veal cooked in Dubrovnik Style sounded enticing. It is not a dominant cuisine, but the waiter explained that onions and mushrooms are sautéed in butter and seasoned with thyme and bay leaves. Rice and chicken broth are added, then cooked in the oven until the rice is tender. It is then puréed, and egg yolks, unsweetened whipped cream, and grated Parmesan cheese are added. The escallopes are sautéed in butter, sherry is added, and the liquid reduced. The sauce is added, the rice mixture is spread on top, and Parmesan cheese on top of that. The dish is heated quickly under the broiler till golden brown.

If the chefs were going to spend that much time cooking this dish, I thought it was only fair to order it. I did so after considering first a Slovak specialty—pork chops with apricots—and second a German dish—baby chickens with sauerkraut. The birds used are very small, the size of the French *"poussins,"* and I knew that Cornish game hens are used in this dish in the USA.

The Stanton Walburgs had come in meanwhile and were interrogating the waiter about the menu. I noticed that Karl Kramer was not present, then realized that I had never seen him in the dining coach.

Then came the grand entrance. Magda Malescu, with Dr. Stolz once again in attendance, paused dramatically in the doorway, lit up the coach with a smile, and swept down the corridor. She smiled delightfully at me in passing, and the doctor bade me a good evening. She wore a gown that she must have kept after performing in *Madame Dubarry.*

My pâté was excellent, with just the right addition of Cognac. It was served on small crackers of indefinable origin but unobtrusive, as they should be. The *Rollmopse* were as mouth-puckering as expected. I drank San Pellegrino with those two courses as a wine would be ruined, completely overwhelmed by the vinegar, the onions, and the dill pickles. I chose the Italian sparkling water as it is high in minerals and less gassy than many of its competitors.

With the veal, I had ordered—at the waiter's recommendation—a bottle of Szamorodni, a Hungarian white wine. A light red wine would go well with the veal, too, he said, but this was a white more assertive than most and was equal to the task. Both dry and sweet wines are offered with the Szamorodni label, and this one was pale golden in color and very much like a good Riesling.

The Veal Dubrovnik was a rich, satisfying dish. The escallopes were small, maybe two inches in diameter and tender enough to cut with a fork. The use of pureéd rice is unusual, a clever way of avoiding the cream so loved by Middle European chefs, while the liberal application of Parmesan cheese gave it substance. A few tiny roasted potatoes came with it and just a spoonful of slim green beans, cooked then sautéed quickly in seasoned oil.

I wasn't really watching the table where Irena Koslova and Paolo Conti were sitting facing each other, but I could hardly help noticing that they were having some long conversations. They were eating and drinking, too, though I couldn't see what had been their choices.

My waiter came, highly recommending the desserts. "The pastry chef is from Vienna," he told me. "He spent many years at Sacher's."

I knew the restaurant. It played a prominent role in one of the most publicized incidents in the history of cuisine. In the heyday of the Austro-Hungarian Empire, the famous *Sachertorte* had been a dessert that no visitor to Vienna could leave without tasting. Sacher's Restaurant, where it was served, became world-renowned.

Then the Café Demel began serving it, too. Sacher's claimed that Demel's could not do that—it was their specialty. Franz Sacher had concocted the confection for Prince von Metternich, they said. Demel's kept on serving it, claiming they had the original recipe.

A huge court case began, and most of Europe hung on every line uttered by the learned counsels. Fortunes were spent by the protagonists—and presumably fortunes were made by the legal profession. Demel's went bankrupt and was sold to a conglomerate, while Sacher's general manager committed suicide. Dessert can be a tough business.

Sacher's is still there today though. It's on Philharmonikastrasse, and much of the secret of making *Sachertorte* has been leaked. It is a chocolate sponge cake and, after baking, it is sliced in two and filled with apricot jam.

"I don't suppose he bakes—" I began, and the waiter smiled.

"No, *Meinherr,* he doesn't bake *Sachertorte* but he does make an excellent *Salzburger Nockerl.*"

That is another outstanding Austrian dessert, and I opted for it without hesitation. It is a soufflé that offers the diner the chance to feel righteous as it contains only eggs, flour, lemon, milk, and a little sugar. Raspberry syrup is offered on the side, but may be declined if one wishes to avoid shattering that righteous image.

It was indeed superb, and I told the waiter that he could convey my compliments to the pastry chef. I stole a few more glances in the direction of that other table. Conti was giving Irena his Italian smile. She was listening intently to what he was saying. I reflected on the excellent meal I had just enjoyed and pushed out all other thoughts—except the one about Magda Malescu and her visit to the kitchens and the food storage coach. That should tell me a lot, and I kept turning it over and over in my mind to find the kernel of knowledge in that nut . . .

CHAPTER SEVENTEEN

Tiny lights pulsed by, fleeting fireflies in the coal black night. I watched for a while from the seclusion of my compartment. A spatter of rain came, miniscule drops flung at the glass so suddenly that I jerked back. It was during one of those moments when I felt a pang of nostalgia for the old days of train travel—the thump of the wheels over the rail joints, the shriek of the wind past ill-fitting windows, and the rolling of the coach. All gone now, eclipsed by technology, which gave us instead, quiet, calm, and balance.

I thought I remembered the rhythmic thump, the steely rattle and the hypnotic sway of the coach as being conducive to sleep, but maybe nostalgia was overplaying its role. I pulled the curtain and must have been asleep within minutes.

The seductive aroma of coffee filled the air of the dining coach the next morning. Many passengers preferred to have breakfast in their compartments, and there were empty tables as I entered.

I was enjoying a glass of Italian orange juice while I contemplated the breakfast choice. It is different from the orange juice of Spain or Israel, the two leaders in the field, as it is bloodred. First-time visitors to Italy who order orange juice send it back when they see it, complaining that they have been brought tomato juice instead. It is, in fact, squeezed from the blood oranges that the Italians prefer.

I selected a bowl of Swiss muesli with pineapple and pumpernickel bread with butter made earlier on the train. The waiter looked disappointed, but I was being prudent after the excellent meal of the previous night. He offered me a choice of newspapers—Paris *Matin*, Frankfurter *Zeitung*, Zurcher *Tagblatt*, and the London *Times*. He had others, he said, but to carry all exceeded his lifting capacity. He mentioned the papers of Vienna, Budapest, Berlin, Rome, and was prepared to go on, but I stopped him there. I took the Zurich and the London papers and saw that they were both that morning's edition. I had expected no less from the ever-efficient Danube Express, but I asked the waiter how they received them so promptly, and he told me that they were downloaded into the train's computer and printed out almost simultaneously.

I was partway into a juicy scandal in Switzerland and finishing the muesli when I became aware that Irena Koslova was standing there. "May I join you?" she asked.

She was wearing a casual light-wool dress in mauve and russet colors, and her hair looked as if she had come directly from the beauty shop.

"Certainly," I said.

She sat opposite me and ordered a half grapefruit and black coffee from the waiter, who appeared as if by magic.

"That's all?" I asked.

"That's all I ever have for breakfast. So—did you enjoy your dinner last night?"

"It was very good indeed. All German-Austrian dishes."

"Mine was very good, too. I had fish."

"You looked as if you were enjoying yourself," I said.

"I was doing what you told me to do."

"Me? What did I tell you to do?"

"You said I would make a good detective."

I took a final mouthful of muesli. There was just enough milk. "I didn't say that," I protested, "you said that."

"No, I asked you if I would make a good detective, and you said I would if I weren't so attractive."

"Did I say that?" I reached for the pumpernickel and the butter.

She waved her grapefruit spoon. "Well, something like that—anyway, that's what I was doing last night. I was being a detective. I decided you need an assistant."

She gave me a triumphant look.

"Good," I said, perhaps a little faintly. "What did you learn?"

She attacked the grapefruit with vigor. It didn't stand a chance. "Paolo Conti is something of a mystery man. He told me about his writing for the *European Wine Journal* but when I asked him what other magazines or newspapers he writes for, he was vague. I asked him about wine festivals and wine fairs, and he says he attends some of them but on an irregular basis."

She put the spoon down, having achieved the complete demolition of the grapefruit. "I asked him about VinItalia—you know, the Italian Wine Fair they have in Verona every year—"

"Yes, I know it, I have attended a few."

"I said he must know the president, Luigi Barcarolli."

"And did he?"

"He hesitated, then he said he didn't exactly know him but he had met him."

"Maybe he had," I suggested.

"I've only attended the fair once," she said, "and that was six years ago. Don't they change presidents more often than that?" She produced the statement with all the flair of a conjuror bringing a white rabbit from a top hat.

"I would think so. Or he could have been re-elected."

She smiled. "Still, did I do well?"

"Very well. Anything else?"

"Conti does seem to travel a lot. I tried to find out why because he doesn't seem to do enough writing to justify it. He wasn't helpful though."

"Did he say where he travels?" I asked.

"France, Italy, Spain, and he mentioned Germany, Hungary, and the old Yugoslav republics."

"All wine-producing areas," I pointed out.

"Yes," she said thoughtfully. "So that supports his story, doesn't it?"

"Did he say where he lives?"

"A village near Venice."

That fitted with Karl Kramer's information. What now, I wondered? Irena was looking at me hopefully, awaiting a gem of investigative wisdom from the pride of Scotland Yard. I couldn't disappoint her.

"For the moment, we have to shift our attention to other suspects," I said resolutely. "We will come back to Conti when we get further information on him."

"Do we have other suspects?" she asked. It was "we," already. Scotland Yard had just gained another recruit.

"Everybody is a suspect," I said portentously, hoping that her inexperience as an investigator meant that she hadn't heard that old chestnut a hundred times.

"So whom do you want me to interrogate next?" she asked eagerly.

I reached for another slice of pumpernickel and applied butter deliberately.

"We can't rule out the possibility that the murderer is a woman."

She looked disappointed. "I think I would be better at interrogating men."

"Mata Hari used to travel on this train. Did you know that?"

"Yes. I'll bet she preferred interrogating men, too, although, as you probably know, she had her own techniques."

"So I've heard, but I'm not suggesting that you have to seduce every man on this train," I told her.

"I might not have to go that far," she said, and took a slice of my pumpernickel from the basket. "Not every man, anyway."

"It could be dangerous," I said.

"Is that the only reason you don't want me to do it?" A pout accompanied the question. It was a tough one because I wasn't sure of the answer myself.

"It's enough of a reason," I temporized. "If you were the next victim because of something you found out, I'd lose a valuable assistant."

She was smiling faintly as if she had just learned an interesting fact. "I wouldn't want that to happen."

"Helmut Lydecker may be the next one on the list," I said.

"He knows Magda Malescu," Irena said thoughtfully, "so he may have had some connection with her mysterious disappearance. But did he know Talia, her understudy?"

"Yes, he did. He may have had an affair with her."

"As a way of getting back at Malescu?"

"That's a shrewd observation. It could be a reason."

"H'm, all right, I'll put Herr Lydecker on the list. What about Larouge? He's not much of a mystery man, but if he's trying to avoid suspicion, he wouldn't want to appear mysterious, would he?"

"Good point. I'm a little bothered about him myself—though I admit it's mainly because there's nothing to be suspicious about."

"So he's the next on the list," she said briskly. "Who else?"

The waiter came with an offer of fresh coffee, and we both accepted. "Look," I said, "I don't want to spoil your trip—you didn't come on this train to be sleuthing, you should be—"

"Oh, I love this," she assured me.

"There's a woman we don't know enough about—Elisha Tabor."

"That's more in your line, isn't it?"

"Are you suggesting that I seduce every woman on the train?"

"It sounds as if we're both going to be very busy, doesn't it?" she asked, her eyes dancing.

"I wasn't serious," I told her, even as I realized I was being a little pompous. I quickly thought of another candidate for investigation.

"Have you talked to Herr Vollmer?" I asked.

"No. He's in some sort of business, isn't he?"

"He is with *Nord Deutscher Energie*. He says he is going to discuss offshore oil drilling in the Black Sea."

"I don't know much about oil," she said, shaking her head.

"I'm sure you know enough about men," I told her, and she smiled as if I had complimented her. Maybe I had.

"Oh, and I'm forgetting one other. The Swiss fellow, Reingold." She did not look enthusiastic. "He doesn't look too interesting."

"You can't pick only the ones you want to seduce," I said.

"Of course not, but he can't be a murderer surely?"

"Anyone can be a murderer," I said, plucking another bon mot from the files of Scotland Yard.

"This is getting to be a long list," she complained.

"Have another slice of pumpernickel," I suggested. "You may need to build up your strength."

She smiled and took a slice. "Pass the butter, please."

We separated after breakfast. I watched the scenery as the train swept effortlessly up the steep bank of the Danube River. We had passed Bratislava during the night and Slovenia was on our left. The river along this stretch winds and weaves like a wriggling snake and only the superb balancing mechanism and brilliant engineering kept us from being travel sick. It also meant that our progress was slow. In places, the riverbank was sandy and, in others, stony. Rooks and gulls swooped low in search of food.

"Roman ruins are just visible from the other side of the train," a voice advised me. It was Professor Sundvall.

"They are?"

"Yes, the *Heidentor* is a massive arch, and near it is the ancient Roman city of Carnentum."

"That's interesting," I said. "I don't know this area."

"Yes, Carnentum has sulfur springs where the Fourteenth Roman Legion used to rejuvenate themselves after a long march when returning from subjugation of the barbarian tribes. Marcus Aurelius lived there for many years, too, and wrote several of his *Meditations* during that time."

"I am on the wrong side of the train," I said, and he laughed.

"Soon," he said, "we will see the March River. It is very wide here and flows in to swell the Danube. Here also, is the *Hutelberg*, the 'Hat Hill.' It is from a later period than the Romans—it is a huge mound that was formed by the inhabitants who brought earth in their hats. It was their way of raising a memorial in remembrance of the expulsion of the Turks."

"You are a mine of information, Professor," I told him.

"Now I must go," he said. "My little talk on Mozart was, it seems, very popular, and I have been asked to say something about Johann Strauss."

"I must hear that," I said. I had a secondary reason for that—it would be a good opportunity to rub shoulders with the passengers. Including, surely, a murderer?

As he left, Henri Larouge came along the corridor. He nodded pleasantly, but, before he could pass by, I asked him, "How are you enjoying the food on this trip? As you are in this business, you must be well qualified to give an opinion."

"It is very good indeed," he replied. "I have traveled on other luxury trains, and I cannot recall one of them that served finer meals. The produce is fresh, the cooking is imaginative, the meals are satisfying, and the service impeccable."

"High praise," I said.

"It is justified. Also, they are very clever at introducing the cuisines of the various regions we are passing through."

"I have to agree with that, too," I said. "What about the wines? Do they come up to expectation?"

He gave a Gallic shrug. "Austria, Hungary, Romania, Slovakia—they are countries that offer good wines but few great wines so there are few outstanding vintages. The DS Bahn has done well in selecting the wines they have served so far; all have been very pleasing."

I noticed that he used the word "pleasing" as the French do when they are being grudging with their praise. The situation is analogous to the English use of "interesting" as applied to works of art. It usually means that the speaker finds it hard to find suitable compliments but does not wish to offend with critical comments.

"The *Veltliner* was better than most I have tasted," I said.

"Yes, the ones they serve on the train are from the northern regions of the Wachau. They are very good. The *Gumpoldskirchen* is a more renowned wine, of course,—"

"But it's a little too sweet for most tastes," I said, "especially with food."

"True," he agreed.

"Tell me," I said, "do you think these vines that we have on board will be successful in reviving the Romanian wine industry?"

He turned pensive. "From what I have heard of them, they have the potential," he said slowly.

"You sound doubtful."

"I have no doubt that the vines could revive the industry in that country, but I was talking to Paolo Conti—you have met him?"

"Only briefly," I said, wanting to squeeze out of him all I could.

"He is very concerned over the safety of the vines."

"In what way?" I tried to sound obtuse.

"There have been rumors of threats, it seems."

"Why would anyone want to damage or destroy them?"

"Conti wasn't willing to speak outright and tell me where the threats were coming from—if he knows."

"Surely not rival vineyards," I said in my most ingenuous manner.

He gave me a scornful look. "It is possible."

I agreed with him there. The French *Huitième Bureau* is an operation set up to investigate crimes affecting the wine business in France. The famous *Deuxième Bureau* is the Secret Service, and only those in the inner circle of the French government know in which pies the third to the seventh bureaux have their fingers, but certainly the Eighth, the *Huitième Bureau,* is a powerful if shadowy organization with uncounted finances to back it. Larouge must have had dealings with them, and certainly he would know of their activities—as much as anyone on the outside ever did.

I wondered how much more Larouge knew that he was not telling me. I probed a little further. "Rival vineyards in Romania or in other countries?"

"Both are possible," Larouge said decisively.

"Would a revived Romanian wine industry be that much of a threat?"

"Certainly. The 'Wine Lake' is already overflowing."

The "Wine Lake" is the expression used to encompass the wine production of the countries in the European Community. The inclusion of the former Eastern European countries in the European Community is resulting in an ever-expanding capacity.

"What's the latest estimate on the volume of the 'Wine Lake'?" I asked casually.

He gave an equally casual shrug. "Twenty thousand million liters, probably more."

Larouge was better informed than I had expected. I should pay more attention to him. Perhaps he was not as peripheral a player in this deadly game as I had supposed.

"You will excuse me now," he said. "I would like to hear the professor's words on Johann Strauss."

He went past me as I stood, thinking.

CHAPTER EIGHTEEN

I had no time to deliberate. Gerhardt Vollmer, the oil man, came along and greeted me. He looked dapper in a light tweed jacket, light slacks, and brown-and-white shoes.

"I'm going to hear Professor Sundvall on Johann Strauss," he told me. "I don't usually listen to talks like that, but my wife is an enthusiastic pianist, and Strauss is one of her favorite composers—so I thought I should know more about him. Are you going that way?"

I agreed, and we passed through the train into the lounge coach where Professor Sundvall was just starting.

"The Strauss family consisted of five musically gifted members," the professor began. "Johann Strauss I, 'the Elder,' was passionately involved in music from an early age. He began composing waltzes at the age of twenty-one and, after delighting Viennese audiences for some years, toured Europe on several occasions." Professor Sundvall's eyes twinkled as he referred to Wagner's account of Strauss as a conductor, " 'he conducted with a mad passion'. He wrote 150 waltzes and over a hundred other pieces," said the professor as he continued.

"His eldest son, Johann Strauss II, was known as 'the Younger,' and it is his works that we know best. *The Blue Danube, Tales from the Vienna Woods, Voices of Spring,* and *Wine, Women and Song* are the outstanding examples of the elegant and charming waltzes he composed while 'Die Fledermaus' and 'The Gypsy Baron' are among the sixteen operettas he composed. His father was opposed to his taking up a musical career, but music seemed to be in the blood of the Strauss family.

"Strauss the Elder had two other sons, Joseph and Eduard, who both composed and conducted, while Eduard's son, Johann III became director of the court balls in Vienna and later Berlin."

Professor Sundvall clearly had a love of his subject. He was one of those educators who sincerely enjoyed passing on his own ardor to others.

The crowd was not large but listened attentively. Franz Reingold, the Swiss with the ski lift inheritance and the train hobby, was there, and I saw Mr. and Mrs. Stanton Walburg who, I was willing to bet, never missed any entertainment of any kind. Dr. Stolz came in late and stood at the back. The Australian couple was there, too, and clapped loudly.

I had hardly expected Herman Friedlander to attend, and he did not. But he came in just as Professor Sundvall was finishing. Maybe his timing was deliberate. I went over to him to find out, and said, "You missed an interesting talk, Herr Friedlander, but then perhaps your opinion of Johann Strauss is similar to your view of Mozart."

I am not usually that confrontational, but persons who are that way themselves are not usually aroused by others who display the same attitude to them, so I felt safe. My confidence was borne out as Friedlander turned a slightly sour look toward me, and said, "Johann Strauss writes powder puff music. Now Richard Strauss—no relation, of course—there is a *real* composer."

"I have always found Strauss's waltzes to be lighthearted and uplifting," I said. "Surely no music portrays its place and time as accurately as does that of Strauss and nineteenth-century Vienna."

Friedlander's sour look showed no sign of being sweetened by my words. "Music has the power to stir our deepest emotions," he said. "That is how it should be used—not to sugarcoat life and make the masses happy."

I could see we were about to get into a political debate and I was not sure if I wanted to mix music and politics. I was still juggling an answer when Karl Kramer appeared and saved me.

He gave me a rare and clearly a professional smile as he said, "*Meinherr*, I wonder if I could have a few words with you?"

He took me by the arm, and we walked through the lounge coach. When we had passed through the automatic door connecting to the next coach, Kramer turned to me as we entered the corridor of the next coach. We continued to walk, but Kramer's step quickened and took on an urgency.

"I have ordered the stewards in each of the coaches to be particularly alert since the death of Fraulein Svarovina," he said. "One of them has just reported that Signor Conti did not come into breakfast in the restaurant coach, nor did he order breakfast in his room."

"He could have spent the night in another compartment," I suggested. "After all, several young women are on the train and—"

"I had the stewards check the other passengers. None is unaccounted for, and all have had breakfast in either the dining coach or their compartments."

We went on through the train while, outside, pleasant green countryside spun by, copses and dense woodlands, occasional gently rolling hills or a periodic church steeple poking above the treetops. It was hard to believe that we were in a train, as the sophisticated gyroscopic devices on the Danube Express compensated and adjusted to the deviations in angle and curvature of the track.

Kramer came to a stop. A steward stood on duty by a compartment door, trying not to look too obviously like a guard. Kramer reached into his pocket and took out the wallet-like piece of apparatus that I had seen before. Punching in numbers, he pulled out the cylindrical key electronically prescribed. Before inserting it in the lock, he knocked, gently at first, then louder. There was no response, and he tried a third time.

He shrugged when there was still no response and inserted the key in the lock. He turned it once, then again. The door opened.

It was dark in the compartment. I started to follow Kramer inside, but he held up a warning hand. He glanced up and down the corridor. No one was in sight. We went in and closed the door behind us.

It was dark and silent. Kramer called out Conti's name. The silence continued. He snapped on the light.

The layout of this compartment was different from both mine and from Magda Malescu's. It was not as large as Malescu's and, though about the same size as mine, the design was different. Kramer went through the small anteroom and into the living area. It was tidy but empty. Kramer gave me a quick wave to follow him and went into the bedroom.

Conti lay on the bed in blue pajamas. His arms and legs were at awkward angles. His face was pale, and there was no sign of life.

Kramer felt at his wrist and throat. He shook his head. "I can't find any indication that he is alive," he said, still trying. Finally, he gave up and shook his head again. He moved around the room, lithe as a cat, quickly looking in the closets and the bathroom.

"No one here," he said, his voice normal.

I was looking carefully at the body. No signs of violence were visible. Nothing else was on the bed. I went around the room sniffing like a bloodhound.

"Anything?" Kramer asked.

"No," I said. "Nothing recent—and certainly no aroma of bitter almonds."

Kramer took out his phone and spoke rapidly into it. He was calling Dr. Stolz and asking him to come at once.

We both searched the room more thoroughly. The closet was full of clothes; the bathroom was not unreasonably untidy. Nothing looked out of place. Nothing looked like a clue. The compartment appeared completely typical except for one item—the body sprawled on the bed.

A knock came at the door, and Kramer let in Dr. Stolz. He had his habitual solemn face; it was probably part of his medical persona. He carried a small black bag and placed it at the side of the bed.

He showed an instant of recognition as he looked at the face, then he was all business. He went through the whole procedure—

pulse, eyes, mouth, carotid arteries, and heart. Kramer and I continued to look through the room while the doctor conducted his examination, but neither of us was finding anything helpful.

The doctor took his stethoscope out and used it extensively. He produced a magnifying glass and used it, too, then pulled from his bag a small instrument with a green dial and small probes.

A knock came at the door. Kramer went to it but did not open it, calling out, "Who is there?"

A voice, evidently that of the steward who had been left on duty outside, said something that I could not hear. The steward replied, and Kramer unlocked the door and opened it just barely enough to admit Erich Brenner.

Kramer closed the door quickly and locked it again, motioning toward the bed, where Dr. Stolz was still taking readings. Brenner's eyes opened in astonishment. He went to the bed and stood beside the doctor, who ignored him.

In a voice that was very different from his usual strong baritone, Erich Brenner asked Kramer for details. Kramer quickly ran through the sequence of events he had given me. Brenner shook his head. "This is terrible. Well, it's terrible for poor Signor Conti, too, of course but I mean, coming after the other . . ."

The doctor was still bent over the body, oblivious to Brenner's entry. Brenner said to Kramer in almost a whisper, "Has he learned anything yet?"

"He hasn't said anything."

Stolz was still using the small meter, and Brenner looked at him expectantly, but the doctor continued without speaking. The three of us waited expectantly. At last, the doctor reopened his bag and dropped the meter into it.

"Well, Doctor, what have you found?" Brenner asked.

Stolz stood looking at the body contemplatively. He seemed reluctant to answer. Finally, he said, "Most of the signs are the same as those of the young woman, Talia Svarovina."

Silence fell. The hum of the train's movement was all that could be heard. Not even the reassuring *thunk-thunk* of steel wheels over rail joints could be heard as in the golden days of the railroad. We were all assessing the significance of the doctor's words.

"This is too much of a coincidence," said Kramer. His voice was decisive, a welcome shaking-up after the numbing effect of Dr. Stolz's statement.

"It will be difficult to explain this in Budapest tonight," Brenner said, shaking his head. "The Hungarian authorities would have let us continue after the death of the unfortunate young lady—but now, it is very doubtful."

Dr. Stolz snapped his bag shut with a loud click.

"The *Donau Schnellzug* should be able to continue past Budapest," he said and there was something in his tone. All three of us stared at him. Kramer was the first to voice our perplexity. "Why do you say that, Doctor?"

The doctor evidently enjoyed his small moments in the spotlight. I recalled that he had been similarly dramatic after the death of Talia Svarovina when, for a moment or two, we had all thought that Magda Malescu was dead.

He looked at each of us in turn, as if inviting us to guess his next words, but when none of us spoke, he said "Signor Conti is not dead. He should recover in a couple of hours."

CHAPTER NINETEEN

Kramer was the first to recover. "I could find no life signs," he snapped.

"I had difficulty at first," the doctor admitted. "I had to use this new device—it detects movement of the blood in the circulation system. This continues even when the nervous complex is dormant, the pulsing of the heart is too weak to be detected, and the respiration is too infrequent for measurement."

"You mean Conti is in some form of suspended animation?" asked Kramer.

"No, no," the doctor said. "He is merely in a reduced state of being. All his systems are operating but at very low levels." He looked for a blanket, found one, and laid it over the body, adjusting the sprawled position of the legs. "Need to keep his temperature up," he explained.

"The cause of this condition, Doctor?" Brenner demanded, anxious to bypass the medical trivia.

"It would be necessary to analyze the contents of Signor Conti's stomach to be sure . . . but I would be fairly certain that he has ingested the same herb, Farfalia, as Fraulein Svarovina. In her case, it proved fatal, but Conti's much stronger male constitution has resulted only in complete incapacitation for a short period."

"How long ago did he ingest these drugs?" Kramer wanted to know.

"Several hours ago; it is not possible to be more precise."

"When do you suppose he will recover, Doctor?" Brenner asked.

"Recovery will probably be rapid," said Stolz. "There is no sign of it at the moment, but as soon as any of his vital signs shows an increase, then he will be back to normal soon after."

"So, Doctor," I interjected. "you mean that both Fraulein Svarovina and Signor Conti were given a dose of this Farfalia."

"Apparently," the doctor said.

Kramer was the one frowning now. "I don't like this. Two people on the same train and within a few days of each other . . ."

"Following Herr Kramer's comment," I said, "does it seem as if someone may have killed Fraulein Svarovina and attempted to kill Signor Conti?"

"No, no," Brenner said heartily. I could see that he didn't even want to have such an opinion aired. "Other explanations are more likely." I noticed that he made no effort to tell us what they were.

Kramer was frowning. "Have you heard any reports or comments that might indicate other passengers on the *Donau Schnellzug* have been affected in this way?"

The doctor shook his head firmly. "No."

Kramer was also looking unconvinced by Brenner's words, but he decided this was not the time to debate them. He gave a brief nod that was more a termination of the discussion than any kind of agreement. "Thank you, Doctor," he said to Stolz. "Please prepare your report, and you and I will talk again." He turned to Brenner, "Be assured, Herr Brenner, that our colleague from Scotland Yard and I will have more information very speedily."

I tried to look both modest but competent at the same time and wondered how successful I was. Brenner looked satisfied that Kramer was taking an optimistic approach. Brenner and Dr. Stolz went out and Kramer said a few words to the steward in the corridor to continue his watch. Then Kramer locked the door from the inside, and said briskly to me, "We have been wondering about this Conti fellow with his strangely uninformative background, have we not? Well, here is an excellent opportunity to try to learn something."

Was it invasion of privacy, I wondered? Kramer intercepted my involuntary glance at the body on the bed, now partially covered by a blanket. He interpreted my look correctly. "We are continuing our investigation in the presence of the occupant of the compartment," he explained with a straight face.

We both went to work, starting at opposite ends of the compartment. I went through the wardrobes. Conti's clothes were expensive and mostly Italian. It was hard to judge if that was because he considered them the best in Europe or it simply meant that he spent more time in Italy. I searched through every pocket of every garment.

Kramer meanwhile was opening the drawers, which were also full of clothes. He subjected every item to a detailed scrutiny. He moved into the bathroom, and we went on with our search, as thorough as it could be without ripping out the wall panels.

Kramer returned to the bedroom, and we looked at the recumbent figure. "No change," Kramer reported, then he thrust out a hand. He held a cashmere jacket. I looked at it, seeing nothing unusual. Kramer gave me a moment, then, holding up the jacket, turned back one lapel.

A tiny badge was there. I bent closer. It looked like gold and had an emblem of a single black grape with a green leaf underneath it. Both were picked out in colored enamel. Some tiny letters were at the bottom of the badge, and Kramer held the jacket higher so that I could read them.

"Do you see what it says?" he asked.

I could just read them. "*Amici della Uva.*" I said the Italian words out loud. Some tiny numbers followed.

"You would say 'Friends of the Grape' in English, would you not?" Kramer asked.

"Yes," I said.

"Do the words mean anything to you?"

"Yes, they do."

Kramer nodded complacently. He returned the jacket to the wardrobe. "Tell me," he ordered.

"France was the first country to appreciate the enormous significance of the wine industry in their economy," I said slowly, putting the thoughts together as I went. "When any business gets big and powerful—and wealthy—it attracts crime. The French have had an espionage organization for nearly two hundred years—they call it the *Deuxième Bureau*. A direct translation would be the 'Second Department' but that is merely a name and it is operative today."

"I am aware of their existence, of course," Kramer said. "Please continue."

"France has set up other organizations, but their precise activities are kept secret. One of them, however, the *Huitième Bureau*, or the 'Eighth Department,' has had a very limited amount of publicity. Problems have arisen in France because of the necessary involvement of the government in a major industry's affairs. Because of that, another organization has been formed in recent years and it—"

"It is called *Amici della Uva*." Kramer completed the sentence for me.

"Yes. It is not specifically French although the French are one of the larger participants. It is composed, in fact, of members from all the European Community countries who are wine producers. The name is Italian, but that does not mean anything—it's just a name that trips off the tongue."

"I have heard of them," said Kramer, "but I know very little."

"That's all anyone knows. They operate clandestinely and have no visible presence. The power of twelve countries is behind them though, and they undoubtedly achieve much, even if little—if any—of it gets into the media."

"And our friend, Conti, here, is a member—or should I say, an agent—a representative?"

"I don't know what they call them," I admitted. "I have heard bits of gossip about them here and there in my work but not what you would call hard facts."

"Scotland Yard must know about them," Kramer said.

I had to remind myself that I was the delegate—in Kramer's eyes anyway—of that august body. "Ah, yes," I temporized, "but England is too small a wine producer to be a member. So, er—we know very little of *Amici della Uva*."

He accepted that, I was glad to note. "His cover as a wine journalist presumably enables Conti to move around Europe on the business of this organization," Kramer continued.

"And his presence on the *Donau Schnellzug* must be due to the cargo of vines for Romania," I added.

"That seems probable," he agreed. "Perhaps threats have been made or whispers heard that might mean some attempt may be made to steal the vines."

"Or destroy them. Yes, it does."

Kramer let out a sigh of exasperation. "That makes Conti a target, does it not? If some persons are determined to steal those vines, they may have found Conti an impediment to their plans. So they tried to kill him."

"And Fraulein Svarovina? Is she a victim of this murder plot, too?"

"*Ach!*" He grunted. "So complicated! There is still much that we do not know."

"At least no difficulties should result when we arrive in Budapest later today," I said.

"That is one ray of sun in this whole affair," Kramer agreed. "If Conti had been dead, the Hungarian authorities might well have detained the train in Budapest."

"Surely Herr Brenner will employ his silver tongue to good effect?"

Kramer paused a moment as he searched for the right words. "I am quite sure that Herr Brenner will succeed in convincing the people in Budapest that the train should continue its journey." He glanced around the compartment. "I do not believe there is anywhere else in here for us to search. I must go now and talk to the stewards to see if any of them has heard or seen something that could be helpful."

"I'll do the same with as many passengers as I can," I said.

We both headed for the door, and as Kramer opened it, there came a loud groan from the bedroom.

"He is recovering," Kramer said unsympathetically, and we went back inside.

CHAPTER TWENTY

Y ou have some explaining to do," said Kramer, and there wasn't a hint of sympathy in his voice. Conti looked as if he had expected at least a little. He pulled himself up in the bed so that he reached a sitting position. He looked weak, tired, and vulnerable.

"I feel terrible," he said. "What happened to me?"

It was true he didn't look good, but he appeared to be recovering fast, just as Dr. Stolz had said he would. His eyes, foggy at first, were clearing, and his pale complexion was taking on a trace of color.

Kramer's obvious answer should have been, *That's what we want you to tell us,* but he avoided the obvious, and said, "Please tell us the last events you recall."

Conti blinked. His eyes were focusing, but recall seemed to give him a problem, his mental processes evidently affected. He tried to say something, stopped, then tried again. "I was in the bar after dinner—" were the words that finally emerged.

Kramer looked disappointed. I certainly was.

Conti licked his lips. The drug had probably dehydrated him, but Kramer didn't offer him a glass of water. Conti's eyes were steady by then, and he was reapproaching normality.

"That's the last I remember," he said slowly.

"You were drugged?" Kramer put it as a question not a statement.

"I don't know." Conti tried to shake his head but thought better of it after a wince or two.

"Who were you drinking with?"

"No one in particular . . ." His voice trailed off.

"You think the bartender drugged you?"

"I don't know."

"Is there any reason why someone should drug you?"

Conti looked at Kramer as if he found him unfamiliar.

"I—no."

I knew what was making Kramer antagonistic. He didn't like the idea of an undercover investigator secretly at work on the train of which he was the security chief. I had been lucky and slipped under Kramer's radar screen before the boom was lowered. The Scotland Yard connection had stood me in good stead, and, once again, I hoped it would hold.

Kramer wasn't going to tell Conti that he had searched his compartment and found his badge. He was giving him the opportunity of admitting his mission. Maybe when Conti recovered further, he would do that; but so far, it looked as if he intended to hold out.

"If someone drugged you, we need to know who it was and why?" Kramer continued remorselessly.

Conti smoothed out the bedclothes with his outstretched palms. It had the appearance of a placating gesture but Kramer was not being placatable.

"You might have died," Kramer said. "You came very close to it. Who drugged you?"

Conti dropped his eyes. He looked as if he were thinking, trying to remember. Then he looked up, and said, "I don't know. I hadn't drunk anything for some time before I went into the bar, just wine at dinner. I spoke to a few people there. Had a drink then I—yes, I had another. I didn't feel well. I stayed a while longer. I was tired and decided to go back to my compartment. That's all I remember."

"Who was in the bar at that time?"

"Let me see—Lydecker was there, Reingold, the Swiss fellow, was talking about the Swiss railway system, oh and Friedlander came in but didn't stay long. The Romanian girl, Koslova, was there talking to Larouge."

"Who else?" demanded Kramer.

Conti's brow wrinkled as he made an effort at recall. "Elisha Tabor was getting friendly with the oil man—"

"Vollmer?"

"Yes. I think there were one or two others I didn't know."

"Which bartenders were on duty?"

"I—I'm not sure."

"Tell me, Signor Conti, do you take medication?"

"When I need it."

"Have you taken any on this journey?"

"Not up to now."

"Do you have trouble sleeping?"

Conti frowned. "Sleeping? No."

"Have you taken any sedatives?"

"No."

Kramer wasn't finished with him yet though. "What have your researches on the *Donau Schnellzug* brought so far?" he demanded.

"My researches?"

"You are researching for an article on wine, aren't you?"

Conti looked uncertain. "Well, yes," he said, "it's going to be an article on the Express with emphasis on wine and the wine regions that the train passes through."

"You will be mentioning the vines for Romania?"

"No, I don't think so."

"Why not? Are they not important?"

"Yes, but they would make a separate story."

"You are writing such a story?" Kramer continued to press.

"No, I have it in mind and it will come later."

"You don't write very much, do you, Signor Conti?"

Conti sat up straighter in the bed. I made a mental note that a person in bed is at a definite disadvantage in an interview. Still, I realized that it is rare that the investigator can contrive such a juxtaposition with his victim.

"I usually publish four or five articles a year," Conti said.

"Two last year and three the year before." Kramer's tone was impersonal but his investigational precision stung Conti.

"That's my business," he said angrily. "I can write as much or as little as I want."

"The *European Wine Journal* is satisfied with your output?"

"You can ask them yourself," was the retort.

Kramer nodded. It conveyed the message, *You can bet I will*, and Conti didn't miss it. "Are there any more questions you want to ask me, Herr Kramer?" he asked testily. "If not, I am feeling tired and would like to get a little sleep."

"Just a few more questions," Kramer said, ignoring the hint.

Conti sighed, and his eyelids drooped, but it looked like a touch of acting to me, and Kramer went ahead with a disregard of whether it was histrionics or physical distress.

"Is there anyone on the *Donau Schnellzug* who would have a motive for trying to poison you?"

"When you write material and have it published, there could always be someone who objects to what you say."

"That is true in your case?"

"In the past, I have had complaints."

"What kind of complaints?"

"One vineyard owner felt that my comments influenced public opinion concerning his product and that might adversely affect his business."

"Could he not have sued you?" asked Kramer.

Conti sighed. "He threatened to do so but changed his mind."

"Has there been anyone who might have felt strongly enough about your written comments that he might want to kill you?"

"I can't think of anyone."

Kramer regarded him for a moment. He might have been digesting that answer or merely preparing the next question.

"Do you know anyone on the train?"

"Er, no. There is no one on the train I have met before."

"Herr Brenner—you did not know him?"

"No."

"So you maintain that you are not aware of any person on this train who might want to kill you?"

"No. I am not aware of any such person."

Kramer asked him more questions, but they were inconsequential and probably more for the sake of irritating Conti than for any other reason. Kramer finally concluded his interrogation. "Very well, Signor Conti. I suggest that you get some sleep now." He gave the Italian a condescending nod, got a glare in return, and we both left.

Outside in the corridor, the steward gave a salute and resumed his duty. We moved a little farther away and Kramer said, "So it seems that someone is using the herb Farfalia as a poison."

"It does," I agreed. "A little more, and Conti would be dead. He has a leisurely lifestyle, don't you think?"

"Yes, I must have Thomas check on him in greater detail. It looks though as Conti's cover of being a magazine writer is just a convenient way of hiding his activities as an agent for *Amici della Uva*."

"Yes," I agreed. "It would be a good mask, and it certainly explains why his history has so many gaps in it. I suppose it might be possible to list all the known wine frauds, scandals, and crimes of the last few years and try to match them against those gaps in Conti's past."

"That is a good idea," Kramer said. "I will have Thomas work on it."

"I wonder if Conti will recover sufficiently to join us this evening in Budapest?" I said, and Kramer shrugged.

"Are the arrangements similar to those in Vienna?" I asked. "Limousines take us all directly from the station to the banquet room in Budapest?"

"Yes. Special arrangements have been made for the train to go into the *Keleti Palyaudvar*, the Eastern Railway Station. The banquet is only a short distance only from there."

"That's the old station, isn't it? Built during the imperial days?'

"Yes. A magnificent structure. Herr Brenner thought it very compatible with the concept of the twenty-fifth anniversary of the *Donau Schnellzug*."

We separated, and I walked into the lounge coach. The panoramic windows were popular viewing spots, and most of the seats were taken. We were presumably leaving the section of track that had views of the Slovak Republic to the north, our left, and we were now entering the track with Hungary on both sides. Green, wooded islands studded the Danube and the river itself pursued a serpentine route. The bends were so close together that the river appeared to be more like a string of small lakes, closed at each end.

The banks of the Danube were sometimes stony, sometimes sandy, and many areas were the subject of hopeful scrutiny by flocks of gulls and rooks. The water of the river must be plentifully stocked with fish, too, and where the water was shallow near the banks, the birds dived into the water, usually emerging drenched but triumphant with a wriggling silver fish.

On the right, the land began to rise from the Carpathians. Ruined castles, one after another, perched precariously on craggy hilltops within a short distance of the train. I had not noticed Professor Sundvall before, but then I saw him, surrounded by a small entourage. He was describing the passing countryside and was pointing to a towering ruin, more than three hundred feet above the river.

"The Castle of *Paszony*, or Pressburg as it is known in the West," he said. It was a squat quadrangular mass, and at its foot, near the river, was, said the professor, the ancient town of the same name. ". . . and once," the professor continued, "the capital city. At the four corners of the castle itself, you can see large square towers—those were its principal means of defense. It looks old and not particularly attractive from this viewpoint, but if you should come through this area by river, you should certainly stop here. The narrow, tortuous streets, the sudden appearance of flights of steep steps, and the quaint old houses are a delight, and perhaps you will be fortunate and visit it on market day, when the lively crowds will fill the town."

The castle was visible for quite a while. The rail track zigzagged and the Danube twisted and turned almost as much—the convolutions of the two seldom coinciding.

"Twice," said Professor Sundvall, "this town, Pressburg, has been responsible for establishing the Hapsburg Dynasty on the Austrian throne, and its cathedral, which you can just see—has been the coronation site of most of the kings of Hungary. Pressburg, in fact, became such an important town that it was thought more prudent to move the capital farther from the frontier. That was how the honor was moved away from Pressburg, and Budapest became the capital."

The Danube Express rolled smoothly on, making easy going of the weaving railbed and ironing out the kinks in the Danube River.

"And so we continue our journey to Budapest, one of the most romantic and exciting cities in Europe," said Professor Sundvall, and everyone craned closer to the window, eager to catch the first glimpse . . .

CHAPTER TWENTY-ONE

The *Donau Schnellzug* unloaded us at the *Keleti Polyaudvar*, the Eastern Railway Station, a Gothic structure with a distinctly imperial look and a soaring roof. It is neither the oldest nor the largest station in Budapest, but it has been restored to a level of efficiency that make it suitable for international train traffic. Its neo-Renaissance façade is flanked by statues of two pioneers of the railroad—James Watt and George Stephenson.

As in Vienna, we boarded a fleet of limousines and I found myself with the Australians, Herman Friedlander, Elisha Tabor, a couple of jolly Tyroleans, a Japanese couple with perplexed expressions arising from their incomplete knowledge of any European language, and Franz Reingold, the Swiss ski lift heir.

The limos took us on a mildly zigzag route to enable us to see a few of Budapest's more famous sights. It was a pity that the first of these was the Square of the Republic as it is surrounded by the grimmest, drabbest buildings I have ever seen. The solid concrete block edifices formerly housed the Communist Party headquarters. They are too ugly to conceal and too massive to blow up.

Our small cavalcade rolled on to the *Kapel Szent Roch*, the St. Roch Chapel, a delightful yellow church built in the eighteenth century. Its charm is increased by the traditionally garbed peasant women selling lace and embroidery all around the church.

The streets were busy and the sidewalks crowded with people. The Hungarians had supplied a guide in each limousine, and we listened to comments and explanations as we passed the various sights. Our guide was an elfin young lady with a serious demeanor and an unmistakable aura of academia. She was, she told us, a professor of history at the university, but she led guided tours for the city whenever a special occasion such as this brought important visitors.

Oh, everything was much better now that Hungary had abandoned Communism for the capitalist way of life, she assured us, but the country still lagged economically behind the standards of Western Europe.

We passed the *Operahaz*, the Opera House, guarded by two large marble sphinxes. It was built in the 1880's but badly damaged during the siege of 1944–45. It was now fully restored, explained Renata, our guide, and she said it was regrettable that we would not have time to see its impressive interior, with its grand staircases, wood-paneled corridors, and its green-and-gilt salons. Four tiers of boxes are supported by figures of helmeted sphinxes under a magnificently frescoed ceiling.

We saw the Liszt Memorial Museum and the Liszt Academy of Music, for Franz Liszt was one of the city's most famous citizens, and we drove through Heroes' Square with several impressive buildings including the Museum of Fine Arts and the Palace of Exhibitions. The former contained Raphael's masterpiece, *Portrait of Youth*, retrieved after one of the most spectacular heists in art history. That, however, was another story, Renata said primly, and left us all wanting to hear more.

By then, though, we were crossing the Lanc-hid, the first of the five permanent bridges that now span the Danube, although, Renata reminded us, the Romans built a bridge connecting the military outposts in Pest on one side and the civil town of Aquincum on the other. Aquincum, she said, had been extensively excavated recently, and the amphitheater that had been restored was one of the finest in Europe.

One of the Australians wanted to know why the bridge had a kink in the middle. Was it a mistake, construction from both sides not meeting in the middle? Certainly not, said Renata indignantly, the Danube currents are so strong that each half of the bridge has to be exactly vertical to the current on that side. We all admired the bridge, with its massive stone supports and the huge crouching lion statues at the entrances.

Sculptures, statues, and carvings abound throughout the city as well as old churches, chapels, and gateways. The famous Fisherman's Bastion has seven beautifully carved turrets representing the seven Magyar tribes.

"The Soviets loved statues," commented Reingold, who said he had not been there in many years. "They must have put up a lot of them. Aren't any left?"

"Just one in the entire city," Renata said. "A column in Liberty Square."

After crossing the bridge, we were now in Buda. That and Pest combine to comprise the modern city of Budapest. We climbed up Varhegy, Castle Hill, where the biggest concentration of major sights can be found. It is a long, narrow plateau of cobblestone streets packed with remarkably well preserved Renaissance, Gothic, and Baroque houses. On top of the hill is the Royal Palace. The entire area has a fairy-tale appearance, spoiled only by the presence of cars that are banned but manage to be there anyway.

"One building that you might expect to be obtrusive here," said Renata, "is the Hilton Hotel. It is coming up now on our left—" There were a few gasps of surprise as we identified it, and Renata went on, "As you can see, it has been very cleverly incorporated into the oldest church here on Castle Hill—the church built by Dominican friars in the thirteenth century."

"Not like any Hilton I ever saw," said one of the Australians.

We drove up the Bem Rokport, the boulevard that runs along the west bank of the Danube, going north past a string of other imposing buildings, although all were dwarfed by the magnificence of the view across the river.

The Parliament buildings in Budapest, spectacularly arranged along the opposite bank, are, by universal agreement, the most beautiful in the world. They are similar in general appearance to the Parliament buildings in London but stretch over a much more extensive length at the historic location where three towns, Buda, Pest and Obuda, have been joined to make the city's capital.

"Twenty-four towers adorn the building," Renata said, and we eyed them appreciatively, each one graceful and slender. We drove on up the riverbank, where fishermen, idlers, lovers, schoolchildren, nurses, and policemen strolled as they do by all of the world's great rivers as they run through capital cities.

"One thousand workers spent seventeen years building this bridge," said Renata, as our limousines crossed the Margit Hid, the bridge named after Margaret, the daughter of King Bela IV, 1235–1270. She entered the Dominican convent there, Renata told us, so as to fulfill the vow made by her father to have her brought up as a nun if the invading Tartars could be forced out of Hungary.

Our limos deposited us at the main entrance of the Parliament buildings, where banners waved and flags fluttered as a contingent of Hungarian guards in resplendent uniforms split into two columns. We walked between them and into the main building.

"There are seven hundred rooms and eighteen courtyards in this building," said the indefatigable Renata. We all looked around in astonishment. It is an amazing mixture of styles and designs that ought not to blend, but do so very well. Renovation was going on everywhere, and Renata explained that the surfaces were made of a local limestone that is unfortunately porous, so that the renovation work may have to be continued perpetually.

Inside, the walls were lavishly covered with paintings, frescoes, murals, and tapestries. Alert-looking guards stood around, their extravagant uniforms in amusing contrast to the Kalashnikov automatic rifles, cradled under their arms.

"Most of the works of art show scenes from Hungarian history," said Renata. We walked into a great room, with massive timbered ceilings and a fireplace on one wall through which the Danube Express could have easily driven.

It was a dazzling sight, but our immediate attention was captured by the contents of a large glass case. Renata stopped in front of it.

"You are very fortunate," she said. "This is a special exhibit, being shown here before it goes overseas."

No one spoke. Jewels glittered like a miniature bright-colored night sky—ruby red, emerald green, diamond white. Their setting of soft gold was almost of secondary note.

"The Crown of St. Stephen," said Renata in a reverent tone.

In the case, sitting on purple velvet, was a two-part crown. On top was a cross, which looked to be crooked. Pendants hung down either side, and enameled plaques were richly decorated with gems, too.

"According to legend, Asztrick, the first abbot of the Benedictine monastery at Pannonhalma in Transylvania presented it to King Stephen as a gift from Pope Sylvester II," said Renata.

"When was that?" someone asked.

"About the year A.D. 1000," said Renata.

"Nice gift," murmured a voice.

"It legitimized the new king's rule and also assured his loyalty to Rome rather than Constantinople," Renata explained.

"Isn't that cross bent?"

"The crown disappeared several times over the next few centuries," continued Renata, evidently accustomed to that question and probably many others. "But it kept reappearing. During the Mongol invasions in the thirteenth century, an attack on the city was expected and in the haste to transport the crown to a safe hiding place, it was dropped." She met the gaze of the questioner. "That is how the cross became bent."

She went on, her small audience raptly attentive. "At the end of World War II, fascist troops fleeing the Soviets took it to Austria. Shortly afterward, it fell into the hands of the U.S. Army occupation forces and was placed in Fort Knox, Kentucky. In 1978, a great ceremony was held here when the crown was returned. It has always been considered a living symbol of Hungary, and all legal judgments are still handed down with the statement 'in the name of St. Stephen's Crown.' "

"Is it kept here now?" came the question.

"No. Currently, it is kept in the Sandor Palace in the Castle District. With the crown here, you see the ceremonial sword, the orb, and the tenth-century scepter."

We stared at them in wonder. The crown itself had been so imposing that we had hardly noticed the other objects.

"Is that crystal?" asked one of the Australians. She was referring to the scepter, which had a scintillating head.

"It is, pure crystal. It is the oldest item in the regalia."

We stood, still admiring the sparkling, shimmering collection, until Renata reminded us that we were due in the banquet room. We moved reluctantly. The thoughts buzzing through my head were of the extraordinary array of treasures I was being exposed to on the trip. I had expected a pleasant journey through Middle Europe and the opportunity to enjoy various different cuisines along the Danube.

First, had been the vines going to Romania—far from priceless but certainly valuable. Then had come the Mozart manuscript, its worth incalculable. Both of these had intangible value, they were worth whatever someone coveting them might be willing to pay. The jewel collection starring the Crown of St. Stephen also had intangible value, but, in addition, it had very tangible worth. The items could be broken down and sold for their gem and gold content, should anyone be barbaric enough to do that. Still, I reflected, not much doubt about that. Plenty of people around would be willing to do so.

We walked between two more hard-eyed guards, each with a Kalashnikov held in a grip that showed a familiarity and a willingness to use it without compunction.

CHAPTER TWENTY-TWO

The banquet room was as spectacular as the other rooms in the Parliament building complex. Over the centuries, the rooms had clearly fulfilled a variety of functions. Some of them had probably been witness to scenes too terrible to record. A flamboyant but very appropriate touch came from banners hung around the walls proclaiming the famous restaurants of Budapest—the *Alabardos*, its name recalling the halberd, an ancient edged weapon; the *Lou Lou,* one of the most popular eating places for some years; the *Muveszinas*, medieval and romantic; the *Vadrosza* which means the "Wild Rose"; the *Feszek,* home of the Artist's Club; and the *Udvarhaz*, the restaurant with the unrivaled hilltop view.

They were resplendent with images of fruit, shanks of veal, vegetables, and wine bottles, and Renata reminded us that all those restaurants had combined to put on the banquet.

"Isn't that unusual?" asked Franz Reingold and Renata smiled.

"Yes," she agreed, "Hungarian restaurateurs are extremely competitive and rarely cooperate. Such an occasion as this was needed to persuade them to do so—as you can see." She motioned to a huge multicolored banner that portrayed the Danube Express in all its power and majesty roaring out of a tunnel and into the Danube Valley with picturesque blue water and a white steamer. The latter, however, were small and the train enormous.

My banquet attendance in Vienna had been brief and interrupted. I hoped this would be different. At the table with me were Herman Lydecker, Elisha Tabor, Dr. Stolz and Eva Zilinsky. A Hungarian guide—Renata in our case—was at each table to provide interpretation and information. So, with me, there were six at the table, and all the other tables had the same number.

Drinks were served at the table. "You must all try the Hungarian aperitif, *Palinka*," said Renata. "The most popular one is *Barackpalinka*—it is apricot schnapps."

"Evian water for me," Elisha Tabor ordered. "I don't take alcoholic drinks before dinner."

Lydecker and the doctor gave their assent to the apricot schnapps, and I joined them. "Scotch on the rocks," said Eva Zilinsky peremptorily, "Famous Grouse." Renata hesitated, then ordered the apricot schnapps, too. Perhaps the guides were expected to remain teetotal, and Renata was hoping she was not under observation.

Violinists strolled around the edges of the table area, playing Hungarian folk music. They were audible but stayed far enough away that they did not intrude upon conversation. "Those are the famous Lakatos family," Renata explained. "They are legendary in Hungary".

As we sipped the drinks, Eva Zilinsky was eyeing the adjoining table. "Magda Malescu appears to be in good form," she said. "She's our principal export after paprika, you know," she added to me.

We could not hear their conversation, but it was evident from the waving arms, the flashing eyes, and the animated faces, that Magda was entrancing her captive audience. Laughter burst out after one of her stories.

"She must be talking about herself," Herman Lydecker, and Elisha Tabor added tartly, "Who else?"

"She made a remarkable recovery from her death," commented Lydecker, and a few chuckles came from around the table. I was watching Magda Malescu at that moment, though, and I thought I detected a slightly hysterical exaggeration in her motions. Perhaps we were doing her an injustice—maybe she felt the death of her understudy more deeply than we realized.

Waiters came, bringing menus. It seemed the meal was to be a compromise between a fixed menu and a wide choice. The participating restaurants were shown as offering three of their finest recommendations for each of the seven courses.

"Seven courses!" commented Dr. Stolz.

"Why not?" asked Eva Zilinsky gaily. "Do you advise dieting to your patients, Doctor?"

"Only when it is strictly necessary," he replied. "Hungarian meals are known to be—well, let us say, robust."

"Still," I was obliged to point out, "these dishes appear to have been chosen very carefully, and I am sure that excessive fat, starch, and carbohydrate contents have been avoided."

"Oh dear," said Elisha Tabor. "Have the abstemious ways of Western dieting finally reached Hungary?"

"I think that the world is now accepting the need for using dietary guidelines," Dr. Stolz said. "It is possible to enjoy meals and be prudent too."

"How boring!" Eva Zilinsky sighed.

"Not at all," said Lydecker, who seemed ready to shift his argument wherever he could find the opportunity to disagree. "It is easy for a good chef to serve food that satisfies the gourmet and yet is healthful."

I was ready to debate that—not the desirability of the achievement but the description of it as being easy. Chefs trained in the ways of preparing rich, traditional foods have had to work hard to find ways of reducing saturated fats, calories, and cholesterol. Instead of crossing swords with Herman Lydecker, however, I let the moment pass in the interest of harmony at the table.

Eva Zilinsky ordered an apricot schnapps, and Elisha Tabor had another Evian water. The rest of us passed—in my case, the decision was made after looking at the list of wines we were to be offered. Most were Hungarian, and several vineyards were represented whose wares are rarely seen outside that corner of Europe. The banquet would be an unusual opportunity to sample some of them.

Ordering the meal was an interesting study in tastes and attitudes. Soups have declined in popularity in the Western world—perhaps it is a class-conscious reaction, and soup is considered a peasant choice. In countries with Eastern connections, though, soups are still popular, and this is certainly true in Hungary.

Lydecker and I both ordered *Meggyleves* to start. It is a cold soup made with sour cherries, a truly Hungarian specialty. Dr. Stolz ordered a soup, too, a hearty one consisting of beans and cabbage, laced with smoked pork, while Elisha Tabor went for a simple beef consommé. Eva Zilinsky chose the *Oborka Salata,* a salad of sliced and pickled cucumbers, and Renata took the mixed salad.

The cherry soup was excellent, the cherries being sufficiently sour to give the dish a sharp edge that made it a true appetizer. Brandy and cinnamon rounded off the taste and concealed the sweetness of the sugar that must have been added. The doctor praised his soup, too. Elisha Tabor made no comment on her consommé but was the first to finish the course. Eva and Renata nodded approval of their salads.

No attempt was made to offer wine. That was a good decision, for all the first course items would affect its taste—especially the sour cherry soup and the acidic salads.

Next, we listened to the waiter describe the dishes to be offered for the second course. The *Kehli* restaurant in old Buda had contributed one of their famous dishes, he said. It is bone marrow on toast and very highly regarded since the renowned Hungarian novelist, Gyula Krudy, did a moonlighting stint there as a restaurant critic. He then highly praised the dish in his column in the Budapest *Times.* We listened impassively, but no one ordered it.

The next item drew close attention though. The animal most beloved by Hungarian epicures, said the waiter, is the goose. All summer long, young girls and old crones feed corn to the geese until they become fat and their meat tender and sweet. They can be roasted or braised, and the cracklings made from the skin and the layer of fat beneath it are widely used as a flavoring in many dishes.

However, it is the liver that is the most eagerly sought part of the goose. Large and unbelievably delicious, it can be eaten baked, smoked, or sautéed, but the culmination of the chef's art comes when it is made into pâté, known as *Libermaj* in Hungarian. Paprika, pimientos, scallions, capers, hard-boiled eggs, and white wine are added, cooked, seasoned, and blended.

The waiter ended his spiel and looked around the table. We all nodded approval. For a moment, I thought Lydecker was going to demur and demand chicken liver instead, but he went along with the rest of us.

The pâté arrived on a shining silver platter and was placed in the middle of the table. Very thin sliced rye bread was recommended with it, the waiter said, and brought a tray of it plus some black pumpernickel. Specially shaped silver knives were provided.

We were served a light, dry white wine with this. It was from the district of Eger in the Northern Uplands of Hungary. It was labeled *Leanyka*, which means "Little Girl." It was just tasty enough to be assertive but did not detract in any way from the magnificent goose pâté. Our table was silent as we all enjoyed this. Renata commented that, as a girl, she had often eaten goose liver pâté but never one as good.

The noise level in the huge banquet room had dropped—presumably all the other tables were concentrating on enjoying the Hungarian specialty as much as we were. The tables were well separated, too, which is a consideration often overlooked even in the best restaurants.

For the third course, we were offered a range of fish dishes. The waiter spoke highly of the *Fogas*, which comes only from Lake Balaton and is highly prized. In some countries, they are known as the 'Zander'. Their meat is white and delicious, and they resemble a small trout, although many liken them to perch. *Fogas* was being prepared in three ways that night—*Kalocsa* style with *lecso*, which is a mixture of stewed onions, tomatoes, and paprika; or *à la Gundel*, a light spinach-and-cheese sauce; or simply grilled as fillets.

The women at our table decided on the plain grilled and the men on *Kalocsa* style. With it we drank a white wine from Badacsony, a volcanic area that rises from the northwest shores of Lake Balaton. The waiter suggested the unique wine known as Blue Stalk. Many of the wines from this region are of the Riesling type, but the Blue Stalk, "*Keknyelu*" in Hungarian, has a distinctive mineral taste from the volcanic soil yet retains its basic wine flavors. "This one is from the Szeremley vineyard," said the waiter proudly, "one of the finest in Hungary."

To continue, we were told that the Hungarian staple dishes of goulash and *porkolt* were available at all the local restaurants. For such a special occasion as this, though, the chefs were determined to uphold their reputations and offer the finest in their repertoire. Duck is a very popular in the country and *Hacsa* is prized as the best way to prepare it. At our table, it was universally agreed that to be the best choice.

When it arrived, it was superb. The duck is stuffed with quince and roasted until very crispy. The chefs had felt that they should be traditionally Hungarian in the serving of accompaniments, however, and *Toltott Kaposzta*, stuffed cabbage, was served with it, along with noodles with poppy seeds. The stuffed cabbage, the waiter explained, was an elaborate dish and elevated above the simpler version found in country taverns. Ground pork, rice, garlic, onions, and sour cream are in the stuffing that fills each carefully rolled cabbage leaf, which is then placed in the sauerkraut seasoned with paprika, chopped bacon, and caraway seeds.

The country version of the dish may contain a mixture of beef and pork and can be considered a main course. In our case, we were served a modest portion, and an excellent adjunct to the crispy duck.

A choice of wines came with that course. In addition to a white from the renowned Thummerer vineyard, the chefs wanted to be sure that we tasted some Hungarian reds. A *Kadarka*, a late-ripening red, was described as being the wine that Franz Schubert drank while composing his *Trout* Quintet. The waiter suggested that we try tasting several reds, and we did so, this one being from the Ferenc Takler vineyard. Almost as much praise was heaped upon a wine from the Vesztergombi vineyard and it was the wine variety known as *Bikaver*.

Drinking different wines in succession is not considered a good idea by wine aficionados. That is why, at a wine tasting, the wine is not swallowed. The spitting out that is necessary would, of course, be frowned on during a meal, so it is only on rare occasions that different wines are consumed, and the twenty-fifth anniversary of the Danube Express fell into that category. Still, the morning-after effects can be unpleasant, and I wondered if all at the table—and indeed at the other tables also—were prepared for that. But I didn't want to be a spoilsport and tried to rationalize that at least the Hungarian red wines we were drinking here were from approximately the same varietal, and so the effects might be minimal.

Everyone at the table was in a happy mood, and even Lydecker was mellow. We were being allowed plenty of time to sample as many wines as we wished, and the atmosphere was jovial. Renata was smiling, in contrast to her previously prim manner, and Eva Zilinsky was pushing her glass forward for another serving of Attila Gere's unusually complex-flavored Cabernet Sauvignon when Elisha Tabor unexpectedly turned to Dr. Stolz.

"So, Doctor, tell us how the murders occurred."

CHAPTER TWENTY-THREE

It was a conversation-stopping remark, and our table was an oasis of silence in a vast room vibrating with chatter. Eva Zilinsky looked at Elisha Tabor with a half-amused, half-admiring expression that suggested she wished she had said it.

Herman Lydecker paused with a wineglass partway to his mouth. Renata looked interested in hearing the answer but was understandably less involved than the passengers. All eyes were on the doctor.

Dr. Stolz completed a sip of his wine, and I thought he savored it longer than usual. He dabbed his mouth gently with his napkin, and said, "Murders? I know of one death only, and it is that of Fraulein Talia Svarovina." He gave Elisha Tabor a direct look. "Do you have reason to believe she was murdered?"

The cool rebuttal might have slowed some women, but Elisha Tabor replied, "Two deaths. Magda Malescu was described as being dead, wasn't she?"

"Erroneously as it happened," said the doctor.

"That was strange, wasn't it?"

"Yes," the doctor agreed equably, but Elisha Tabor was persistent.

"I mean, to be declared dead and then to be found very much alive."

"Which we were all very glad to find was the case," the doctor said.

"So Malescu wasn't dead, but her understudy was."

"Are you suggesting that there was a connection between the two?" Eva Zilinsky had joined the conversation now. Elisha Tabor gave her a look as if she were about to tell her to mind her own business, but Zilinsky was not likely to be receptive to that kind of advice, and Tabor must have realized it.

"I don't believe in coincidences," said Tabor. "It's too much to believe that the two events are unrelated."

"How do you think they are related?" asked Zilinsky.

"I don't know."

"What about you, Doctor? How do you think they are related?"

The doctor was busy attracting the attention of the waiter so that he could get another glass of wine. Then he turned to Zilinsky. "I am a doctor, not a detective. It would be better if you spoke with Head of Security, Herr Kramer."

"But we have a detective right here with us," Lydecker said slyly. "A detective from Scotland Yard. Why don't we ask him?" All eyes switched toward me.

The waiter had left, so I was not able to use the doctor's delaying tactic. I decided on the aloof, we-know-a-lot-that-we-can't-reveal attitude. I drummed fingers on the pristine white tablecloth in lieu of twisting a wine glass stem.

"I am skeptical of coincidences, too," I said. "It seems likely that there is a connection between the two events, and we are investigating that connection very closely."

Zilinsky didn't intend to let go. "Svarovina was, after all, Malescu's understudy. Malescu was known to be jealous of her."

"Is that so?" murmured Tabor, leading her on.

"Yes, it certainly is so." Zilinsky was warming to her role now. "There was an incident in Belgrade last year when Malescu was late for a performance. Svarovina was dressed and ready to go on as her understudy when Malescu arrived. She insisted on holding the curtain until she was ready despite a very restless audience. She was furious at Svarovina. The Budapest *Times* had a great time with that story, had it going for days."

"In the column of Mikhel Czerny?" I asked.

"Of course," said Zilinsky.

"But is that motive for murder?"

"It could be," Zilinsky said. "There was a case in Prague last year of a man who killed his wife because she smoked in bed. There is no limit to the acts that are trivial to one person but desperately important to another." She regarded Dr. Stolz. "Tell me, Doctor, Svarovina was poisoned, was she not?"

"She had ingested a poisonous substance."

"What about Malescu?" Elisha Tabor wanted to know. "Did she take the same medications?"

"If she did, they did not affect her in any lasting way."

"Or did Malescu take something else?" asked Lydecker.

I recalled the strong smell of cyanide when I had first entered Malescu's compartment. It had been bothering me ever since, and I was still perplexed. Malescu could not have taken—or been given cyanide—or she would be dead. I waited for the doctor's answer.

"I have asked her that," the doctor said. "She does not recall taking anything potentially dangerous."

"Oh, well," said Elisha Tabor, the woman who had started it all. She fluttered one hand in a very feminine gesture. "I just thought I'd ask."

Eva Zilinsky looked disappointed. Dr. Stolz was probably relieved but didn't show it. Lydecker appeared indifferent, and Renata had had her interest piqued and looked eager to hear more. I tried to keep up my there's-a-lot-I'd-like-to-tell-you-but-I-can't front.

The waiter came, timing impeccable. "Hungary is famous for its desserts. I urge you to try one even if you are not usually a dessert-eater."

We probably had two or three of those, but everybody decided to be a sport and have a dessert. *Palacsintas*, flambéed pancakes, thin enough to be called crêpes, were high on the list and the *Muveszinas* restaurant in downtown Pest had prepared them. "They are a specialty there," the waiter explained. "They are famous for them."

Tabor decided on *Palacsintas* with chocolate and walnuts. I had them with apricots. *Retes* are strudels and come filled with a variety of fruit. Dr. Stolz chose them filled with *szilvas*—plums. Zilinsky, ever adventurous, selected tender fried Camembert cheese covered with blueberry jam. Lydecker chose *Dobostorta* that he said he had eaten previously in Hungary. It was a layered cake with a crispy caramelized top. Renata ordered a thinner cake with chestnut cream.

The violinists played on, unobtrusive and melodious. We all ordered coffee, three asking for the Café Diablo after the waiter had described it—served flaming from a liberal amount of Grand Marnier.

Conversations were occupying the others at the table when Zilinsky leaned toward me. "I think you know more than you are telling us," she murmured.

"More?" I said. "You mean about the murders?"

Her eyes widened. "Ah, so you agree there were two?"

"There certainly appeared to be one when the Budapest *Times* reported it."

"Yes." Zilinsky's tone was musing. She was an attractive girl, though her polished veneer suggested a lot of living. "So what else do you know?"

"I am sure it will all become clear in a day or two," I told her.

"I'd like to know now," she said softly, leaning closer. "We must talk about it when we get back to the train tonight."

I barely had time to nod an agreement, for a few of the guests were moving to other tables to talk to friends and acquaintances. Franz Reingold came over to ours.

"Wasn't that a wonderful meal?" he asked, eyes shining.

There was universal agreement. "Still," Reingold went on, "I'll be glad to get back to the *Donau Schnellzug*. I just love trains!"

"I thought you liked the toy trains," said Lydecker.

"I do, but I love the big ones, too. Have all my life. When I was a boy, my greatest thrill was to ride on a train."

"You have many of them in Switzerland," remarked Renata. Perhaps she had done her homework on the passengers, or perhaps she picked up on his accent.

"Yes, we do," said Reingold. "When I grew up into a teenager, I rode them all over the country. My friend Albert and I knew every station in the country. I could tell you many stories about what we learned. One thing, was how two can travel for the price of one."

Lydecker voiced the thought of others of us at the table, though he did so more harshly. "I thought you came from a rich family. You didn't need to do that."

Reingold giggled. At times, the boy that was still in him emerged. "Of course we didn't, but we liked to—just for the fun of it."

"So tell us, Franz," said Dr. Stolz, who had evidently come to know him a little better than the rest of us, "how did the two of you travel for the price of one?"

"When the conductor came through the train collecting tickets," Reingold said, still giggling, "Albert and I would go into the toilet. "Naturally, conductors knew the trick of hiding in the toilet if you didn't have a ticket. But, you see, I had a ticket—and when the conductor came and rapped on the door, I would open it a little and hand out my ticket. He never suspected there were two of us!"

Chuckling at his own cleverness, Reingold moved on to another table. Lydecker watched him. "Tell me, Doctor—you seem to know him—is he as uncomplicated as he sounds?"

"Yes," said Dr. Stolz, "I believe he is."

Renata got up to go and talk to a colleague at another table. Elisha Tabor saw someone she knew, waved, and the two met mid-table. Professor Sundvall walked over, and we had a review of the meal, comparing dishes. "Wasn't that goose liver pâté superb?" he asked, and we all agreed.

Conversations started, finished as people moved around. The violinists gave up trying to compete or maybe they were dry and had sought temporary respite at a bar.

It was close to midnight as we returned to the limousines at the door. The huge building was almost empty. The jewel case containing the crown was brilliantly lit in the darkened room, and the guards were still on duty everywhere and looking just as alert.

The city was still bright and busy as the luxurious limousines swept through the streets. We passed a few sights that we had not seen before, and Renata dutifully described them to us. We passed the Medieval Synagogue, the Matthias Church, with its strangely lopsided front caused by its having one tall and one low spire, and the Holy Trinity Square, surrounding the Baroque column erected in 1712 as gesture of thanksgiving by the population for being spared the plague. "This is a favorite place for large numbers of Budapest citizens to gather," Renata told us, "in order to watch the wedding spectacles that take place every weekend in spring and summer."

The Liberation Memorial was easy to spot. The 140-foot tower is visible from many parts of the city, and it honors the siege of Budapest by the Russians in 1945 and the Russian soldiers who died to liberate the city. On top is a young girl holding an olive branch high, her robe and hair flying in the wind.

"The memorial was embellished by statues of Red Army infantrymen, peasants rejoicing at their new freedom, and giants slaying dragons—symbolic of Communism's defeat of Nazism," said Renata. "In recent years, the city government has worked towards a lighter approach, and most of the older statues have now disappeared."

We passed numerous museums—Budapest seemed to have an awful lot of them—then Renata announced proudly that we were entering People's Republic Road. "It is considered by most to be the most elegant and attractive thoroughfare in Budapest," she said. "It was modeled after the Champs Élysées in Paris and has had numerous names."

The buildings were a bizarre blend of a dozen different styles, and Renata pointed out Number 60 in particular. It did not look unusual, and we waited for her to tell us about it. "It was Gestapo headquarters when the Germans were here, and then the headquarters of the NKVD, the Soviet secret police," she said. Several buildings had mosaics on the outside; courtyards were visible inside iron gates, and some of them had fountains.

At the end of People's Republic Road, Renata told us we were crossing Heroes' Square. It was built to celebrate Hungary's millennium in 1896. A semicircular colonnade is divided by an immensely tall column on the top of which is a winged figure rising in the center. Statues of Magyar chieftains on horseback surround the column.

We rolled on through the old city of Pest, where most of the city's sights are located, and finally slowed to a stop in front of the station.

The orange globes cast an unhealthy tinge on our complexions, I noticed, as we walked the short distance from the limousines. I saw Karl Kramer standing on the cavernous platform, looking down toward the far end. I detached myself from our group and went to join him. He greeted me with a nod.

"Your meal was good, I hope?"

"Very good indeed," I told him. "You are waiting to see us all put to bed?"

"No," he said seriously. "We have a shipment arriving that we must take on to Bucharest. It is late."

At a nearby platform, a train shrieked a whistle, then began to pull slowly out of the station, coaches half-filled with passengers. We watched it leave, and after the few waving good-bye to the train had left, the ensuing silence was almost palpable. Most platforms were bare, and on one, a cart loaded with mail sacks was being pulled along, one wheel squeaking harshly.

An evening breeze surged in, and newspapers blew and floated like lazy birds. The train that had just left sounded a double-note whistle as it picked up speed for its run out of the city.

The other passengers had all boarded by then. Kramer and I stood alone on the dimly lit platform. He looked at his watch even though there was a large clock high above the platform.

"Still, they are late," he complained.

"What is the shipment?" I asked.

"It is going to Bucharest National Museum, some ancient artifacts. We only just heard about it, and we warned that we must leave on time, but they assured us it would be here." He looked at his watch again. "We had a telephone message that it was delayed, but it should be here by—"

He broke off as a man in overalls appeared with a crate on a small, powered wagon with a snarling engine.

"Finally, it is here," Kramer said with relief.

"Ancient artifacts," I said. "Not another cargo of interest to villains, is it?"

"I don't know," Kramer said. "I must see the manifest." He started forward, and I followed.

"Is it valuable, do you know?"

"It may be," he said grimly.

A gray-haired man in uniform and a peaked cap who was evidently the stationmaster had emerged and was talking to the man with the wagon. They were producing papers, and there was conversation. One of the train stewards was unlocking the door of the freight coach.

We stopped a few paces away. Kramer was nervously scanning the platform we were on and also the adjoining ones. "This is a vulnerable time," he said to me. "I don't like to see the coach opened."

I could understand his concern. The stationmaster and the steward were nodding agreement. The door of the coach slid open, and the man with the wagon and the steward lifted the crate and carried it inside.

A voice on another platform called plaintively. It sounded like a name and echoed from the enormous vaulted roof. Kramer was looking to see where the voice came from when there was a cry, a different voice. It was difficult to determine its origin, but it must have come from another platform.

Kramer moved closer to the freight coach. The steward was nodding and speaking to the other man, who climbed back onto his wagon and drove away. Kramer watched wagon and driver closely until they were out of sight, then he went to the steward and was asking him questions. Kramer returned to me.

"All is well," he said.

"You were worried," I commented.

"I like to consider all possibilities," he replied.

CHAPTER TWENTY-FOUR

The Danube Bend' is a unique blend of geography and history and one of the most historic places in Central Europe. It is flecked with medieval villages and thousand-year-old castles. Hungary's turbulent past is inextricably mixed with it.

As the great river winds its way out of Budapest eastward, it then turns south. That section of it, more than any other perhaps, has been a major transportation artery, starting in prehistoric times. Caesar's armies built one of their most powerful fortresses there as a defense against the barbarian hordes. Traders have used the same route for countless centuries, and the roads visible on both banks of the river have served in both peace and war.

Professor Sundvall was explaining all of this to us the next morning. It was a packed house—or at least, a packed coach. Everyone on the train seemed to be aware of the extraordinary significance of the region and was eager to learn about it.

"We are still in the Alfold, the great Hungarian plain, the largest plain in Europe," the professor was saying, "and we are crossing the Tisza, its largest river." Gasps were audible as the passengers looked down into a chasm that seemed a mile deep. It wasn't, but its steep, rocky banks made it look that way. The bridge curved, too, so that we could see the graceful but spindly arches supporting it.

"The south bank—that is, to the right, is of greater interest. You will see three large towns—Szentendre, Visegard, and Ezstergom. On the left bank, the only town of any size is Vac."

Within minutes, Szentendre came into sight. "A Roman fortress was here, too," said the professor, "and it was a Hungarian settlement in the tenth century. It was totally destroyed three times but always rebuilt."

It was a colorful town, with medieval shops and houses painted in greens, yellows, and pinks. Small gables, towers, and spires protruded here and there. The professor pointed out Castle Hill, rising above the town and glinting in the morning sun.

The previous evening, Kramer and I had inspected the freight coach and found everything in order. It was the first time I had been inside it. The coffin-shaped container that held the vines, the large crate holding the Mozart manuscript, and the cargo for the Bucharest National Museum were there. There were also a number of mail and small freight items, most of them on shelves, the larger ones on the floor. The coach was about three-quarters full. Kramer prowled through it like a tiger, but finally professed himself satisfied.

When he had personally locked the coach, he tried to find out who had called out on the platform just as the wagon appeared and where the second cry came from, but none the few people on the station admitted to it. We agreed that it could have been a means of diverting our attention, had an attempt at theft followed.

So the *Donau Schnellzug* left Budapest on time. Kramer looked vastly relieved and told me that we should talk the next morning. I had not seen him and presumed that he was still cleaning up details from the previous night, so I felt free to listen to the professor's fascinating talk on the Danube Bend.

The train purred along in its usual imperturbable manner. A flight of wild ducks soared past us and settled in the willows by the Danube's edge. Birch trees grew in abundance, and we saw groves of yellow melons and blue cornflowers. An occasional church spire stood tall and slender, and the professor told us that we might see the cornfields that cover much of the area.

"Another ruined castle," commented some jaded passenger. It stood on a promontory by the edge of the river and looked to have been built of several cubes of stone. A couple of fishing boats drifted lazily, satisfied to go with the leisurely movement of the Danube. The fishermen gave us a disdainful look, probably convinced that we were disturbing the fish.

Irena Koslova was one of the professor's attentive audience, and when he took a break she saw me and waved. I went to join her. She looked eye-catching in an azure blue light sweater and white pants. "Enjoy the meal last night?" she asked.

"Mine was very good. And you?"

"Loved it."

"The goose liver pâté was exceptional, I thought, and so was the duck."

"They were."

"I was trying to spot you, but you must have been at one of the tables on the opposite side of the room."

"I was with Herr Vollmer, Monsieur Larouge, Paolo Conti, an interesting Spanish lady, and a lawyer from Berlin," she said.

"Did you have a chance to do some more detecting work on Signor Conti?" I asked.

"As much as I could." She gave me an arch look. "I haven't forgotten that I'm an assistant to Scotland Yard now."

"We had, er, better keep that between ourselves," I told her hastily.

"Of course," she said blithely. "I can keep a secret."

"Besides," I added, "I wouldn't want to put you in any danger." I didn't want to frighten her, but I didn't want the "Scotland Yard" connection given too much publicity.

She smiled. "Don't worry. I'll be careful. Anyway," she went on, "I can't believe I'm in any danger from Paolo Conti. He seems nice enough although he is paying a lot of attention to Elisha Tabor."

"Did he tell you that someone poisoned him?"

Her eyes widened. "No!"

"Yes."

She reflected for a moment. "He said he had to choose what he was going to eat very carefully at the banquet, but I thought maybe he had a stomach upset or something."

I gave her a sketchy account of the incident. "So who do you think poisoned him?" she immediately wanted to know.

"It's hard to say at the moment."

"You think it was the same person as the one who poisoned Talia Svarovina and Magda Malescu?"

"I would leave out Magda Malescu," I said. "She's very much alive—you must know that, she was giving a bravura performance last night."

"I saw her," Irena said. "She's always onstage, isn't she? So what about Svarovina?"

"She was poisoned," I conceded. "Maybe it was the same person."

"If it was the same poison both times, then they must have been given by the same poisoner."

"Very perceptive," I told her.

She looked scornful. "You mean it's logical, and you don't think women can be logical."

She was being perceptive again. It was true, I had been thinking that logic is not the female character's outstanding trait—but I wasn't going to admit it.

"When something seems obvious, a detective needs to re-examine it," I said.

"Good," she said. "Let's reexamine—you say that Conti may have been given the same poison as Svarovina."

"That's right."

"But not the same poison as Malescu," she persisted.

"Probably not. That's why I said we should leave out Malescu."

She pouted. "That's because you like her."

"She's a wonderful actress and—"

"Ha!" There was a world of contempt there.

"Well, okay," I conceded. "She is good-looking, I admit."

"You should have stomach-pumped her," Irena said callously.

I ignored that and continued. "The strange thing is that there was a strong smell of bitter almonds in her compartment."

"So?"

"It is usually associated with cyanide—the deadliest of all poisons."

"If it's that deadly, why didn't she die?"

"You're being logical again," I told her. "But you're right. That's the puzzle."

"How does she explain it?"

"She doesn't."

Irena looked thoughtfully out of the window. "There's a Bulgarian herb called *Sayiya Vanesta*. Do you know it?"

"No," I said. "Tell me about it."

"It could be translated as 'Acid Essence of Almonds.' It's cake flavoring. Bulgarians love cakes—they make them with all kinds of nuts. Almonds are one of the most popular, and they use *Sayiya Vanesta* to increase the almond flavor. There's so much sugar in the cake that you need the acid to balance it."

"How do you know all this?" I asked.

"When I was a girl, I worked in my aunt's bakery in Craiova. It's in the south, near the Romanian border with Bulgaria, and my aunt used lots of herbs as flavors."

"Irena—you continue to amaze me!"

She looked pleased. "I do?"

"You may have provided the clue that solves part of this case."

"Really? Which part?"

"I'm not sure of that myself yet, but I think it moves us along. Tell me more about Conti—did he say much at the banquet?"

"Not much at all. He was very subdued. I suppose it was the after-effects of the poisoning?"

"Evidently."

"I can talk to him again," Irena said. "He must be feeling better today." She was examining me intently. "What is it?"

"What is what?"

"You're wondering whether or not to tell me something. If we're working together, I think you should tell me."

She was getting altogether too intuitive. "I am going to tell you," I said. "I'm trying to think of the right way."

She waited, her hands folded in front of her and her eyes shining—how could I keep anything from her? I tried to assume a Scotland Yard image. Did they tell their helpers everything? Probably not, but if it might help elicit further information . . .

"Conti is an agent," I said. "An agent of a secret organization called *Amici della Uva*. They work for the European Union in the area of crimes relating to the wine industry."

"So why is he on the *Donau Schnellzug*?"

"You must know about the shipment of vines going to Romania?"

"Of course; it's been in all the news programs."

"Well, he may be protecting them, but he hasn't told us about it. We found out in—er, well, in another way."

"He doesn't know you know?"

"Right. Now I don't see how that is connected with the death of Svarovina, but it may be. Anyway, see what you can find out from Conti."

"I will. Anything else?"

"You were talking to Larouge at the banquet. Did you learn anything from him?"

"Nothing that seemed interesting. He said he found me very attractive."

"I can understand that. Anything else?"

"Well, I did talk to the oil man—"

"Gerhardt Vollmer?"

"Yes. He found me attractive too—"

"I don't doubt it. What else did he say?"

"He seemed to know a lot about Malescu."

"What does that tell us?" I asked.

"H'm, well . . . if he knows her as well as he says, he must have been another one of her lovers."

"Do I detect a note of censure there?"

"What does 'censure' mean?"

"It means criticism—or disapproval."

She shrugged, a dismissive shrug that suggested she thought she had every right to be critical.

"All I'm saying is, if he was one of her lovers, he might have some motive to kill her."

"But she wasn't—"

"She wasn't killed, I know, but you said someone may have tried to kill her." She flashed me one of her derisive glances.

"What's Vollmer's attitude toward her? Angry, bitter, does he sound resentful, discarded . . . ?"

"Not exactly bitter, no. Not vengeful either but very definitely not friendly toward her."

"So why did he admit being one of her lovers?"

"He didn't—but he knew so much about her—and anyway, a woman can tell."

That was the final word as far as Irena was concerned. *A woman can tell.* The aggravating thing was that in her case, I believed it.

CHAPTER TWENTY-FIVE

Professor Sundvall had resumed his duties by the time Irena and I had finished talking. "This used to be known as Petervarad," he was saying. "It has always been described as the Gibraltar of the Danube."

A massive fortress stood high on a rock, one of those ancient piles of stone that looks as if it has been there a thousand years—and, of course, this one had. Its perch, about two hundred feet above the river, overshadowed a small town at the foot of the cliffs.

"In the Empress Maria Theresa's day," the professor said, "every member of the male population had to spend three weeks out of every month on active military service. That service consisted of defending the land against attack by the Turks. This fortress was the keystone of their defense line."

Someone wanted to know why it was called Petervarad. "Isn't that a little like Petrograd?"

"Exactly," said the professor with a satisfied beam, "but Petrograd was named after Peter the Great of Russia. Petervarad was named after a much earlier Peter." He looked expectantly around his audience, giving anyone who wished the chance to shine. No one did.

The professor beamed again anyway. "Peter the Hermit," he explained. "Many centuries earlier."

"The monk who traveled all over Europe preaching the First Crusade," said the questioner.

"Yes. Peter had visited the Holy Sepulchre in Jerusalem and was strongly moved by the plight of the Christians there. Pope Urban II was massing the European nations, their armies, and their money, for a Crusade to recover the Holy Land for Christianity. In Peter the

Hermit, he recognized a vigorous and dedicated prophet. He summoned him to Rome, applauded his intentions, and promised him all the support he needed."

"And he came here?"

"He traveled throughout France and Italy, where the greatest support could be expected, then he expanded his efforts into the surrounding Christian countries. This was one of the places where he visited and preached."

"Is this myth or history?" The questioner sounded dubious.

"Oh, it's historical fact," said the professor. "The story of Peter's visit here is carved in stone inside the fortress you are now viewing."

"And this was in what year?" asked another voice.

"The year 1096."

I looked at the wooded islands dotting the Danube and the woodlands and hills sloping away to the south. We slid past them and over another bridge giving fine views of the Danube. A cruise ship, gleaming white, passed underneath us. Then I left and walked through the train to Kramer's compartment.

A steward was outside. He was not obviously on guard, but I knew that was his mission. He identified me and knocked, telling Kramer that I was there. Kramer unlocked and opened the door.

"Come in. Perfect timing," he said.

I sat opposite him across the desk. His blond hair looked even more impossibly blond than usual, and again I marveled at how ultratypically German he looked.

"I have a number of reports here but nothing helpful."

"That means we still have the problem of who poisoned Talia Svarovina," I said.

He nodded. "Yes."

"We are in agreement on that, aren't we? It wasn't accidental or an overdose."

"I think we can proceed on that basis. As soon as all the passengers were in the limousines and on the way to the banquet, the vehicle arrived and took her body to the city morgue. They have promised me that they will give top priority to her examination."

"No problem with letting the train continue on to Bucharest?"

"Only a little. Svarovina is a Hungarian citizen, so her body should be left in Budapest. Of course, Herr Brenner did his usual masterly job of diplomatically smoothing the waters."

He sat back and studied me. "Any news from among the passengers?"

"It appears that Gerhardt Vollmer was probably one of Malescu's lovers."

"Another of them?"

"Yes," I said.

"H'm," he murmured. "I am still puzzled by that event. Who tried to poison Malescu and why? Also why did they fail?"

"That's still puzzling me, too," I admitted. I considered telling him about Irena's information about the Bulgarian herb but decided to wait until I had something more definite.

"La Malescu seems to have had so many lovers that if we consider them all suspects, we may have to bring in another fifty men," I said, and he smiled one of his mirthless smiles.

"I understand that Conti attended the banquet," Kramer said.

"Yes. He said he didn't feel his usual self, but he attended anyway. His table companions said he was quiet, didn't say much."

"He still doesn't want to tell us of his position as an agent for *Amici della Uva*, does he?" said Kramer.

"No. Still, it is an organization that likes to keep an extremely low profile. Any stories that might come out about the activities of its agents could cause a lot of awkward questions in the governments of Europe. Just one leak could be highly embarrassing—it's something the organization has to work hard to avoid."

Kramer nodded. "We are on the last leg of our journey now. It is also the longest. We must resolve the mystery of the death of Fraulein Svarovina before we reach Bucharest."

"The original intention was to stop in Belgrade, wasn't it?"

"Yes but that was changed before the journey was finally planned.

There will be no more stops now." He raised a finger. "I spoke with the stewards before we left Budapest. I asked them all to be especially vigilant."

"Good," I said, "and I'll increase my circulation and talk to as many passengers as I can. Some clue must emerge."

"I believe so," Kramer said emphatically. "There is much that we do not yet know, and it cannot all be with one individual. Knowing what communication takes place between the passengers may yield that clue."

I left to make my first round of what had to be the last stage of the investigation.

I had time for a conversation with Henri Larouge before lunch, but it was not particularly rewarding. He was critical of the banquet in Budapest.

"It was very good—of its type," he conceded, "but it was not typical of Hungarian food. Not the food that the average Hungarian eats, anyway."

"No goulash, no paprikash, you mean?"

"Yes, that's what I mean."

"But it was a banquet," I said. "Some of the best restaurants in Budapest prepared the food, and I thought they did it very well. At a banquet, you don't expect to eat the food the peasants eat—if I can say that without being accused of classism."

"It doesn't have to be peasant food," Larouge argued. "It could be typical dishes featuring paprika, sour cream, caraway—the food that most people in Hungary eat."

"With top restaurants doing the catering, they are going to do all they can to bring their best efforts to the table," I countered. "Limiting dishes the way you suggest would not let them demonstrate their capabilities sufficiently. As it was, they served that superb goose liver pâté and duck, which are typically Hungarian."

"The average Hungarian can't afford to eat either of those," said Larouge.

"The average Frenchman can't afford to eat the meals served in Paris restaurants though, can he? Except perhaps on special occasions. The banquet was one of those occasions."

Larouge grumbled a while longer, and I assumed he was not in a good mood. I hoped it wasn't something he had eaten. I switched the subject. "Let's hope we have no more excitement on the train for the rest of the journey—Malescu murdered—then returning from the dead, Svarovina dead and not recovering, Conti poisoned and recovering—it's all too much for me."

"Have the police learned anything about Svarovina's death?" he asked. "You seem to be working with them."

I sidestepped the question implicit in the latter statement and concentrated on the former question.

"Her body was taken off the train in Budapest, I understand. The authorities there will be examining it carefully."

"So it was not a murder," he said.

"It is not being handled as proven to be murder," I said cautiously.

"The same as Malescu," he said. "But then, it must be concluded that she was not murdered only because she reappeared—alive."

Everybody wanted to be a detective, it seemed. Well, if I gathered enough theories, I might spot a clue.

"I wouldn't call it 'the same as Malescu,' " I said. "I believe that most of the circumstances are different."

"Svarovina was Malescu's understudy," he said stubbornly. "That cannot be a coincidence surely?"

I gave him an inquiring look and waited for him to go on. This might prove useful.

"I'm not sure what you mean."

"Perhaps someone tried to kill Malescu and failed. They tried again, but this time killed Mademoiselle Svarovina."

"By mistake, you mean?"

"Yes, it's possible."

"That would indicate that someone was really determined to kill Malescu."

"And why not?" he asked, with a sudden flash of Gallic spirit.

"She has had dozens of lovers—there must be an army of husbands and wives out there with sufficient motive. Not to mention the people who don't want her to play Rakoczi's daughter."

"The IMG, you mean? But surely they wouldn't commit murder just to prevent a play being performed?"

"They are a powerful organization," Larouge said in a serious tone.

"Do they have a record of killing?"

"They do not make claims like some revolutionary organizations. As a result, it is difficult to know which crimes can be attributed to them." He looked at me quizzically. "I suppose you are wondering how I know so much about them? It is not really a lot, but perhaps I know more than the average European. Outside of Hungary, the IMG does not get a lot of publicity."

He was right, I was wondering that. I waited for him to continue.

"I was in Szeged, in the south of Hungary one time. It is, as you may know, a major production center for paprika. From there, they export it all over the world. I was there to discuss a large shipment of paprika to Paris. I was in the Central Post Office when a bomb exploded. I escaped with only cuts and bruises, others died. It was attributed to the IMG. From then on, I read about their exploits whenever they appeared in the press. I suppose that every time I did so, I thanked God for sparing me."

"Yes, I can see that having a personal involvement like that would make you particularly interested in the IMG's activities," I said.

He looked at his watch. "Now you must excuse me. I have some things to do before lunch."

I also had something to do myself before lunch. I headed for the restaurant coach, went through the bakery, full of glorious aromas and hot steamy flavors, and into the coach with the storage rooms. I was seeking Herr Hofstatter, the Austrian head chef.

CHAPTER TWENTY-SIX

The genial head chef was tasting a slab of butter. He was grimacing just slightly and as he reached to dip for second taste, he saw me and smiled.

"Too much salt?" I asked.

"When we make so many foods right here on the train," he said, "it is inevitable that slight variations creep in."

"The amount of salt in butter is always a difficult decision."

"It is indeed. In this case, I must go back to the salt supplier and make sure that the product they provide us remains constant."

He replaced his long tasting spoon, wiped a hand on his spotlessly clean apron, and held it out for me to shake.

"I just wanted to clear up a detail or two," I told him. "I hoped that before lunch was a suitable time."

"Of course, of course," he assured me. "How can I help you?"

"When I was here before, we talked about your stocks of fruit and nuts," I said. That had not been the precise progression of our discussion, but I wanted to approach my point tangentially.

"Ah, yes," he said immediately, "I told you that Fraulein Malescu asked about fruit and nuts—she said that it must be difficult to keep a fresh stock of both at all times."

I hid a smile. He was aware of the direction in which I wanted to steer the conversation. Well, that might save some time.

"Did she examine any of your stocks?" I asked.

"Examine? Not exactly examine, no. She looked at many labels."

"Did she appear to recognize many of them?"

"Some were familiar to her, some were not. *Ach*, I would say that most were familiar to her."

"Did any of them appear to be of special interest to her?"

His wrinkled brow developed a few more wrinkles. "Let me think . . . well, yes, as she looked along the shelves, she paused at some—I suppose they were those that were less familiar to her."

"Could it have been that she was looking for one in particular?"

He frowned still more, trying to recollect.

"Not that I recall," he said finally.

She is an actress, I reminded myself. *She would be adept at concealing her intention.*

I made one more attempt. "Could you say that she spent longer looking at any one product than the others?"

He made a genuine try but shook his head. "No, I could not say that."

I approached from another angle. "Do you have any nuts in the form of essence?"

"Yes, we have coconut essence, we use that in cakes. Let me see, we have also Essence of Almonds—we use that in cakes, too."

"Is that Acid Essence of Almonds?" I asked casually.

I thought I saw a glint in his eye. He was a shrewd old bird. He might spend all his time cooking on trains, but he knew a thing or two outside the railroad. He might be right there alongside me in his thinking . . .

"It is sometimes called that because the cakes it flavors are usually very sugary, and the acid essence balances the sugar."

I was formulating my next question when he asked, "Do you wish to know if Fraulein Malescu showed more interest in those two—the coconut and the almond?"

I smiled involuntarily. He returned the smile, we were like two conspirators.

"I might ask that, yes. Did she show more interest in those two?"

"No, she did not," he said promptly, and laughed a booming laugh that echoed in the confined space. I was obliged to join him.

He wiped his eyes on his apron.

"Do you have any more questions about Fraulein Malescu's visit to my domain?" he asked.

"Not at the moment," I said. "I certainly want to thank you for your time though. And I have enjoyed sharing a laugh with you."

"Anytime, anytime," he said jovially. "Please come again soon."

He was escorting me to the door, a friendly hand on my arm. I was opening it and about to exit when he spoke again.

"The next time you are here, you may wish to ask me about Fraulein Svarovina's visit."

It was a great exit line except that I was the one making the exit, and he was the one with the line. I grasped the doorknob, opened the door, and went back into the coach. Facing him, I said, "Svarovina was here, visiting, after Malescu?"

He was enjoying this, the son of a gun. Through his happy smile, he said, "Yes, she was indeed." His smile began to fade. "The poor lady, she died, I know." A look of alarm appeared on his face. "Of course, her visit here had nothing to do with her death."

I waited a moment, letting that thought crystallize in his mind. He was working on it, I could see.

"Acid Essence of Almonds smells like bitter almonds," he said. "Not exactly but similar—and while cyanide is a deadly poison, Acid Essence of Almonds is quite harmless."

I nodded and let him continue. "You see, when Fraulein Svarovina came after Fraulein Malescu, I gave her the same tour of our facilities here. When we reached the fruit and nuts storage, Fraulein Svarovina had a little trouble speaking and asked me for a glass of water."

I looked around. "So you had to go into the next coach to do that—I see no water supply here."

"That is correct. So she was here alone for perhaps a minute or a little less—" He broke off with another of his engaging smiles. "That is what you were going to ask me, isn't it? Was she alone in here at any time?"

"That is what I was going to ask you," I conceded. "My next question was going to be—but you probably know that, too."

"Was anything missing? That would be your next question—well, no, I didn't think that, not at first. I mean, she is—she was—the understudy to a famous actress, so I would not expect her to be taking anything." He spread his hands in a helpless gesture. "But then you can never be sure—there was a Spanish cabinet minister on one of our trips, and he was constantly taking oranges. He didn't need to do so, we could have—still, never mind."

"So later you noticed that a jar of Acid Essence of Almonds was missing." I had had enough of Herr Hofstatter second-guessing me. It was time for me to pull that on him.

He smiled good-naturedly. "My pastry chef noticed that a jar was missing."

"Thank you for telling me this."

He looked anxious. "It is true, you know. Acid Essence of Almonds is quite harmless."

"Don't worry. I appreciate your confidence. There is no blame to be attached to the kitchens on the train in any way."

"Come and see us again," he urged.

"I will," I said, "and thanks again."

On my way back through the train, I was still putting the pieces together. The aroma of bitter almonds that I had noticed in Malescu's compartment had bothered me. If she had taken cyanide, she would have been dead. She was not dead—therefore, she had not taken cyanide. Until now, that had remained a puzzle, but it was no longer the case. The aroma I had observed had been from Acid Essence of Almonds and not from cyanide. From there, it was only a short step to a major breakthrough in the case.

I was still working on that short step when I met Herman Friedlander. The conductor looked unhappy. "Is anything wrong?" I asked him.

He shook his head angrily. "I cannot get it right. I keep thinking I have it, then it goes wrong."

He noticed my perplexed look. "My symphony; I compose it as the train progresses, you see."

"Sounds like a hard way to do it."

"No, no, I often do this," he said.

"Did you enjoy the banquet in Budapest?" I asked.

"It was very good," he said, but without enthusiasm.

"Authentic Hungarian dishes," I prompted him, but he just shrugged.

"I gather you won't be conducting when the Mozart manuscript we are carrying is played in Bucharest?" I said innocently.

"Bah! Of course not."

"Still, some think the manuscript is valuable," I said. I wasn't exactly trying to get his goat but he did offer a tempting target for a few digs.

"I can't imagine who they could be," he said scornfully.

"The manuscript has not yet been authenticated," Friedlander added.

"You think it is a fake?"

"Until it is authenticated—it could be. Although that does not matter. Even should it prove to be actually written by Mozart, that does not make it a worthwhile work. Much of his music is weak, spineless, deficient in true musical content."

"A lot of people like his music," I said, still trying to goad him.

"People who like Muzak—not music." Friedlander was at his most contemptuous, and I knew when to give up.

"I'll be conducting Salieri in Bucharest," he continued.

"Your ancestor."

"Precisely. It will be a fine concert. Will you attend?"

"I would certainly like to do so."

"I will send you a complimentary ticket."

"Thank you; you're very kind."

He gave me a bow and went off, his head no doubt filled with the music of a large string section, and I hoped he was getting it right.

I stopped in the nearest toilet room and washed for lunch. It was a casual affair, strung out over about three hours so that the dining coach was sparsely occupied throughout. I presumed the magnificent repast of the previous night had temporarily satiated appetites.

The afternoon followed much the same pattern. I talked with as many passengers as I could but could not discern any useful information. Most apparently wanted to forget the earlier events and keep the topics trivial.

The views out of the window were of cultivated land with lots of activity. River traffic increased as we neared the town of Mohacs, and after it, village after village on the riverbank was pursuing its busy routine. We passed several vineyards as we rolled on southwards toward Belgrade.

When dinnertime came around, the passengers' lethargy looked to be yielding to a more positive attitude. As I went into the dining coach, there were half a dozen there already, and Erich Brenner waved for me to join him. With him were Dr. Stolz and Eva Zilinsky.

Herr Brenner had ordered a bottle of *Moriezerjo,* a wine not seen outside of Hungary, he said. As the Danube Express was still inside the country, he wanted us to taste the dry, golden wine. "It was first produced here in the eighteenth century," he told us, "by refugees from Bavaria who hacked down the trees and planted vines. The refugees knew how to make wine, and they recognized the soil here to have a high mica and quartz content. This is a very unpleasant combination for the dreaded *Phylloxera,* the bug that loves vine roots."

We watched the waiter pour the rich-colored liquid. "The efforts of the refugees prospered, another reason for their success," said Herr Brenner, "being that they located their vineyards on mountain slopes, where they are protected from winter frosts yet have a complete absence of shadow in summer."

It was dry, surprisingly so in view of its strong color, and with a satisfying and lingering aftertaste rare in a wine suitable for accompanying a meal.

At another table, I saw Paolo Conti with the Sundvalls and Helmut Lydecker. At another, the Australians and Henri Larouge were ordering already when Irena Koslova came in and joined them.

At our table, Eva Zilinsky ordered a cold grape soup and carp in horseradish and sour cream sauce. Herr Brenner nodded approval. "Very Hungarian," he agreed. For himself, he had a ragout soup, which he told us the Hungarians made from the gizzard, liver, and heart of a turkey. He looked around the table to see who wanted to emulate him, but there no takers. He followed with a sirloin steak with mushrooms.

Dr. Stolz took an asparagus salad and baked pike, while I had a cucumber salad and red mullet cooked on a spit. Dill and paprika are the only spices used by the Hungarians on the salad.

The conversation was desultory. Herr Brenner gave us a few reminiscences of earlier trips and the eccentric passengers occasionally contributed, but the doctor was not communicative and concentrated on his meal. Eva Zilinsky tried to live up to what she evidently considered to be her reputation and tossed in a story now and then. I referred to some train journeys of the past, including one or two where the train blew real black smoke and the rails clicked and clacked.

Herr Brenner's recommendation for wine was heartily endorsed by all of us, and the waiter brought another bottle. "Dessert," announced Herr Brenner. "We will all have a Hungarian dessert to mark our last meal in Hungary."

No one was inclined to refuse such an invitation, and Herr Brenner called the waiter. "We want a really typical Hungarian dessert," he said. "What do you propose?"

The waiter had several suggestions. He began with *Dios Pite,* a nut cake, then *Dobos Torte*, a chocolate layer cake. He continued with *Kepvisolofank*, a very different version of the cream puff. Various fruit or cheese strudels were available too as well as crêpes in a variety of guises.

It was a tough decision. The waiter mentioned another Hungarian specialty, golden dumplings, and we considered those but eventually, we all went for the Hungarian cream puffs. Served with a glaze of raspberry syrup, they were light as air and scrumptious.

The wine had gone by the time we had eaten dessert, and I noticed Herr Brenner exchange a few quick words with the waiter. The reason became obvious when the waiter appeared with small, elaborate glasses and a crusted bottle.

"The pride of Hungary," Herr Brenner said theatrically. "It is particularly appropriate to serve it now as, at this very moment, we are passing through the region where this is produced. It is the great wine of Hungary—Tokay."

Everyone had heard of it, and I was sure that some of us had drunk it, but I had no doubt that Herr Brenner's description was about to entertain us.

"There is a condition called 'noble rot'—it is a fungus that affects grapes. It gives them an unpleasant taste and oxidizes them. Amazingly though, with suitable climatic conditions at the end of the season, it contributes a unique taste to the wine, the reasons for which still cannot be adequately explained.

"This was first discovered more than a century ago when Prince Rakoczi, the ruler of Transylvania, delayed the harvest on his estate because he was busy with one of his wars and all his workers were fighting. He managed to win that war, and the harvest could not be brought in until late November."

"Doesn't that mean," asked Eva Zilinsky, "that any vineyard could make Tokay? All they have to do is wait until the weather gets cold—like the *Spatlese* wines from Germany."

"They are simply sweet wines, gathered late," said Herr Brenner. "Tokay has a taste that is like no other wine—but you can see for yourselves." He motioned to the waiter. He handled the bottle reverently, with a cloth with colored edges, clearly a special one.

"This grade is known as *Essencia*," said Herr Brenner. "The grapes for this are not pressed, the juice is allowed to drip from the grapes into a tub. It is one of the factors that make Tokay unique. Very few wine producers want to invest that much time in a wine. This is the finest grade of Tokay."

It was immeasurably sweet. Little wonder the glasses were tiny and not filled. There was a hint of fruit, a little like apricots but not quite identifiable. The remarkable thing about Tokay—and I had noticed it before—is that its sweetness changes to a dry finish so that the mouth is not left with the cloying sweetness of sugar. It is truly a taste experience quite unlike any other in the wine realm.

After the Tokay, my dinner companions drifted away one by one. I was left till last because I was observing the table where Irena Koslova sat. The Australians had left already. I watched Larouge speaking to Irena, and she was shaking her head. The Frenchman tried again but finally gave up and left. I thought Irena was looking in the direction of my table, and I walked over to hers.

"Enjoy your last meal in Hungary for this trip?" she asked me.

"Yes, it was excellent."

"Did you notice that La Malescu is not here?" she asked.

"Yes," I said. "I hope it doesn't mean that she has disappeared again."

"Elisha Tabor is not here either."

"That's true. A good thing you are here—brightening up the room."

She smiled an acknowledgment and rose. I went with her to the door, which a steward opened for us.

Irena hesitated. "Let me see now—I still have a problem remembering which direction my compartment is."

"It's this way," I told her. "May I escort you?"

At the door, she produced her key and inserted it in the lock.

"A pity we couldn't sit at the same table," I said.

The door swung open. "Larouge and that nice Australian lady waved to me to join them," she said.

"Like I say—a pity."

She looked into my eyes. Hers were deep and inviting.

"Doesn't matter," she said, "you're here now."

She placed a hand at the back of my neck and pulled me into the compartment, adroitly kicking the door closed at the same time.

CHAPTER TWENTY-SEVEN

Irena was still sleeping the next morning when I woke. She opened her eyes briefly, smiled, turned over, and went back to sleep. I dressed, returned to my compartment to change, and went to the dining coach with a healthy appetite.

I started with a bowl of fresh fruit, which included plump cherries, juicy apricots, aromatic pears, fat blackberries, and tangy grapefruit slices. One of the chefs was Italian, I knew, and he and his chrome-plated monster of a machine produced a *caffe latte* that put all its imitations to shame. I asked for a cup of the magnificent brew it produced, then I was ready to order.

The waiter ran through a tempting array of possibilities. "I want to stay with Hungarian dishes as long as we are still in Hungary," I told him.

He motioned out of the window. The rail line was running along the edge of the Danube Valley, looking down two hundred feet or more at the slowly flowing river. The surface was broken by numerous small islands. A castle that was in no worse repair than a score of others we had seen slipped by, and, as we climbed even higher, a vineyard stretched away to the horizon.

"We travel more slowly at night," the waiter said, "so we are still in Hungary, though we will be leaving it very soon. Zimony will be the last Hungarian town we pass."

"Didn't it used to be an important frontier station?" I asked.

"Yes, it did, very important." He was at least ten years older than I and he smiled with a touch of nostalgia. "But in these days of harmony, frontiers are no longer the exciting places they were in the past. Passports are no longer the vital documents they were—officials would delay a train for two or three hours to examine passports, then the customs people would come through the train with forms and documents and searches and questions."

"The good old days?"

"Ah, you are right. Perhaps some things have changed for the better, what used to take hours now only takes minutes."

"Still, all the romance has gone out of it, hasn't it?" I said. "Frontier guards with their uniforms and guns, the flags, the barriers, the languages—now one frontier is just like another, and the thrilling moments of passing from country to country have vanished."

"That is unfortunately true."

"At least the *Donau Schnellzug* maintains a semblance of romance," I said. "The periodic whistle, the puff of smoke, the slower speed . . . not to mention these coaches."

"It is a wonderful train," he agreed and waited patiently for me to make a breakfast decision, his pen poised.

"Tell me about the Crêpes with Ham."

"Certainly. Flour, salt, eggs, butter, and milk are blended until thick. We let this batter stand at least an hour, then we bake small crêpes. We mince ham and add beaten egg yolks. In another pan, we beat sour cream with white pepper and tarragon and add it to the ham mixture. We spread some on each crêpe and fold into small squares." He smiled, took a breath, and continued.

"Each crêpe is then dipped into beaten egg, then into flour, then into egg again, and finally into bread crumbs. The crêpes are then fried until crisp and served at once."

"I wouldn't dare order anything else," I told him. "It sounds irresistible."

It was. The tarragon and pepper had been added by a sure hand at spicing, and the crêpes were golden brown and thin, just on the edge of crispy.

"Something else, *Meinherr*?" the waiter asked when I had finished.

"One more cup of this delicious *caffe latte*," I said.

I looked down on a small market square, full of stands and people. It was evidently market day, and the farmers had brought in their wares for sale. Our train moved past it at a reduced speed so that we could take in the full view. It was an animated scene and a Gypsy band was unpacking its instruments. The *Zigeuner*, the Gypsies, are making a comeback in Hungary after so many decades of repression and brutality by two ruthless totalitarian regimes in succession.

Now we were approaching the junction point where the broad Save River joins the Danube and widens it considerably. The great War Island sits in the middle of the conflux, and the railbed here runs high along the riverbank. The town of Zimony was coming into sight, surrounded by trees and green hills. This is Croatia once again, after being part of Yugoslavia for so long and Austrian before that. We rolled smoothly past the town and as the waiter brought my second *caffe latte*, he glanced out the window, and said, "Now we approach Belgrade." It was the Serbian capital once again after it, too, had been absorbed by Yugoslavia.

Ferocious battles had been fought many times in history over this crucial bend where two great rivers meet. I knew that such conflicts had persisted since Celtic times and decided that, after breakfast, I would seek out Professor Sundvall and ask him to fill in the details.

I was watching boats on the gently flowing Danube when the door to the dining coach opened with an unusual abruptness. A steward burst in, looked around the tables. He evidently did not see the person he was looking for, but at that moment the door at the other end of the coach opened and Karl Kramer entered.

The steward immediately approached him, and the two spoke in low tones. The steward was clearly agitated and, over his shoulder, Kramer saw me. He exchanged a few more words with the steward, then the two of them came to my table. The adjacent tables were empty, but even so, Kramer's voice was kept low.

"You had better come with us. Werner here tells me we have another dead body."

———

I almost choked on the coffee. Werner, the steward, was a small man with streaky gray hair and an alert manner.

"Tell us," Kramer invited.

"It's a young lady," Werner said. "I'm afraid she's dead."

I felt a freezing cold grip me. After carefully swallowing the mouthful of coffee, I took another sip for restorative purposes. It didn't help. Fortunately, Kramer looked so disturbed by the news that he didn't notice my alarm, and the steward was so upset he was not in an observant mood either.

"Where is she?" Kramer asked.

"In her compartment. I think she—you had better come and see," said Werner.

We walked out of the dining coach, all endeavoring to look calm. I wasn't sure any of us were convincing. Werner led the way through the adjacent coach and into the next. My heart was pounding, my brain filled with disbelief and anguish.

When had this happened? After I had left Irena's compartment? But such a short time had elapsed. Would she admit anyone at such an hour? Perhaps she had thought it was me returning. Who else would she admit?

When the steward stopped in front of a compartment door and Kramer produced his master key, my stomach flipped over, my head was in turmoil—but now the reason was different.

I had been rehearsing my answers. "She was alive when I left her . . . Certainly, I had no reason to harm her . . . No, I had never met her before this journey . . . What time had it been? . . ."

Now my brain was settling. I was still puzzled, but knew I didn't need my defensive answers.

It was not Irena's compartment.

My utter relief must have showed in my attitude, but neither Kramer nor Werner the steward noticed. My relief was that Irena was all right—but Werner had spoken of a dead woman. Who was it?

The door opened and we entered. She sat in a chair at a table for two. She wore a sky-blue dressing gown and puffy slippers. It was Elisha Tabor.

She was in a normal sitting position, though her head rested on the chairback, her eyes closed. She was not breathing, but her face appeared relaxed. Kramer pressed his fingers on the inside of her wrist, then shook his head. He placed his hand flat on her forearm. "She has been dead six to eight hours," he said.

An empty wine glass was on the small table in front of her. I sniffed at it but could detect nothing. All was orderly and completely normal.

Kramer moved restlessly through the room, looking, peering, probing, and Werner took his lead from the security chief and did likewise but touched nothing.

I went into the bathroom. In front of the large mirror, an array of cosmetics was spread and several bottles and small boxes of pharmaceutical products. I looked through them—headache remedies, sleeping pills, cold remedies. Kramer came in, and I shook my head.

"Then it is far beyond coincidence," he said. "It is murder."

We continued our investigation, but none of us found anything unusual. Werner glanced out of the window as we were concluding our third tour of the compartment.

"We are leaving Hungary," he told Kramer.

I knew that he was reminding him that the train was no longer under the official jurisdiction of Hungary and that would make it easier to continue on to Bucharest without hindrance. The multinational nature of the Danube Express blurred those lines of delineation anyway, and the blurring was compounded by the diplomatic leverage that Herr Brenner could exert.

Kramer had his phone out and called Dr. Stolz first. I could hear that there was some amazement at the other end of the connection. It was understandable that the doctor should be bewildered at being called upon to attend to yet another dead body. It was clearly not turning out to be the relaxing journey he had anticipated.

Kramer then called Thomas, and I could hear that he was asking him to check what messages had gone out in the recent hours. Next, he called Erich Brenner and broke the news to him. He didn't do it gently—there was no way to do that.

He had hung up, and we had patrolled the compartment once more without seeing any item that was unusual, when Herr Brenner arrived. He was out of breath and bordering on the incredulous. He stared at the body, then listened to Kramer and shook his head sadly. "Two women dead. I can't believe it."

He and Kramer had a discussion on the political ramifications and agreed that it should be possible to continue the journey to Bucharest and turn over the investigation to the authorities there. The possibility of stopping in Yugoslavia because the crime had been discovered there was dismissed as quickly as it arose.

"Besides," Kramer said grimly, "we intend to solve both deaths before reaching Bucharest." He looked at me and I nodded vigorously. "That's right. We will."

Herr Brenner looked relieved. He and Kramer put together a short message to send back to *Donau Schnellzug* headquarters in Germany and secure strong backing there first for the train's continuation, then another to send ahead to Bucharest to have them prepare a forensic team to bring on board.

"We will have this solved before then," Kramer said, "but we need to have Bucharest believe that they will have authority over it."

Brenner left, and, as he did so, Kramer's phone buzzed. He listened, then, the phone still in his hand, said to me, "A message went out from a cell phone just before midnight. It went to the Budapest *Times*."

"Czerny?"

"It could have been." He shook his head. "What a pity we are not permitted to have a full trace on every call that goes out."

"Can you have Thomas have a look at the morning edition of the Budapest *Times*? See if there was a story that could have gone out?"

He talked with Thomas, then shook his head at me. I held up a hand. "Don't hang up—one other thing." I took out my notebook, ripped a page from it, and scribbled a short message on it. I riffled through the notebook pages and added an e-mail address. I handed the message to Kramer. "Have Thomas send that."

He read it out into the phone. First, he gave Thomas an e-mail address in Geneva, Switzerland. There was a note of perplexity in Kramer's voice as he read my message.

" 'Emil—one, before you drink your next glass of Pinot Noir, ask 121 ADU for full physical description. Two, potential cargo buyer beside original? Urgent response vital.' "

Kramer had to repeat it for Thomas. It must have sounded just as mysterious to him. Kramer slapped his cell phone cover back in place.

"It's a wild idea," I told him. "A long shot—but it's worth a try."

" 'Long shot,' " he repeated, "ah, yes, from the days of horse racing, yes?"

"Correct."

"And so wild, you don't want to tell me what this is all about?"

"On the nose," I said.

He nodded wisely. "Another horse racing expression."

"Precisely," I said.

CHAPTER TWENTY-EIGHT

I was still feeling an immense relief as I left Kramer's office—relief that it had not been Irena who had been killed. I regretted that Elisha Tabor had to be the victim but I did not feel ashamed of being glad it was not Irena.

That she had been killed was no longer in doubt. The conclusion was that the same person had killed both victims, and it was probable that the motives were closely linked.

I returned to the restaurant coach, and the first person I saw was Irena. She was sitting alone, and I joined her. She smiled brightly, then her expression changed.

"Is something wrong?"

She was very intuitive, I had learned that.

"I'm afraid so," I said, and told her of Elisha Tabor.

Her face clouded. "Oh, no! That's terrible! The poor woman! How did she die?"

"The same poisons that were used on Talia Svarovina and Paolo Conti."

She shuddered. "I hope it was a quick death."

"It was, and a painless one," I assured her.

"I didn't know her really well, but we talked a number of times." A glint came into Irena's eyes. "So now we have to find out who killed her—and before we reach Bucharest."

"Yes, we do."

She saw me eying her breakfast. It was a boiled egg, a slice each of salami, ham, and cheese and a roll. She had only just started on it. "I felt hungry today," she explained, eating quickly. "We have to go to work. What can I do?"

"Have you seen Magda Malescu this morning?"

"No, why?" She caught her breath. "You suspect her?"

"Not especially, but a lot of questions still hang over her head."

"I haven't seen her in here. Maybe she takes breakfast very late or more likely in her compartment."

"In her compartment probably. Tell me, did you learn anything at the banquet in Budapest? I didn't have a chance to ask you last night."

"Neither of us had much chance for talking about murder, did we?" she said with a mischievous smile. "After the banquet, I talked to Helmut Lydecker."

"What did you talk about?"

"Making women disappear."

"I hope he didn't think you were volunteering."

"I'm sure he didn't. No, he talked about Magda Malescu though."

"Why her?"

"Because I asked him."

"Good for you," I said with a smile. "What did he say?"

"Oh, he said she was a very good assistant for the act. She was a fast learner and willing to practice as long as was needed."

"Did he say anything about her on a personal level?"

"I tried to get him to do that, but he steered away from it. I reached one conclusion though—"

"Go on," I urged.

"I think he's still in love with her."

"After all this time? Surely he—"

"What do you mean, 'after all this time'? How long is love supposed to last?"

"Well, it's thirty years ago, isn't it?" I said weakly.

"So? Couldn't he be in love with her still?"

"I suppose so. You think he is?"

"Yes, I do."

"I'm trying to figure out what that might mean," I said.

Irena cooled off a little. "He's a magician, isn't he? Makes women disappear? Maybe he had something to do with her disappearance the time we all thought she was dead."

"I wonder how well he knew Talia Svarovina," I said. "I also wonder just what was the relationship between Malescu and Svarovina."

"I thought you interrogated Malescu on that subject?"

"Herr Kramer and I did talk to her, and we asked that specific question. Naturally, Malescu said they were good friends. What else would she say?"

Irena looked pensive. "There are many strange relationships between people on this train. Malescu and Doctor Stolz are another— he was once her lover, too, and he's a doctor, so he has drugs and medicines, doesn't he?"

"We have no evidence against him at all though."

Irena tossed me a look of disdain.

I shook my head sorrowfully. "Centuries of barbarian ancestors and decades under Nazism and Communism have given you a disregard for some of the conventions of democracy like evidence and proof, I'm sorry to say."

"Well, it does sometimes protect wicked people when we have to produce silly things like those," she protested.

"Do you know any good tortures?" I asked. "Perhaps that would be our best method of getting truthful answers to all our questions."

"Ha-ha," she said.

"But as we can't do that," I said, "we have to resort to more sophisticated methods."

"By 'sophisticated,' you mean clever."

"Clever would be good. Do you have any ideas?"

"You're the detective. What would Scotland Yard do?"

"Kramer and I are going to have to talk to Malescu again. There are still some things she hasn't told us."

Irena nodded emphatically. "Torture—you're right. This may be the time for it—and Malescu would be the one to try it on, perhaps you should—"

"We'll try a normal interrogation first," I said.

She pouted in disappointment. "It may be a mistake. She is a devious woman."

"Nevertheless, we'll try it first."

Her shrug said, *All right, go ahead and make your own mistakes.* Aloud, she asked, "What can I do?"

"Larouge still sounds suspicious, probably because we don't know much about him. Friedlander has more motive than anyone to want to get hold of the Mozart manuscript—"

"I thought he was a famous conductor?"

"Well-known, if not famous."

"Then he can't be a crook, can he?"

"Even famous people can be crooked."

"H'm . . ." She digested that for a moment. "I suppose I can talk to Herr Lydecker again. He knew both Malescu and Talia Svarovina."

"All right. Maybe some connection exists between those two women that we haven't found yet."

"And I suppose," she said, with a toss of her head, "that while I'm interrogating the men, you'll be interrogating the women?"

"Sounds like a sensible division of labor."

"Who comes after Malescu?"

"Eva Zilinsky."

"You like her, don't you?"

"She's refreshing to talk to and—"

"Refreshing!"

"Yes, you know what I mean—lively."

"I'm sure she is," Irena said tartly. She paused to glance out of the window meditatively. "Two women murdered. Both of them sort of attractive . . ."

"I'm glad you said that. It's been bothering me. A pattern of some kind might be suggested although two women are not quite enough to reach any conclusion."

"Would you like more women to be murdered so that your 'pattern' could become more definite?"

"Of course not, but it worries me when I think there may be an association I'm missing, that's all."

She had a charming smile, and she displayed it. "I know what you mean." She pointed out the window. "We're approaching the Iron Gate. Do you know it?"

Sloping, tree-grown hills rose on the left bank, up to high sand-hills on the Romanian side. On the Serbian side, large expanses of green grass unfolded like well-kept lawns.

"The Iron Gate is a series of cataracts, isn't it?" I asked. "I have heard of it but never seen it."

"Yes, it is. It used to be wild and rushing water, shallow and with huge rocks but a lot of work has been done to clear it and make it safer for boats. I remember learning in school about the stone bridge that crossed the Danube here. It was built by the Romans, but then the Emperor Hadrian destroyed it so the invading Goths couldn't use it. You can still see a few pieces of the original bridge though, sticking up above the water."

"The Danube must be shallow all through here."

"It is, but you can often see dredgers at work—they keep it just deep enough for the passenger boats." She started to rise. "I'll see you later, I—oh, I meant to tell you, Elisha Tabor was having an affair with a man on this train."

"What?" I exploded.

She looked at me innocently. "Yes, she—"

"How do you know this?"

"Oh, I don't exactly *know* it."

"Then why do you say—explain yourself, Irena," I said sternly.

"I mean, she didn't tell me, and I didn't see her with any particular man—but I knew."

"Intuition?"

She shrugged. "If you want to call it that."

"Your Gypsy ancestors?"

"Don't make fun of me," she said with mock anger. "I know that I do, well, sense things."

"So what else can you tell me? Who the man was, for instance?"

"Just because she was having an affair with a man on the train doesn't mean that he was the one who killed her."

"It puts him high on my suspect list," I said.

"I suppose so. Oh, if I knew who he was, I'd tell you."

"Can't you intuit?"

"What's that?"

"Use intuition to work out who he was."

She looked out of the window for inspiration. "I don't know," she said after a moment.

"Care to guess?"

She pondered. "I don't think so."

This investigation is in a sorry state, I thought to myself, *when here I am asking a girl I had never even met a week ago to guess who had murdered two women.*

She saw my doubt. "Does this help?"

"I can't say. Are you really sure about it?"

"I'm sure that I know this is what I feel. I already told you I don't actually *know.*"

"Why didn't you tell me about it before?"

"Before when? No, you don't need to answer that—no, it was a sort of confused mixture in my mind, and it all just came together now."

"Suddenly?"

"I suppose my mind had already registered Elisha's change of attitude. The shock of hearing that she was dead must have been what sparked the realization that she was having an affair. Does that sound strange?"

"To be honest, yes."

"I suppose it would to you. After all, you're a man."

She said that with a finality that was inarguable. She smiled and resumed her departure. I sat alone thinking.

If she was right, I was inclined to think that any man who had been having an affair on the train with Elisha Tabor was a hot suspect. I debated how much to tell Kramer. It was not that I wanted to withhold any useful information from him, but his reaction when I told him that my "information" came from intuition was predictable. He would scoff. I decided to hold Irena's suspicions for a while and see if I could make anything of them.

The Danube Express was still following a serpentine route as it wove its way along the track high above the river. Rocks gleamed dully in the desultory sunshine, though they had been cleared from the river's main course, and their appearances were confined to the shallower edges.

Farms and villages dotted the scene as far as the eye could see, and, in the distance, another of the tall graceful church spires pierced the air.

As I entered the next coach, Kramer and Dr. Stolz were coming toward me. We paused in the corridor. No one was near.

"The doctor finds the cause of death to be undoubtedly the same as before," Kramer told me, and the doctor nodded agreement. "The symptoms are identical."

He looked from one to the other of us. "I must leave you. There is a sore throat in Coach 6 that requires attention."

He left, and Kramer said, "I have some answers from Thomas. First, he has learned that our Swiss friend, Franz Reingold, is a major stockholder in *Ostdeutscher Eisenbahn Gesellschaft*—a very prominent railroad company in Germany. They would like to have the contract to run a luxury train similar to this one. If we were severely behind schedule or if we suffered an accident or if various other things happened—we might lose our contract, and the OEG might be able to pick it up."

"Might be a motive," I conceded, "but I don't see Herr Reingold as a serious suspect."

"Nor do I," said Kramer, "but I cannot afford to overlook anything. Further, this morning's edition of the Budapest *Times* gives its daily report of the progress of the *Donau Schnellzug*. No revelations, but there is a strong recommendation that readers who are following the daily reports should be sure to read tomorrow's paper for another sensational story."

"Another? Does that mean even more sensational than the murder of Malescu and her miraculous reappearance?"

"One would presume so."

"So Czerny—or someone very close to him—is on the train?"

"It looks that way," Kramer said harshly.

"I have a suggestion . . ."

"Yes?" Kramer looked at me hopefully.

"Let me talk to Malescu alone."

He frowned. "I had intended that we should interrogate her together. Surely it would be—"

"We can still do that—but let me talk to her first. I have some half-formed theories, and if I can talk to her on a sort of personal basis, I believe I might learn something helpful. I am sure she feels intimidated by you, but she might open up to me."

Kramer looked doubtful.

"We don't have much time left," I urged. "We need to try anything."

"I am not sure," he said reluctantly. "When do you propose to do this?"

"Now," I told him, and the immediacy in the one word was enough to convince him.

"Very well," he said officiously. "Proceed."

CHAPTER TWENTY-NINE

She opened her compartment door in response to my knock and gave me an inquiring smile. I came right to the point.

"Herr Kramer and I were going to interrogate you further," I said, making it sound as heavy as I could. "I asked him to let me talk to you first." That removed the smile.

"What is this about?" she asked, not being too confrontational but not hinting at a lot of cooperation.

"It's about Acid Essence of Almonds."

The great actress came on display at once, but it was a fifth of a second late. A momentary flash of alarm had shown for that length of time, and I had been watching carefully for it.

"When do you wish to do this talk?" she asked, her composure returning rapidly.

"Right now would be convenient."

She paused, then pulled the door open, and I entered.

The compartment was much more untidy than when I had seen it before. Clothes of every description were everywhere. She wore a beige pantsuit and she had fluffy slippers on her feet. Her face showed only a little makeup although she looked surprisingly good that way. "I was getting dressed to leave the compartment," she explained, and I made no comment. She cleared a small armchair by sweeping an armful of clothes on to the chest.

I sat and she took a similar chair opposite. She had now donned a conciliatory facial expression, which I guessed meant she intended to find out what I knew.

"The circumstances surrounding the episode of your murder as reported in the Budapest *Times* have clouded this investigation," I said in my most official voice. "It is time to clarify it."

"I have told all I know," she said before I could continue.

I shook my head. "Not all, not all by any means. You have not, for instance, told us of your visit to Herr Hofstatter's storage room next to the kitchen coach. Nor have you told us that you sent your understudy, Talia Svarovina, there after your visit."

She looked away. She might be a great actress, and she might be a woman who could control her emotions in personal situations, but I had given her to believe that I knew a lot that she thought she had concealed.

"Why don't you tell me about it?" I invited. I was about to smile to set her at ease, but I had the feeling that it might be a sharklike smile and set the wrong tone.

"It—it was supposed to be a publicity stunt," she said. Her voice faltered just enough. "We have tabloid newspapers in Hungary just as melodramatic as you have in England or the United States. They supply wonderful stories that get a lot of attention, and it doesn't matter if they are proved to be false days later. I arranged with one of them to run a story that I had been poisoned, then to run a retraction later. They felt that having it all take place on the Danube Express would make it an even bigger story."

"Where does your understudy fit into this?"

"I discussed it with her, of course. We were very close."

"So," I said, "you went to the storage area on the train and saw the Acid Essence of Almonds. You sent Talia Svarovina to steal a jar of it. You know the odor of bitter almonds is characteristic of cyanide, a lethal poison—and that the two are very similar except for one being deadly and one being harmless. You thought that an aroma of cyanide would add to the appearance of death. But tell me, you must have planned this before leaving Munich—but you didn't steal the Acid Essence until you were on the train."

She was gaining confidence now. "I had planned on leaving an empty bottle of aspirin on the bed to make it look as if I had taken all of them. The tour of the kitchens was something I often do—

but seeing the Acid Essence of Almonds, I decided to make the apparent death so much more dramatic."

That, at least, was probably true. A chance to add more drama would be irresistible to her.

"As it happened, though," I said, "the first appearance of the story in print did not appear in a tabloid, did it? The Budapest *Times* carried it."

"I had not reckoned on the resourcefulness of Mikhel Czerny," she said, a touch of anger in her voice. "I don't know how he got the story so quickly."

"Could it be because Czerny or one of his informers is on the train?"

I tried to discern if that surprised her or not. I was alert for any clue, but I wasn't certain of her reaction.

"I don't know," she said softly.

I switched tracks, hoping to catch her off guard. "You said you and your understudy were very close. Did you often have her impersonate you?"

"Of course. Many stars do that."

"For what reason?"

"To avoid crowds, to replace them at boring events, when they don't feel well—many reasons."

"To take risks for you when you think you might be in danger?"

She hesitated. "Some stars do that. I don't; I would not risk Talia's life."

"But surely you have done so when you have been in danger from the IMG? Didn't they threaten your life if you played Rakoczi's daughter?"

"I have never endangered Talia—not knowingly."

"Didn't you endanger her when you had her replace you in this enactment of a phony murder?"

"Not at all," she said promptly.

"Yet she was murdered."

"There was no connection," she said forcefully.

"You say that you and Talia were very close, but surely you had your disagreements, arguments?"

"Of course. Such a relationship is not always smooth—especially between two women."

"Arguments about men?"

That took her unawares. "Men? No, not about men."

"Surely not about theatre?"

"She was my understudy—there was nothing to argue about there. No, if we had arguments, they were about clothes, makeup, style—"

She stopped. My skepticism must have been transparent.

"All right! Trivial matters to you," she snapped.

"Far from a motive for murder."

"I didn't murder her!" she shouted.

"Do you know who did?" I asked sharply.

"No, I have not the slightest idea."

She sat back and stared out of the window. Her profile was perfect. Outside, there was a striking view, although I knew that was not why she had adopted that position. The Danube Express was snaking around a bend, and, ahead of us, a high suspension bridge soared loftily over the river, which was still brown. Neither of us had a camera though, or, at that moment, the photographic urge.

I had a sudden outrageous notion. I decided to give it a try. "I don't believe your story about a tabloid. Furthermore, I think you set up this whole scenario with Mikhel Czerny."

It didn't matter if it was true or not, I was thinking while I said it, the sheer provocation of the statement ought to be enough to pull something out of her.

Her attention jerked back toward me. "That's the most preposterous thing I ever heard," she said. But somehow, I felt I was onto something. I wasn't sure if it was in her words or her attitude or her face, but it was worth following up.

"Maybe this antagonism between you and Czerny isn't real," I said, trying to use a silky tone. "Maybe it's just another good publicity gimmick."

"That's nonsense!" Her response was fiery enough to make me wonder if I was wrong, but I plunged ahead, making it up as I went along.

"Taking it a step further, if you and he are not in conflict, then perhaps the opposite is true. Perhaps he's your lover."

Her reaction surprised me. She burst into laughter. "That's absurd—" Another thought struck her, and her laughter subsided to a giggle. "Not impossible, I suppose but still—" She quickly became serious. "If only you knew how—but never mind, I understand that you are only doing your job and trying to find out who killed Talia and Tabor."

"We will be in Bucharest tomorrow, and the journey will be over," I told her. "The only chance of finding the killer of those two women is to do it before we arrive. Don't you want to help to do that?"

"I can't help you," she said simply.

"I think you can. Do you mean you don't want to?"

She gazed out of the window again. Clearly there was some dilemma she was trying to resolve. Maybe I could spur her on . . . add some pressure.

"Naturally, there is some suspicion that you may have killed Talia," I said. "She was your understudy, and it would be understandable if she was jealous of you. So if she might have a motive to kill you, might you not have one to kill her?"

"I suppose you could think that," she murmured, still looking out the window at an expanse of green grass dotted with stands of birches, "but I would have no motive to kill Tabor."

"Maybe you did have a motive," I said sharply.

"Even if I did, I certainly did not kill her."

"You realize that you are under suspicion, and if you have a motive, we will find it."

Was she debating what to tell me? If so, she had something to hide. What could it be?

"Did you know Tabor before this trip?"

She paused a long time. I knew I must be onto something else.

I put on more pressure. "Better tell me. We'll learn about it anyway."

She paused again then made up her mind. "Yes, Tabor almost killed me twice."

It was the "twice" that rang a bell in my memory. Who was it who had almost killed somebody twice . . . ?

"When you were with Lydecker," I said slowly, "your early days in the theatre—his other assistant made mistakes during your rehearsals, she caused two accidents—you say they almost killed you . . . Lydecker let that other assistant go—that was Elisha Tabor, wasn't it?"

She didn't answer at once, then she decided.

"Yes," she breathed. "She was jealous of me. I was better-looking than she, I was better in the act."

"She denied all that, though, didn't she? She said you set up those accidents to get rid of her."

She flashed me an angry look. "Lydecker told you that? It's not true!"

I had my own ideas about who was telling the truth, but I didn't express them. Instead, I said, "So you and Tabor have had this feud all these years? I find that hard to believe. Have you both been arranging accidents for the other all this time?"

"She has been harassing me."

"In what way?"

She hesitated, but knew that she had gone too far now to stop. "In print," she said.

"In print? You mean she was passing information to Czerny?"

"No, she didn't need to do that."

"Why not?"

She paused, no doubt a natural actor's pause for dramatic effect. "She WAS Czerny."

CHAPTER THIRTY

Several components slotted into place after I had absorbed that startling revelation.

"You faked your own death. You have had lots of practice at dying—on the stage. You sprinkled Acid Essence of Almonds around your compartment and summoned Czerny." A thought struck me. "How did you summon Czerny, by the way?"

She raised her chin defiantly. I was thinking quickly and discarding possibilities just as quickly. "My guess would be by a phone call, probably saying something like, 'Someone has killed Malescu—go to her compartment at once—you can get the story of a lifetime. If you hurry, you can get there before anyone finds her.' "

I looked for some reaction but could see none. "If you want to help yourself avoid being suspected of the murders of Svarovina and Tabor, you'd better cooperate," I said harshly.

She swallowed and looked away. "All right. Yes, it was something like that. I used a deep voice, sounding like a man."

"When Czerny arrived, you put on the typical death rictus associated with cyanide." I had in fact, on one occasion found the body of a man poisoned that way and had never forgotten the snarling, tortured features. "You looked so frightening that Czerny would have bolted out of the door at once."

"I am quite sure I looked frightening," Malescu murmured. "Still, the desire to splash the news across the front page would have been overwhelming. She couldn't wait to send in the story."

"And then you did your disappearing act."

"No one was harmed by it." She shrugged.

"I appreciate your frankness," I said. "At this point, I regret that the interview has to become official. I must bring in the Head of Security, Herr Kramer, and have him hear this."

She shrugged, and I picked up the phone and called Kramer. He came at once, and I recounted the disclosures of the past minutes. He listened without interruption until I finished.

The faint whoosh of air past the windows of the Danube Express was the only sound in the compartment. The scenery was a meaningless blur. Magda Malescu must have been aware of the effect of her bombshell, but to her credit, she didn't exploit it. She sat, impassive but imposing.

"So that is why Czerny's columns criticized you so severely and so frequently," Kramer said.

"They did more than that. They reviled me, they did their best to ruin my professional reputation." Malescu's words were calm, matter-of-fact, but underneath was a simmering anger.

"I understand now why you did not want to tell us this," I said, and she nodded.

"Yes, it is a perfect motive for wanting to kill her, isn't it? I realize that. But I did not. I did not kill her—or Talia."

I could imagine the curtain falling to loud applause as she delivered those lines on the stage. It would be a memorable moment in the performance. She made no effort to dramatize it, but I had to remind myself, as I had so many times before, that she was an accomplished actress. Just as she could act, she could act as if she were not acting.

Kramer looked impatient, anxious to press on with the investigation.

"So Fraulein Svarovina took your place in this charade?"

"No. I must explain. I didn't know Czerny—Elisha Tabor—was going to be on this train. It was on the platform at Munich *Hauptbahnhof*, that I saw her about to board."

That clicked in my mind. "So it was not the letter that the steward, Hirsch, handed you on the platform that startled you so. You looked past him and saw Elisha Tabor."

"You led us to think that it was a death threat from the IMG," snapped Kramer. "You said they were determined to prevent you from playing Rakoczi's daughter."

She raised her chin defiantly. "I have been receiving threats from the IMG. That is true."

"But you cannot produce any of them," Kramer said.

"I destroy them. They are contemptible."

"Then there's the so-called cyanide," I added. "You could not have had plans for putting on this show for Czerny before the journey because you didn't know he—or she—was going to be on the train. You went to the kitchen storage and saw the Acid Essence of Almonds and returned, sending Svarovina to steal a jar of it."

She nodded haughtily.

"No doubt you could not resist the drama of a strong aroma of bitter almonds—normally considered a deadly poison," I said.

"I was in a play. It was good, it lasted almost six months. It was about a man trying to poison his wife. For extra effect, the director had the idea of releasing an aroma of Acid Essence of Almonds into the theatre. The audiences loved it."

"What do you suppose are the circumstances surrounding the death of Fraulein Svarovina?" Kramer demanded.

Malescu's demeanor changed. I was sure she wasn't acting this time, I felt there was genuine sorrow for her understudy.

"We had agreed to change places after I had allowed Tabor to 'find' my murdered body." She permitted herself a faint smile. "Talia enjoyed the few occasions when she played me, and she also admired this compartment—it is much larger and more luxurious than hers. I can only guess that she used the opportunity to entertain a man—and he killed her."

Kramer leaned forward. "Who was the man?"

"I don't know." Her reply was unequivocal.

"I ask you to guess," Kramer said forcefully.

"I cannot guess. I don't know."

"You are sure it was a man?" Kramer went on.

"Oh, yes, quite sure. I knew Talia too well."

"Poison is more often a woman's weapon than a man's."

Malescu made no reply.

"I have another question," I said. "Did Talia Svarovina know that Elisha Tabor was Czerny?"

"I have told you how close we were, Talia and I," said Malescu. "Over the years, personal details came out—it was inevitable."

"Including your earlier acquaintance with Elisha Tabor?"

"That, too, of course."

"And your knowledge that she had become the renowned journalist, Mikhel Czerny."

"Yes."

"We will talk with you further, Fraulein," Kramer said in his most officious voice.

We left and walked to his office. "You did well to extract those admissions from her," he said, when we were seated.

"They clear up the early mystery of the dramatic headline and the disappearance, but I'm not sure how they help us learn who killed Svarovina and Tabor—or why."

"If Svarovina had an assignation with a man after Malescu's faked 'murder' act, she presumably had had earlier contact with him," Kramer said.

"Agreed."

"Did she appear particularly friendly with any man?"

"I haven't come across any evidence of one—" I hesitated. Kramer looked at me keenly. "Go on."

"It may be that Tabor was having an affair with a man. I don't know who, and I'm not certain of it anyway . . ."

"Both women were murdered by the same poison combination, so we may conclude that the same man was responsible for both," Kramer said.

Could I get any more out of Irena Koslova than I already had? Did she know any more? Even subconsciously? Kramer was waiting for me to continue and tell him more about Tabor's lover, I could see. I had to let him wait in vain—I didn't think I could sell him on Irena's intuition. He tapped on his desk reflectively.

"Little did Czerny know that her own murder would be the next sensational story in the paper," he said grimly. "In the meantime, many guests will now be in the lounge coach or the restaurant coach. If you join them, you may learn something. I have the impression that even a tiny clue might complete the puzzle."

"I think so, too."

I talked with Friedlander, the Australians, Professor Sundvall, and the Walburgs. In each case, it was only an exchange of greetings and some small talk, but it was evident that none of them had heard of this latest death.

Lydecker came into the lounge, and we had a brief conversation. "We'll be in Bucharest tomorrow," I said. "You'll be anxious to get your act ready."

"I'm always ready," he said.

"Going to make a woman disappear?" I asked.

He gave me the briefest of glances before he said, "I'm introducing a new variation on that act."

I waited for some elucidation, but he wasn't forthcoming, and I knew it would be a waste of time to press him for his stage secrets. It was difficult to suppress the urge to tell him that his onetime assistant, Elisha Tabor, had reappeared as the dreaded columnist of the Budapest *Times*, but I managed it.

"I believe I'll have an early lunch today," he told me, and headed in the direction of the restaurant coach.

Eva Zilinsky was sitting, drinking a cup of black coffee and reading a Viennese newspaper. She looked up at my approach, smiled, and went on reading. I wished her a good morning, and she acknowledged with another smile. I decided she wasn't seeking company and moved on.

When Irena Koslova entered, I approached her quickly.

"Let's go in to lunch."

"It's early, isn't it?"

"Yes, but I want to talk to you, and it will be quieter in the restaurant coach."

Her eyes lit up. "Is it about our—er, business?"

"Yes, and it's important."

She agreed at once, and we took a table well away from the few diners there already.

"What have you heard?" she wanted to know.

"Elisha Tabor was Mikhel Czerny."

Her mouth opened in astonishment. She became aware of it and promptly closed it. "That's impossible! No, wait a minute . . . no, it isn't. Of course! Why didn't I think of that? She was just the type, and it's quite common for prominent journalists to use another name."

I explained briefly how Malescu had put on her act in order to humiliate Czerny and, when I came to the part about Tabor and Malescu having been assistants in Lydecker's magic act, she started to open her mouth again but this time controlled it.

The waiter arrived at the table, and as Irena saw him approach, she whispered, "We'd better order, or people will get suspicious."

"I think you're just hungry," I told her.

"Exciting news always makes me hungry."

"Maybe some wine will help," I said to Irena. To the waiter, I said "Can you recommend a white wine, Romanian, of course, now that we're about to enter that country? Dry, assertive, a wine with a mind of its own?"

"Romania has a fine Pinot Gris," he told us, "and a Chardonnay that is said to be very close to white Burgundy."

"Let's have the Chardonnay," I decided. To Irena, I explained, "We get very little Romanian wine in England even though Romania is one of the top ten wine-producing countries in the world and number five in Europe. Their problem is that the government has not yet given serious backing to a wine export program."

She nodded impatiently, clearly anxious to get on with detection. When the waiter had left, I said to her, "You realize that this makes your information about Tabor having an affair with a man on the train more significant."

"I can see that. Do you have any idea who he is?"

"No. I was hoping that you might."

"I've tried, really, I have but I can't get any picture of him."

"Is that how it usually works?"

"That's one of the ways."

"Have you talked with Gerhardt Vollmer recently?"

"Just for a few minutes yesterday."

"Did you learn anything?"

"He was more interested in learning my address and phone number."

I avoided the obvious question concerning her response, and instead asked, "You didn't learn anything new from him?"

"No. I led the conversation to Malescu, but he didn't pick up on it."

"Have you talked to Conti?"

"A little. He has fully recovered now, he says. I asked him who had poisoned him—"

I laughed involuntarily.

Irena tossed her head. "Well, it's what you wanted to know, isn't it?"

"It is," I agreed, "and sometimes the direct approach works."

"I don't know if it worked or not. He said he didn't know."

"Did you believe him?"

The waiter arrived with the wine and two glasses. He poured, and I tasted. It did indeed taste like a French white Burgundy, and I complimented him on his recommendation. We both drank, and Irena said, "No, I didn't believe him. He may not have been lying exactly—he may have had just a suspicion but perhaps not enough, you know what I mean?"

"You think he may be trying to figure it out, and he may come up with a decision?"

"Perhaps."

Out of the window, I could see that we were heading for another high suspension bridge. The train was turning sharply to enter the straight run at the bridge.

"This is the biggest bridge we've seen so far," Irena said in an awed voice. "It's enormous."

"We're not in Romania yet, are we?" I asked.

"No, but we're very close. The borders are not as clearly demarcated as they used to be." She leaned closer to the window. "Aren't we going awfully slow?"

The waiter came with a basket of rolls. Tiny wisps of steam arose from them, along with the delicious fresh-baked aroma. He put the basket on the table and peered outside, a puzzled look on his face.

"Something wrong?" I asked him.

"We're going very slow," he muttered. We all looked out at the bridge as we moved toward it. The train slowed more and more.

"This is very strange," the waiter said. "We cannot be stopping here surely . . ."

CHAPTER THIRTY-ONE

The Danube Express moved more and more slowly, as if it was running out of steam. All three of us stared out of the window, and anxious voices farther down the restaurant coach indicated that others were concerned, too.

It was not a view for the fainthearted—the bridge was so high that the river below looked almost miniscule. It was all like a model train set. The bridge was enormously long, too—it crossed the Danube at a diagonal so that it stretched into the distance where the far bank of the river seemed miles away.

We moved still slower, and the view of the land on either side of the train began to fall away. Another waiter came over and spoke to ours in a low voice. I could catch only brief snatches of the conversation, but they were agreeing that this was an unusual occurrence.

I heard someone approaching from behind, and Kramer came hurrying to my table. "We have an emergency," he said in a low voice. "You had better come with me." He ignored Irena, which emphasized the urgency of the occasion.

I followed him past the other tables, where the occupants shot us anxious looks, and on into the next car. As we passed through the other cars, we were asked what was happening, and Kramer gave them a standard, "Nothing to worry about."

We hurried through the lounge coach, then through the kitchen and the storage coaches. We stopped at the locked door leading into the next coach—the freight coach. Kramer reached for his key wallet.

"I had an urgent message from one of the stewards," he said, "just before the train began to slow. He reported voices coming from this coach." He punched keys on the pad in the wallet, activating the master key.

"Voices!" I said. "How can anyone be in there?"

"I don't know but—"

We were aware of someone behind us, and we both turned. Paolo Conti was there, and he had an automatic pistol in his hand.

I should have expected this," Conti said in a bleak voice. "I had a message this morning telling me that one of our agents had stumbled across an informer who warned of an attempt to rob this coach."

Kramer was looking dubiously at the automatic. Conti smiled and lowered the weapon. "Sorry, I guess I reacted a little fast—"

Kramer had still not inserted his key in the lock. "One of your agents?" he asked brusquely.

Conti grimaced. "I should have told you before. I am with *Amici della Uva*—you have probably heard of—"

"Yes, we've heard of you," snapped Kramer. "Why didn't you tell me before?"

Before Conti could answer, into the seconds of silence, came voices from inside the coach. We all stared at one another. It sounded like three voices, probably two men and one woman. They might have been arguing; their voices were strained and tense. The words were right on the threshold of understanding, some were in German, some in English, but the heavy door distorted them, preventing us from hearing clearly what was being said.

"What else did this informer tell you?" asked Kramer.

"Unfortunately, no details, just that a robbery attempt would be made before the train reached Bucharest."

"I wonder . . ." said Kramer. "I wonder what it is they want—the vines or the Mozart manuscript."

"My job," said Conti, brandishing the automatic, "is to protect the vines. I'm not concerned with sheets of music."

"I presume that it was to prevent you from doing your job that the poisoning effort was made?" said Kramer.

Conti nodded. The voices sounded fractionally louder, and all three of us tried to hear what was being said. Finally, Kramer shook his head. "We have to go in . . ." He inserted the key in the lock.

Kramer pushed the door gently. As it opened, the voices became louder, though still unclear. It was more definite now that there were three of them, and they seemed to be bickering over what should be done. Kramer reached inside his jacket and took out a short-barreled pistol.

He kicked the door wide open, holding the pistol in both hands, and went into the coach. Conti and I followed.

No one was in the coach.

We stared at the crate containing the Mozart manuscript, the coffin-shaped chamber that held the vines, and at the shelves stacked with parcels and packages. A number of larger boxes and parcels stood on the floor and in front of them, the crate of artifacts that had been loaded in Budapest. The voices were coming from it. Obviously a tape recorder was concealed inside.

Kramer took a step closer, disbelief showing on his face. From behind us, Conti's voice came, louder than the voices from the crate and sharper—as there was menace in it.

"Place that gun on the floor, Herr Kramer, and do it very, very slowly."

Kramer froze, the gun held firm in his outstretched hand.

"On the floor!" said Conti in an icy tone, and Kramer obeyed.

"Now step over the gun and kick it back here."

Again, Kramer did as he was told. Conti was behind Kramer but within my line of sight. I watched Conti pick up the weapon and drop it into his pocket.

"Now," Conti said, "take that key wallet out of your pocket and do the same with it. Do it slowly."

Again, Kramer obeyed.

I watched Conti examine the wallet. It was evidently still programmed for the door through which we had entered. He used it to lock the door, then turned his attention to the sliding door on the side of the coach and punched numbers. He appeared dissatisfied with the result and did it again. He took two long steps and pressed the muzzle of his gun against my temple.

"Turn this way, Herr Kramer," he instructed. "Stop!" he ordered when Kramer had turned enough to be able to see both Conti and me.

"The code for the key to the side door of this coach is evidently different from the door through which we just entered," Conti said.

Kramer said nothing.

"You confirm that is so? No matter. I know that it is. Now, you will tell me the code for the side door, or I will pull this trigger."

The voices on the recorder were continuing but, with the cold muzzle of the automatic burning the skin on my forehead, they sounded to me like the chatter of goblins, murderous, insane goblins.

Kramer spat out some numbers, his blond hair seeming even blonder and his glare at Conti even more baleful. The gun at my temple did not waver as Conti, one-handed, tapped on the keys. The side door began to slide open steadily.

"I was supposed to have an assistant to do this," said Conti, his mood and tone lighter now. "It's a little more difficult this way but, don't worry, it will still get done."

He took the gun away from my head and stepped away from me, keeping Kramer and me covered as he moved to the open door.

"Fraulein Svarovina must not have liked the idea of being your assistant," said Kramer grittily. "Did she object, and you had to kill her?"

"I had known her sometime ago. When this job came up, I learned that Malescu would be on the train, and I knew that Talia would be with her. I offered her the chance to make enough money that she could give up the menial job of being Malescu's lackey—she was getting tired of being in the shadow of the great star anyway."

He glanced out of the open door. What was he looking for? I wondered. He did not relax his focus on us, however, and he went on. "Stupid girl! She was already blabbing Malescu's intimate details to Czerny—then she wanted a bigger share, otherwise she threatened to spill the story of this job so Czerny could have an even bigger story."

"So, in your guise as an agent for *Amici della Uva*, you developed a friendship with Miss Tabor, to find out if Talia had fed her any titbits on the theft of the vines?" I said. "One of my informers saw you with her a few times."

He nodded, but the gun didn't waver. "Right—and Talia had given her some hints about a robbery. Elisha couldn't wait to get more of the story, greedy bitch. So I had to get rid of her, too—I wasn't sure just how much she knew."

The voices ceased. The tape was probably repetitive and would start up again.

Conti stood by the open door and looked down. From what I could see, all that lay out there was a dizzying drop down a cliffside. At the foot of the cliff would be the Danube, though I couldn't see it. The train was stationary, perched on the end of the high bridge.

"How did you get the train to stop here?" asked Kramer in a conversational tone.

"A length of rail is tied across the tracks," Conti said carelessly. "It was easy to estimate just how far ahead of it the train would stop, then I simply added the length of the train and that gave the position that this coach now occupies."

"You have a boat on the river, I presume," Kramer said. I presumed he was keeping Conti talking until he saw some chance—but of doing what?

"More than one boat," Conti said airily, "just to confuse any pursuit. Now, can I persuade you to push that coffin-shaped crate toward this door?"

I saw the look of surprise appear on Kramer's face. "Sure you don't want the manuscript, too?" he asked.

"Not me," was the prompt reply. "You two can take it if you like and say I took it."

Neither Kramer nor I moved, and Conti shook his head.

"I'm still waiting for you to push that crate," he said, but neither of us responded or spoke.

"A kneecap shattered by a bullet is very painful," Conti said, "and often it never heals."

He held out the automatic and took aim at my right knee. "If the first shot doesn't get you to push that crate over there, the second will."

There was a long silence. Nobody moved. Conti let out an audible sigh. "Too bad . . . very well." His finger curled around the trigger . . .

A *beep-beep-beep* sounded. In the quiet coach, it seemed loud. None of us moved, then Conti lowered the gun. It was the cell phone at Kramer's belt.

If it had not been so dire a situation, it would have been comical. I could almost see the thoughts flickering through Conti's head as if they were appearing on a screen. His first thought would be to tell Kramer not to answer the phone—but then someone would be alerted and a hunt for Kramer initiated. In the confines of the train, that would not take long; in fact, it would take very little time because I recalled Thomas's words that the equipment in the communication center showed which doors and windows were open, anywhere in the train.

On the other hand, if he permitted Kramer to answer, Conti had to risk the use of a code word or even a hurried warning. I had a personal interest in his thought processes, as the consequence in the latter event could involve my kneecap.

Conti must have reviewed both alternatives more than once. He made his decision. He stepped closer to me, took a new aim at my kneecap, and said to Kramer, "Answer it. Answer only with one word at a time."

Kramer looked him in the eye, unhooked the phone and put it to his ear. "Kramer," he said in a voice remarkably close to normal.

There was a pause, and he said, "Yes." After another pause, he said, "No," and immediately closed the connection. As he replaced the phone on his belt, he looked defiantly at Conti.

"Good," said Conti, who had probably been expecting more resistance. He kept the automatic leveled directly at my knee, which had already attracted more attention today than either of Magda Malescu's. To Kramer, he said, "Push the crate to the door."

Kramer resisted to the last second, then did as he was told. The crate was not as heavy as it looked. The vines it contained could not weigh much. Conti waved the gun, telling Kramer to back away. It also took the focus of attention away from my knee, for which I was profoundly grateful.

Conti went to the container that had been the source of the bodiless voices and ostensibly held artifacts for the museum. The facility with which he opened it one-handed indicated that he had probably packed it. He reached inside, pulled out a tiny tape recorder, and thrust it into his pocket. He reached in the container again and took out a nylon net sack with a length of nylon cord attached.

Still keeping us covered with the gun, he draped the sack around the crate of vines and tied the other end of the nylon cord around a handle of the door. It was obvious that he had intended to have an accomplice, for these tasks had to be performed with one hand. He tugged at the cord a couple of times to make sure it was secure, then straightened up and, without taking his eyes from us, pushed the crate with one foot until it teetered on the edge of the doorway.

Holding the frame tightly with his free hand, still covering Kramer and me with the gun in the other hand, he leaned out and took some quick looks down. He was evidently lining up the position of a boat and the bank of the Danube far below.

He seemed dissatisfied, paused, and tried again. "Just a minute or two more," he reassured us, and I presumed that he was mentally cursing the local help and its tardiness.

The hiatus that followed put pressure on all of us. Conti held the gun unwaveringly, pointed in our direction. Kramer tried to shuffle sideways very slowly, evidently with the idea of making it impossible for Conti to keep us both covered at the same time, but Conti saw it and impatiently waved him back.

I was relieved that my knee was no longer such an attraction, but a bullet anywhere else was not much more desirable, and my body was beginning to ache with the tension of keeping still.

Kramer's cell phone beeped again.

Conti made up his mind more swiftly this time. "Tell them you'll call back. Say nothing more than that, or I'll shoot."

Kramer did as he was bid, taking a long time for each movement. Opening the connection, he said the few words as he was told. He closed the phone and replaced it on his belt.

Conti's impatience was beginning to show. He grasped the doorframe and leaned out again. Once more, he took quick glances down.

I had been studying the position of the crate with the vines. It was inches from the edge of the floor. A strong push would send it out. I had also been pondering over Conti's probable future action. If he intended to lower the crate to a boat waiting below, how did he intend to escape? What did he plan for Kramer and me?

One thing appeared obvious—Conti would have to dispose of us. I was trying to catch Kramer's eye, and, when I did, I was reasonably sure he was thinking the same thing. That made some immediate action vital, risky as it might be.

I put every nerve and sinew that I possessed on full alert, concentrating my vision and my mind on Conti while keeping Kramer within peripheral range.

I was ready for whatever desperate measure might be necessary . . .

CHAPTER THIRTY-TWO

Conti's mouth was tight, the engaging grin notably absent. His gaze was wary. He was in a difficult position and he knew it but he was tough and resourceful. He was no doubt willing to make any sacrifice to achieve his goal—unfortunately, Kramer and I were like the proverbial tethered goats.

He looked outside again, scanning the bank of the Danube beneath us, alternating his scrutiny with quick glances at Kramer and me. He was about to duck his head out again when a new sound came. It was a clattering, thumping noise that vibrated the air, a sound no longer unusual in today's world—it was the beat of a helicopter motor and the accompanying pulse of whirring blades.

Conti relaxed visibly. A half-smile showed, and he waved the gun happily. "The alternative route! Reinforcements at last!" He stole a look out the open door, this time upward. I could see the craft, and Kramer turned his head so that he could see out the door, too.

The helicopter came dropping down into our field of view. It was light gray in color, with burn stains streaking back from the engine nacelle. It steadied and began to move closer in a curious, crabwise motion.

The thump-thump of the rotor blades pressed tighter on my eardrums. Kramer and I watched impotently as the chopper grew bigger and bigger in our view. Thirty or forty yards away, it stabilized, no longer moving, just hanging there in the air.

So that was how Conti intended to make his escape—his talk of a boat on the Danube must have been to mislead us in case Kramer was communicating to the outside in some way. It left our fate in the realm of doubt . . .

The helicopter looked large, filling most of the view out of the open door. It began to move. Where was it going? It wasn't moving away. It seemed to be staying in the same location—then it became apparent that it was rotating. It was turning slowly and ponderously. It stopped when it was broadside on to us. Kramer gave a sudden barking laugh.

What was the matter with him? I saw nothing funny. Then I could make out big white letters on the side of the aircraft announcing 'MST'. Between them and the nose, a door slid open, and something poked out, glinting in the sun.

A gun! was my first thought, but why was Kramer still laughing? He controlled himself, looked at me, and saw my lack of comprehension.

"MST!" he shouted over the helicopter noise. "It stands for 'Hungarian Television Service'! You're going to be on every screen in Europe tonight, Conti!"

Conti made an involuntary start at moving away from the open door of the train, understandably camera-shy, but he stopped and stared out. I could not see why at first, then I was aware of the increase in the clamor of engines and blades.

Beyond the television helicopter came another aircraft, similar in general appearance but darker gray in color. It had no markings, and came up past the TV craft in a purposeful sweep. It was so close that the roar of its motor was deafening, and a blast of air funneled in through the open door. For a second or two, it blocked the view completely, then the craft disappeared and a banging noise came from overhead—once, then a second time. The coach rocked slightly; the latest arrival had landed on the roof above us.

Conti had a new awareness now, confident that help was at hand. He held the gun pointing steadfastly at us. He was too far away for us to attempt to rush him. Sounds came from the roof, and a pair of feet appeared in the top of the doorway. They slid down to reveal legs in dark brown army fatigue pants. A voice called out words that were lost as the blades still clattered.

What was there to hold on to out there? I wondered. Besides that, train roofs were curved, weren't they? After the figure had released the helicopter landing rail, what was out there that—I didn't even finish the thought.

There was a cry, and a figure dropped into sight. He was straining to get his legs forward and into the coach. He was too late—his feet hit the edge of the doorway, then he fell backwards. Conti momentarily forgot us and moved to the doorway to try to grab the man, but he was already falling out of sight. If he yelled, the sound was lost.

Kramer had been alert, and now he moved fast. As Conti lunged for the falling figure, Kramer took a few paces to intercept him, but the Italian was fast, too. He swung around, sidestepping and raising the automatic. It was at that moment that another figure appeared in the doorway.

This man had had more practice at entering trains from the roof, and he swung his legs inside the coach and let his body weight propel him into the coach. He was wearing dark brown army fatigues like his unfortunate predecessor, and, as he hit the floor of the coach, he uncoiled and was on his feet like an acrobat. His movement brought him near to Kramer who, despite the speed at which everything was happening, was lightning quick in his reaction. As the man reached in a pocket for a weapon, Kramer leapt at him.

Conti moved to one side, wanting to get a clear shot at Kramer without hitting his ally. That brought Conti closer to me, and, in a rare moment of bravery, I grabbed for the gun in his hand. My knowledge of hand-to-hand combat was limited to watching episodes of *The Avengers*, and I lacked both Mrs. Peel's agility and Steed's umbrella.

Instead of getting hold of the automatic, in my eagerness I hit it with both groping hands, but the impact knocked it out of his grasp.

It bounced and slid along the floor and lay too far away for either of us to risk going for it. We eyed each other warily.

The same thought hit both Conti and me at the same split second—Conti had taken Kramer's short-barreled pistol and dropped it into his pocket, and it was still there.

Two hands rammed simultaneously into that jacket pocket, one mine and one Conti's. It was like the monkey trap, where the monkey, having grasped the banana inside the cage, does not know enough to release the banana in order to extricate its hand through the bars. Both Conti and I knew enough, though, to be vitally aware that whichever of us failed to pull out the gun would be shot immediately.

Both of us strained. The fabric held. Conti brought up a knee to jab me, but I twisted away and took it on the thigh. He followed it instantly, swinging his other arm wildly at me, and his fist connected with the side of my head. I saw stars for a second or two but managed to keep pressure on my hand to keep it in his pocket. The fist changed into two stiff fingers—Conti was probing, poking over my face, trying to jab his fingers into my eyes.

He had all the advantages—height, weight, and training. The longer the struggle lasted, the more likely he was to be the victor. I knew I had to end it and end it fast. We were both straining to get a grip on the gun and pull it out of the pocket. If the gun wouldn't come out of the pocket—so be it, I'd use it right there.

Instead of trying to pull my hand out, I simply plunged it deeper. My fingers slid over the beveled surface of the butt, the middle finger drove on, inside the trigger guard. I felt the trigger and made a supreme effort to slip my finger around it. I pulled, again and again and again.

I had no idea whether Kramer had released the safety catch when he and I had entered the coach. If he hadn't then . . . but he had. As I pulled the trigger, I tried to turn the gun as much as I could in the general direction of Conti's body. I felt his frame jerk violently as three bullets went into the lower part of his torso.

He gurgled horribly and let out a screeching moan as the bullets plowed into him. His hand in the pocket relinquished its grip and I jerked the pistol free as he fell away from me.

I had completely lost track of Kramer's struggle with the other man, but now I saw that they were standing toe-to-toe, gasping and swaying as they fought for mastery of the automatic that was still in the brown-clad man's hand. Kramer had a firm grip with both hands, one on the wrist, one on the gun hand.

"Drop it!" I shouted. "Drop it, or I'll shoot!"

The man had a dark face and glaring eyes. I firmly believe that he sized me up as an amateur with a gun and therefore unpredictable and more dangerous than a professional. He dropped the gun, and Kramer scooped it up. Conti was writhing and moaning piteously, clutching his lower abdomen, which was seeping blood.

A blast of air made us all stagger—the pilot of the attacking helicopter had evidently decided that he had completed his mission, and it was time to go. Hearing the gunshots must have helped his decision. The aircraft bounced once on the roof and soared away, filling the view out of the train doorway for just a few seconds, then dwindling swiftly as it raced out of sight.

The television network helicopter still hovered a short distance away. With the other aircraft gone, it now moved in closer. The crew must have been filming all of this and been highly pleased that they had enough exciting footage to take up at least a half-minute of prime-time news. Their final shot had to be Kramer on his cell phone, rapping out orders for police, an ambulance, and an alert to intercept a dark gray, unmarked helicopter heading north—without a payload.

CHAPTER THIRTY-THREE

The banquet was a subdued affair, though all the assemblage made a creditable effort to make it a successful farewell occasion. Everyone was present except Gerhardt Vollmer, who had to continue his journey to the oil fields on the Black Sea.

Bucharest does not have major hotels in the same quantity and quality as other European capitals. Those of us who were staying over were at the Athenee Palace Hilton, but it lacks a suitable banquet room. Herr Brenner had used his considerable influence to obtain one of the vast chambers in the *Palatul Parlamentalui*, the Parliament buildings. He told us that the arrival of the Danube Express on its twenty-fifth anniversary was providing a lot of publicity for the city, and this had clinched his proposal to them.

From the outside, it is a hot contender for the ugliest building in Europe. This is despite its enormous size—"much bigger than the Pentagon" the guide told us proudly. It is a massive, dull gray edifice that the dictator Nicolae Ceausescu had built as a fortress-palace. We were on the ground floor, but the guide said that five underground stories contained lead-lined bunkers and a train station with an electric train that ran to an undisclosed location elsewhere in the city.

An attempt had been made to lighten the mood in our room with flags and banners and even some tapestries depicting scenes from Romanian history. Two new chandeliers were a start toward proper lighting, and gleaming white tablecloths and shining crystal glasses helped, as did bouquets of fresh flowers.

The passengers were avid for details of the desperate struggle that took place in the freight coach and of all the associated data that contributed to it. The television station showed clips of the action throughout the day, but naturally everyone wanted to hear from the participants.

Karl Kramer was the star of the evening. He kept trying to drag me into the limelight, but I tried to play down my role. If the London newspapers reprinted the story and referred to me as "the man from Scotland Yard," I could expect a polite knock on my door when I returned home, followed by some less polite questions regarding impersonation of a police officer.

The exposure of Elisha Tabor as the infamous Mikhel Czerny was, fortunately for me, a story that was much more important to the Hungarians. The name of Elisha Tabor meant nothing but the fact that the well-known—even hated—columnist was really a woman, coupled with ripping off the mask of anonymity, appealed to the Hungarian love of intrigue.

The day's editions of the Bucharest newspapers played up the story, savoring the chance to take a front-page crack at their neighboring rivals. They implied that the Hungarians placed too much emphasis on sensational exposé types of story, conveniently failing to mention their own predilection for similar "news."

We were all seated at one large oval table which made it easier to converse with most of the guests. I was located between Eva Zilinsky and Irena Koslova. Almost opposite was Magda Malescu, who had received enough attention that one might suppose she had personally struggled hand-to-hand with the villains. Karl Kramer, as a hero of the struggle with Conti and a savior of the day, was there. Erich Brenner was also close by, and so were Doctor Stolz, Helmut Lydecker, and Franz Reingold—the balance of male and female had been thrown out of synchronization by the two deaths. However, they and my other companions on the journey were all enjoying the caviar being served as an appetizer.

"Some Romanians eat as much as half a kilo—that's a pound—of caviar at a sitting," Irena told me, and I resisted a plebeian urge to ask how much that would cost.

"Bucharest's famous '*Ikra* Bar'—'*Ikra*' means 'caviar,' it's a Russian word—serves over forty different kinds of this most precious of all appetizers," explained Erich Brenner. "They have selected the best of the forty kinds for us this evening," he went on. He was in a more jovial mood now that the strain of the past days was removed, and he was determined to make the occasion memorable. " 'Fish eggs,' it may be called by the critics," he said, "but served chilled with slices of lemon, chopped onion, thin crackers, and champagne, it is a superb dish."

All of those accompaniments were on the table, and the starter was proving extremely popular. "I think this table is trying to beat that half-kilo record," I commented to Irena. "By the way, where does this caviar come from?"

Erich Brenner heard the question and cut in with the answer. "The Caspian and the Black Sea provide almost all of our caviar today. The Baltic and the Atlantic used to be suppliers, but dredging and poisonous discharges from factories along the shores have caused the total disappearance from those regions."

"That one," said Irena, determined not to be left out as knowledgeable about caviar and indicating a dish of a light reddish color, "is called red caviar, but it is actually lumpfish. Many people like it better, though its color has tempted some suppliers to blend in salmon, which is much cheaper."

Eva Zilinsky joined in the discussion. "Worse than that is the stuff they sell as 'Romanian Caviar.' It is actually eggplant, flavored with paprika."

"Some people serve that at home for parties," added Irena. "It impresses their friends."

"I've heard of that." I had to make a contribution, and that was as good a time as any. "The trick is to bake the eggplant first, unpeeled, for at least an hour. Then it's peeled, puréed, and mixed with olive oil, lemon juice, salt, pepper, and paprika. Finely chopped onions are added just before serving."

"That's cheating," said Eva Zilinsky disdainfully.

"I know," I agreed. "I was involved in a case once where a group of food enthusiasts put on a monthly dinner at each of their houses in turn. The hosts had to serve one dish that was not what it seemed. This was one of them."

"Why were you involved?" asked Eva Zilinsky.

"Because one of the group was murdered."

"Speaking of murder—" Eva Zilinsky began, then looked around the table at a few reproving glances. "Well, I'm sorry," she said, not sounding sorry at all, "but we have all been through a harrowing time—not to mention two murders. Who'd have thought that nice young Italian man was responsible?"

"That 'nice young man' murdered two women," commented Dr. Stolz acerbically.

"How is he, by the way?" asked Magda Malescu. "I watched him being shot again this afternoon on television."

"He has a 20 percent chance of living and a 95 percent chance of losing his manhood," said the doctor, forgetting his bedside manner in favor of statistics. Several eyes turned in my direction. As the one who pulled the trigger, it was inevitable that some comment was expected.

"I didn't have time to do much thinking," I said. "I just did whatever I could to protect myself against a man with a gun."

"You did it very bravely, too," said Magda firmly, and Irena led a minichorus of approval.

"Killing those two poor girls was unforgivable," added Mrs. Walburg.

"Mikhel Czerny was not a 'poor girl,'" stated Eva Zilinsky loudly. "Many in Hungary are not sorry to have him removed from the pages of the Budapest *Times*."

"A harsh way to go," said Friedlander, reaching for more caviar. "So that story about Conti being poisoned was not true?"

It was not a story that had received wide circulation on the train, and the details had to be explained. "We had investigated him," said Kramer, "and found many gaps in his background—"

"But it wasn't really him," objected Henri Larouge. "Hadn't he taken the identity of a real agent of the *Amici della Uva*?" I realized that as a Frenchman and involved in the wine business, Larouge might well be one of the few who knew anything about that organization.

"He must have realized that the identity he had assumed made him suspicious," said Kramer. "Taking a reduced dose of the poisonous herb himself was, he hoped, a way of removing suspicion."

A phalanx of white-uniformed waiters approached, and a concert group struck up some cheerful music that sounded like Georg Enesco, the Romanian composer. Several of Bucharest's top restaurants had combined to present the meal, and, when the next course appeared, my advisor on matters Romanian, Irena Koslova, explained. "The Greeks introduced this dish to the region. They are called *Mezes*, and a similar word is found in many other languages." It consisted of a bean salad, baked aubergine, raw carrots, and tomatoes, various cheeses, ham, and small sausages.

"It is not very different," said Irena apologetically, "but then cooking in Bucharest cannot be compared to Paris."

We were given a choice of main courses. Irena chose *Ratusca*, roast duck. It looked superb, cooked to a golden brown and with a crispy skin. It was served with dumplings—"very popular in Romania," said Irena. Magda Malescu ordered grilled trout. "I know it's not specifically Romanian," she said, "but I like it."

"I will have something Romanian," declared Kramer and asked for the Chicken Givech. It was cooked with onions, garlic, red peppers, mushrooms, and zucchini. I chose the lamb marinated in vinegar and red wine. It was served with noodles in garlic sauce.

We had a discussion on Romanian wine and everyone knew enough to agree that it was time some official backing was given to wine development.

"Our delivery of the vines today may well be the first step in such a program," stated Brenner.

"I think it was wonderful the way you two fought to save them," said Eva Zilinsky, and proposed a toast to Kramer and me. "*Pofta buna*," she said, and we all echoed it in a variety of bad accents. She went on to Kramer, "I missed something when I was watching it on television. When you answered your phone, what was being said?"

"I had to keep Conti from knowing," Kramer explained, "so I kept my answers simple. Thomas—in charge of the communication center, had alerted Herr Brenner that something was wrong. Herr Brenner's first question was—'Is there a problem?' I answered 'yes.' Then he asked, 'Should we take any action?' and I said 'No.' " As I hoped, these satisfied Conti."

Kramer turned to me. "One thing you have not explained to me," he said, lowering his voice, "is that cryptic message to Switzerland. I gave you a reply this morning that Thomas had received, so I suppose you can now clarify?"

"Ah, yes," I said. "The message went to an old friend who is an authority on wine. Emil is retired now but acts as a consultant, and little happens in the wine business that escapes him. First, I said in the message, 'Before you drink your next glass of Pinot Noir—' That's sort of a code, Emil doesn't like Pinot Noir, so he knows the message is really from me. Then I asked for a physical description of *ADU* 121. '*ADU*' means *Amici della Uva*, of course, and 121 are the numbers on the badge on Conti's jacket. Emil's message said the agent who carries that number weighs sixty-six kilos, is 170 centimeters tall, has gray eyes, and gray hair—that converts to 145 pounds and five feet eight inches tall."

"Obviously not Conti!" said Kramer.

"That's right."

"A pity that message did not arrive earlier," Kramer said drily.

"It is," I agreed.

"So you were suspicious of him?"

"Not especially, but when Elisha Tabor was found poisoned with the same drug as Svarovina, I began to wonder more about the attempt on Conti. The poisoner was so efficient in killing the two women—why was he was so inefficient with Conti and didn't give him enough to kill him?"

"Logical," Kramer nodded. He liked logic. "Now what does the second part of the answering message mean?"

"The second question I asked was 'Potential cargo buyer besides original?' That meant 'Is there someone else who might want the cargo of vines on board the Danube Express?' "

"This Emil knew where you were?"

"Point of origin would be shown on the e-mail, wouldn't it?"

"Yes, of course," Kramer admitted. "And the answer was—?"

"Emil gave me the name of a vineyard that is large and well-known worldwide but has had recent weather problems. They have been involved in a few shady deals and would be likely to pay someone like Conti handsomely to steal these vines. They are wealthy as well as unscrupulous."

"I see," said Kramer. "That is the opposite of what we were thinking, is it not? We were pondering the possibility of another country wanting to prevent the shipment arriving."

"Yes, and the more I thought about that, the less reasonable it seemed. So I turned the question around—it then became, not who wanted to stop the shipment arriving but who would want to get hold of the shipment."

"Logical again," Kramer said. "What will you do about it? Should I—"

"Let me pull a few strings through the *Amici della Uva*. This is their kind of problem. Let them see what connections they might be able to find between this vineyard and Conti. The *ADU* will probably contact you for further information."

"Very good," Kramer said. "I fear that the part of the investigation that we must continue will reveal that the real Conti is dead—killed by this man who took his place."

"I am afraid that must be so."

"Now," said Kramer, "I will have another glass of this excellent—what is it?" He waved to the wine waiter and examined the label. "Ah, yes, *Feteasca Alba*."

"One of the best of our Romanian white wines," the waiter told him.

"The country is about to make great efforts to improve the quality of its wines," said Erich Brenner. "Under the Soviet regime, they were obliged to concentrate their vineyard production on the sweet wines—which the Russians prefer. Now they are going to be producing drier wines, and I anticipate that they will make real progress in the world wine market."

Irena leaned toward me. "I heard your discussion with Herr Kramer. I thought these were just a bunch of vines—are they really so special?"

"Yes, they are. They had to have been very carefully selected as resistant to *Phylloxera*, and they would need resistance to every known disease and virus as well as insects. They would have been grafted on to traditional vinifera vines, and this hybridization process would require time and skill. They must be very special."

When we left the palace, I managed to arrange to move near Irena. "I suppose you are going home now. Are you glad to be back in Bucharest?"

"Oh, yes, but it has been a wonderful journey. I didn't expect that much excitement though."

"None of us did."

Her eyes sparkled in the orange streetlamps. Taxis came and went. We stood there.

"You remember when I said I wasn't sure which direction my compartment was in the train?" she asked. "You said you would walk me there."

"I will never forget it."

"So don't you think it is only fair if I walk you to your hotel?"

"I'm all for fairness," I assured her.

She linked her arm through mine. "Let's go."